ZARAGOZ

THERE WAS A living darkness in the air, hovering above the courtyard and the dancing-floor alike, drowning out the light of the stars and the feeble flames of the candles – an obliteration which erupted from the cracks and crevices of space itself, roiling and writhing as if in indecision over what shape to take, or whether to take any shape at all.

The blackness was filling the air, with a fierce cold and a foul graveyard stink of which Semjaza's odious breath was but the merest echo.

Orfeo's lips formed again the saying which he had repeated to Rodrigo Cordova: *Though the honest strength of men dies with them, their magic may seek vengeance from the grave.*

BUCKINGHAMSHIRE
COUNTY COUNCIL
This
withd
Coun
Price

GW00537525

More Warhammer from the Black Library

· WARHAMMER NOVELS ·

THE WINE OF DREAMS by Brian Craig

ZAVANT by Gordon Rennie

HAMMERS OF ULRIC by Dan Abnett,
Nik Vincent & James Wallis

GILEAD'S BLOOD by Dan Abnett & Nik Vincent

· GOTREK & FELIX ·

TROLLSLAYER by William King

SKAVENSLAYER by William King

DAEMONSLAYER by William King

DRAGONSLAYER by William King

BEASTSLAYER by William King

VAMPIRESLAYER by William King

· THE GENEVIEVE NOVELS ·

DRACHENFELS by Jack Yeovil

GENEVIEVE UNDEAD by Jack Yeovil

· THE KONRAD TRILOGY ·

KONRAD by David Ferring

SHADOWBREED by David Ferring

· WARHAMMER FANTASY STORIES ·

REALM OF CHAOS
eds. Marc Gascoigne & Andy Jones

LORDS OF VALOUR
eds. Marc Gascoigne & Christian Dunn

A WARHAMMER NOVEL

The First Tale of Orfeo

ZARAGOZ

Brian Craig

BUCKINGHAMSHIRE COUNTY LIBRARY	
H J	967343
F	£5.99

A BLACK LIBRARY PUBLICATION

First published in Great Britain in 1989 by
GW Books, a division of Games Workshop Ltd., UK

This edition published in Great Britain in 2002 by
Games Workshop Publishing,
Willow Road, Lenton, Nottingham, NG7 2WS, UK

10 9 8 7 6 5 4 3 2 1

Cover illustration by Clint Langley

Copyright © 1989, 2002 Games Workshop Ltd. All rights reserved.

Games Workshop, the Games Workshop logo and Warhammer are
trademarks of Games Workshop Ltd., registered in the UK and other
countries around the world. The Black Library and the Black Library
logo are trademarks of Games Workshop Ltd.

A CIP record for this book
is available from the British Library

ISBN 1 84154 231 8

Set in ITC Giovanni

Printed and bound in Great Britain by
Cox & Wyman Ltd, Cardiff Rd, Reading, Berkshire RG1 8EX, UK

No part of this publication may be reproduced, stored in a retrieval
system, or transmitted in any form or by any means, electronic,
mechanical, photocopying, recording or otherwise, without the prior
permission of the publishers.

This book is sold subject to the condition that it shall not, by way of
trade or otherwise, be lent, re-sold, hired out or otherwise circulated
without the publisher's prior consent in any form of binding or
cover other than that in which it is published and without a similar
condition including this condition being imposed on the subsequent
purchaser.

See the Black Library on the Internet at
www.blacklibrary.co.uk

Find out more about Games Workshop
and the world of Warhammer at
www.games-workshop.com

ZARAGOZ

Being the First Tale of Orfeo

PROLOGUE

ORFEO RECOVERED CONSCIOUSNESS, slowly and painfully.

Images flickered briefly in his mind as he struggled for command of his memory: turbaned fighting-men leaping from deck to deck, brandishing curved swords...

The tip of his own blade drawing a great gout of blood from a man's neck...

The oarsmen rising up, rattling the shackles which held them in a mad cacophony of delight...

The reek of blood and sweat and fear...

The blinding light... and then the darkness...

He found that he was lying on a stone floor beneath a window, close enough to the wall to be shadowed from the bright light which streamed through it. His hands were bound behind him, and when he tested the strength of the rope the burning pain told him that he had already struggled hard against their confinement, making the skin of his wrists very sore. His head was pounding and his right shoulder was aching badly, as if his collar-bone had been broken.

He could not remember the blow which had knocked him senseless. He had been backed up against the mizzen mast of the galley, defending himself with his slender sword – all too slender, it had seemed, against the scimitars of the pirates. The Estalian sailors had been hopelessly outnumbered to begin with – more so once the attackers had broken the chains which confined the rowers, fully three-quarters of whom were slaves or felons only too eager to join the fight against their masters. The pirates had brought two dhows and a light brigantine from a concealed harbour, and with the wind blowing from the land had overhauled the Estalian galley with absurd ease.

Orfeo remembered that his blade had drawn blood from at least three opponents, one of whom had surely been killed – but that had not made the attackers angry enough to murder him. They fought for profit, not for the pleasure of slaughter, and were well accustomed to sacrificing a man or two of their own in order to harvest a good crop of human flesh, ready for the auction-block.

He wondered whether it might have been better to have received a fatal blow, but he knew that it was only the pain in his head which made him regret being alive. He had been a prisoner before, and a slave too – though never in such an alien land as Araby. In time, he might be free again, if only he could conserve his strength and his cunning.

He had no shortage of either.

He turned over, so that he was no longer facing the blank wall beneath the window. The room was not well furnished, but was certainly no dungeon. It was carpeted, with thicker rugs for sitting upon – which suggested that he was in the hands of men descended from the nomads of the great sand-sea, who had never cared for chairs.

There was one other person present: another prisoner, bound like himself and lying still, facing the other way. It was the youngest of the Estalian sailors, a boy not yet out of his teens. Orfeo had to search his memory for the boy's name, and remembered that his fellows had called him

Maro. Orfeo called out to him, and was glad to see the youth stir in response.

Orfeo tried to get to his feet, propping himself up on his left elbow in order to avoid putting strain on his injured shoulder. He managed to clamber up, and glanced out of the window before going to the boy's side. The window was high above stony ground, in a tower of some kind of citadel which looked over a precipitous cliff. The plain at the foot of the cliff was under cultivation, but the soil was very poor and the region arid; in the distance he could see the rocks and dunes of the Sahra – the great desert of Araby.

When Orfeo stirred the youth's body with his boot Maro opened his dark eyes. They were glazed and very weary, but Orfeo saw that he was not badly hurt. He too had been knocked unconscious by a cudgel, applied with sufficient skill to avoid damaging the goods.

'Where are we?' whispered the boy, the direction of his stare darting about the room as soon as he was able to see clearly again.

Orfeo knelt down, and then moved – not without difficulty – to a sitting position.

'I cannot say for sure,' said Orfeo, 'but I think it is the citadel of Arjijil, which is an infamous nest of pirates. The fortress is said to be impregnable, and it houses the servants of one who styles himself Caliph of Mahabbah and Lord of the Twin Seas. His fame has undoubtedly spread to the Estalian Kingdoms.'

'Oh yes,' said the boy, bitterly. 'I have heard of him. He demands tribute from the vessels which move in these waters – but our own ship was guaranteed safe passage by the Sultan of All Araby himself! The captain carried his seal!'

Orfeo smiled grimly. 'A seal impressed on a document is only as good as the men who will respect it,' he said. 'I do not think the Sultan will be too disappointed by its failure. Our cargo will make its way to him in any case, and I do not think he will care so very much what merchant takes the profit from its sale. Of course, he will send messages to your masters in Almagora expressing his alarm at the loss of their ship, with extravagant promises of revenge to be taken by his armies upon the perpetrators of the vile act – but somehow, I do not think that Arjijil will yet be crushed by his wrath.'

Maro stared at Orfeo while he spoke, not quite able to follow the line of the argument. He tried to sit up, and eventually managed it; he seemed to have gathered fewer bruises than Orfeo, and probably had not joined in the fight aboard the galley in any serious fashion.

'What will become of us?' he asked.

'We will be sold,' said Orfeo, as gently as he could. 'They have put us here together because they do not know quite how to value us. You are young, unseasoned as a sailor, and they may hope to find a cleverer use for you than to put you to the oar. I am an unknown quantity, and they will want to know my skills. They will come soon to question us, and you may care to ask yourself what answers you will give.'

Maro thought about this for a moment or two. Orfeo could see that there would be little point in advising the boy to invent an elaborate lie in the hope of finding easier employment.

With luck, it might not be necessary – the youth had not the power in his arms and legs to make a useful rower, and would probably be sold as a household servant. As for himself, he had no particular need to plan and practise his lies. Improvisation had always come naturally to him, and lies came ever more easily to his lips than the truth.

'What answers will you give?' asked the boy, plainly hoping for a good example.

'I will give them an honest account of my nature and skills,' Orfeo said. 'I will tell them that I was a passenger on the ship, bound for the great cities of Araby, where I hoped to amuse rich men with songs and stories, and learn some new tales which, in the course of time, I might bring back to the lands of Estalia and Bretonnia, and even to the Empire itself.'

And it is an honest account, Orfeo added, within the silence of his own thoughts, as far as it goes.

After a moment's pause, the boy said: 'I beg you, sir, will you speak for me also? I know not what to say.'

Orfeo did not want to be unkind, but neither did he want to accept any responsibility for the boy. He would have said no, as diplomatically as he could, but before he could speak the door of the room was thrown open. As he turned to see who had entered, the thought flitted through his mind that a plea unrejected would seem to the boy a plea accepted, but there was no opportunity to say any-thing further. He could do no more than say to himself that he must do what he was able for the youth, provided only that he did not compromise his own position.

Three men came into the room. All wore turbans after the customary fashion of all the Arabs, and all had the coloured jackets, wide trousers and soft slippers which were worn indoors in these parts. One of the three, how-ever, had garments much finer in quality than the others, and though he wore no jewellery or embroidery of golden thread it was easy to see that he was a man of importance. The others, though they carried no scimitars, were plainly bodyguards; the fact that they carried no weapons was a quiet boast to the effect that their skill in the arts of com-bat was such as to make mere blades unnecessary.

The guards took up positions to either side of the door, while the third man came to look down at the two cap-tives. Orfeo studied him closely. His skin was darkened by the sun and his eyes were equally dark, and to a casual glance he looked every inch the Arab, but Orfeo could see that the cast of his features was somewhat different from the Arab type. Orfeo was not altogether surprised by this. Shipmasters from Estalia and the Border Princes who elected to turn pirate often came to this ragged coast, where there were abundant harbours for shallow boats. In order to be reconciled with the stern priests of Araby they were required to 'take the turban' and swear devotion to the Arabs' single god, but that was no great hardship to men who were used to offering prayers to any deity which seemed appropriate to the moment.

'But this will not do,' said the pirate, in a silky voice. 'We are civilized men and must talk in the fashion of civilized men.' So saying he took a small knife from his sleeve and reached down to cut the bonds which secured Orfeo's wrists. Then he did the same for the boy, and signalled with his hands that they should sit cross-legged in the fashion of Arabic merchants taking tea to mark the conclusion of a deal. Orfeo assumed the position easily, but the boy – who was used to chairs – seemed very uncomfortable.

The pirate also sat down, facing them both. Without turning round he clapped his hands once, and one of his guards opened the door wider, to allow the entrance of a servant carrying a silver tray. Upon the tray were a jug of tea and three shallow cups, each with two handles. No one said a word until the servant had poured out the tea. Orfeo was very thirsty, but he did not reach for his cup until the other man had picked up his own.

Orfeo was not moved by this demonstration of politeness to doubt that he was still a prisoner, intended for a slave. He knew when someone was toying with him.

'May we be allowed to know whose generous hand is thus extended to us, my lord?' asked Orfeo, lifting the cup in mock-appreciation.

'I am Alkadi Nasreen,' replied the other, in the language of the Old World – adding, almost as an afterthought, 'Caliph of Mahabbah and Lord of the Twin Seas.'

Orfeo was surprised, not so much that a man who termed himself caliph should present himself in ungrandiose guise, but that a man who was not an Arab could have ascended to a high position in a land such as this.

Orfeo tried to sip from the cup, but the movement of his arm drew a shock of pain from his shoulder. He would have picked up the cup in his left hand, but knew well enough that among Arabs to do so would have been considered a kind of insult. Alkadi Nasreen noticed his distress.

'It is a pity,' he said, lightly. 'You should not have tried to fight my men, knowing that your situation was hopeless. I have a good bone-setter, but a minstrel must take far better care of himself than this. You will be unable to play the lute for some time, I fear. You *are* a minstrel, are you not, Master Orfeo?'

Orfeo was not suprised that his captor knew his name. The crewmen of the galley who had laid down their arms to surrender would have been quick to buy favour with all the information that their captors could possibly desire to hear. When there is no alternative to slavery but piracy the wise mariner becomes upon the instant the very model of loyalty to the pirates' cause.

'I reserve the title "minstrel" to the elves, my lord,' Orfeo replied, 'as they do themselves. But it is true that I play the lute, and know songs from many lands. I am a storyteller too, and have some little talent to amuse.'

'And you are also a spy for the Lords of Magritta,' said the Caliph, 'sent to gather intelligence in the court of my master the Sultan. So, at least, I have been told.'

'You are far too wise, my lord,' said Orfeo, calmly, 'to trust the fantasies of sailors, who are ever quick to believe that a man is more than he seems. I have been some time in Estalia, and when I amused the merchants of Magritta with my tales of Bretonnia and Albion some were generous enough to pay me in my own coin, with tales of the far lands of Araby – of Kamt and Teshert in the east, and Sud and Songhai in the south – and descriptions of the wonders of the Sultan's court. It seemed to me that a man who could take such tales to the cold northern lands might make a little of them, by way of amusement. So I begged a passage from the captain of the ship from which you took me, who asked so little in terms of coin that when he looked to me for help in defending his vessel against marauders, I could not in all honour refuse.'

'You killed one of my men,' said the Caliph, sadly. 'I do not think that was honourable, as you must have known that he was not attempting to kill you.'

'He intended to make a slave of me, my lord,' Orfeo pointed out, mimicking the playful manner of the other. 'I am content to be the humble servant of all men, but I have a prejudice against becoming the slave of any one. You will understand, I know, that Oldworlders often do have such a prejudice – it is like their reluctance to submit the world to the dominion of one god, though they are ready enough to acknowledge the many.'

'You have a clever tongue,' said the other, lightly. 'I am glad of it, for it will increase your price. I think, if I advertise your skills appropriately, that the Caliphs of Kamt – who value the arts above all men – might compete to buy your talent to amuse. If only you had not hurt your arm... but no matter. I know to my cost that you have a little skill with the rapier – have you perchance any skill in magic also?'

'I fear not,' said Orfeo.

'Yet we took a curious amulet from your pack,' the other countered, 'and a scroll inscribed in letters unknown to me. Are these not magical?'

'Mere trinkets,' Orfeo replied. 'In my hands, at least. No doubt you have given them to your wizards – if they find any virtue in the medal or the script, they will be fortunate indeed, for I never could.'

'But you *can* read,' said Nasreen, his voice becoming somewhat less soft. 'And write too, I suppose.'

'I can read my own tongue,' Orfeo agreed, 'but my fingers are cleverer by far in plucking the strings of a lute than plying the quill. I am a fearfully clumsy scribe, even without the hurt to my shoulder.'

The Caliph smiled, humourlessly. 'A pity,' he said. 'You might in time have risen to a high position had you all the skills of wisdom. Even a slave may become a vizier, if he proves himself worthy.'

'Alas,' said Orfeo, making no attempt to hide his levity, 'my wisdom is a humbler sort, not fit for politics at all, and I do not think I would look so well in a turban as I do in a simple cap.'

The pirate king finally looked away from Orfeo, to stare at Maro. The boy had relaxed a good deal, though the tea had not been to his taste and he had laid down the cup without taking more than a sip.

He had been watching the exchange betwen Orfeo and the Caliph in some perplexity, and had obviously inferred from their apparent ease that his situation was not so desperate as it had seemed.

'What is your name?' asked Nasreen.

'Marcantonio Giraldi, sire,' replied the boy. 'I am called Maro by my friends.'

'I think Maro will suffice,' said the other. 'You will not need your father's name in these lands, and even without it, four syllables would be a luxury for a slave. But you, also, might qualify for a favoured position if the One God wills it. The King of Songhai – who is a powerful ruler indeed – has such eclectic tastes that he has more eunuchs in his harem than wives. I make shift to find him suitable boys whenever I can, and you have a smooth skin, of a colour which he would think unusual. No doubt you served your fellows in the ship as whoreboy, and have some elementary skill in the crafts which he would teach you.'

Orfeo saw that Maro's skin had taken on a paler hue than was usual, but could not tell whether it was merely the thought of castration which alarmed him, or whether the entire prospect laid before him was abhorrent.

He remembered the plea for aid which he had not had time to refuse.

'Do not frighten the boy, my lord, I beg you,' he said. 'This is a mariner, not a catamite, and you would surely do better to train him for a pirate than sell him for a plaything. Let him keep his courage, and one day he may be a captain for you. It is plain to see that Estalian birth is not sufficient to prevent a man from rising in the ranks of Arjijil, even to the Barbary Throne itself.'

The last was said with a very slight hint of insult, to draw the Caliph's attention away from the question of the boy's fate. When the dark man answered, though, his tone was free of any sense of injury or offence.

'Ah yes,' he said. 'My voice will always give me away, when I speak the Oldworlder tongue. My Arabic is very fluent, and the desert men readily take me for one of their own, but you are a travelled man, and can read my features with a practiced eye. Yes, I am of the oldest stock of that world which calls itself old, and I own that I was not above the age of this meek boy when first I took the turban. But I was a fighting man even then, and far more a warrior than a mariner. Little Maro, if I judge him right, is not even an accomplished thief.'

Maro opened his mouth as if to affirm that indeed he was, then suddenly wondered if it was really a wise thing to do. Being unable to decide, he did the worst thing of all, and neither confirmed nor denied the charge.

'You see,' said Alkadi Nasreen to Orfeo, 'no pirate, born or made. I do not train my captains – they earn their station before they humbly beg to join the fleet of Arjijil. But there is no need to hasten to a judgment, for I have already decided that you will be my guests for a while, until I know what is best to do with you. Your broken bone must be set and healed, Master Orfeo, and I am not displeased by the prospect. It is a long time since I was in Estalia, and your talent to amuse will surely find some exercise in reminding me how wise I was to quit its shore.'

'I am certain that you receive regular news from Magritta,' said Orfeo, 'but it is possible that in my travels I have called at other places which you knew. In which of the many principalities were you born, my lord?'

Orfeo saw that the Caliph's face was straitened by this question, as if the memory of his birthplace did not please him.

'I doubt that you have been *there*,' he said, darkly. 'It is but a tiny realm, on the further reaches of the river called Eboro. Its name is Zaragoz.'

Even Orfeo had not sufficient skill to hide his start of shock.

'Say you so?' he said, his voice hardly above a murmur. 'I will confess that I am very surprised to hear it. It happens, my lord, that I have been in Zaragoz, less than two years since. What befell me there is not among my happier memories, though I have consoled myself with the thought that I might one day shape it into a useful story.'

Nasreen's stare was different now in its quality, and Orfeo knew that he was not the only one taken by surprise. It was clear that the Caliph was wondering whether this might be a mere trick intended to win his sympathy, but it was equally clear that the bold pirate king wanted to believe him, and that he would indeed be interested to hear of recent events in Zaragoz. In one sense, this was a good thing for Orfeo to learn, but the matter was not without its hazards.

'And how does Zaragoz fare?' asked the Caliph of Mahabbah and Lord of the Twin Seas, with a curious coldness in his tone. 'Is the son of di Avila well, and do his people love him better than they loved his father?'

'It is a long tale,' said Orfeo, carefully, 'and has more in it than you might expect. I beg your permission to tell it in my own way, when you have made proper time for it. But I will say this, since you ask: Marsilio diAvila, if he is the son that you mean, was called a tyrant by his people. I will tell you also that his reign is at an end... and that my story includes an account of its ending.'

When he had made this speech, Orfeo let his breath out very gently, not sure for a moment or two how accurately he had judged his audience or how cunningly he had planned his advertisement. There was no cause for alarm, for the face of the Caliph of Mahabbah showed plainly enough the extent of his fascination as he came abruptly to his feet.

'You are right, Master Minstrel,' he said. 'I must make time for this, and hear it all. But you must swear to tell me true, for this is a matter which means more to me than you know. I swear by the One God that I will not punish you, should it transpire that you are the bearer of news that hurts me, and I swear also that if I have cause to be pleased in what I hear, then you and this boy will receive fair treatment in Arjijil.'

Orfeo stood up, so that he could look the other man in the eye again.

'I will swear,' he said, 'by your One God or by any of the gods to whom we pay homage in the Old World.'

The Caliph nodded. 'Swear by Morr and Manann,' he instructed. 'The god of death and the god of the sea. Though they are false gods here, I would be content to hear a man like you swear by their names.'

'I so swear,' said Orfeo, calmly. 'By Morr and Manann, I give you my word that I will tell you the truth of that which happened in Zaragoz when I was there. I will give as full and honest an account as any man could.'

The man who styled himself Alkadi Nasreen – but had surely owned another name in his boyhood – nodded in acknowledgement.

'I will send food and clothing,' he said, 'and pallets on which you both may sleep. Water too, so that you may bathe. When the time is made, I will send for you.'

He left the room then, and his guards with him. Orfeo felt his spirits lifting, and was glad to raise his left hand to rub the back of his head where he had earlier been struck down. Then he knelt, to pour more tea from the pot which still remained on the floor.

He heard that two bolts were drawn on the outside of the door, to secure him in his prison, but it did not trouble him at all.

'Were you really in Zaragoz?' asked Maro, in a way which suggested that he hardly dared believe it.

'That I was,' Orfeo replied, in a low tone. 'I could not dare to pretend, even though he cannot have been there for thirty years and more. Nor do I dare invent a tale, when further news might soon arrive from other lips than mine. But I wish I knew what name his father gave him, so that I might tailor the cloth of honesty to suit it. Do not bless your luck too eagerly, friend Maro, for the fate which has entangled your future with mine may yet prove unkind to us both!'

SOME HOURS LATER, Orfeo stood at the window of his lofty residence, watching the sun set over the desert at the right-hand edge of the horizon.

The wind had whipped enough of the desert sand into the air to colour the sun blood red, and that coloured light painted the desert in much darker and more varied hues than the blaze of noon. Long shadows showed where the ridges ran and where the tall palms stood about the wells. He could see a camel-train making its slow way south, making the most of the evening sun after a long afternoon spent sheltering from the day's worst heat. Perhaps it was carrying goods looted from the ship which had brought him unexpectedly to this blighted shore, bound for the King of Songhai and not for the Sultan after all.

The sand-sea of the Sahra was the second of those 'twins' over which the Caliph of Mahabbah claimed lordship, but any such claim was mere fancy. The desert was no man's realm.

Would that I had been a spy for the Lords of Magritta, said Orfeo to himself. For they would have set me aboard a galley with a bombard in its bow, and a troop of pike-men to defend its decks. Alas, a man who has no missions but his own has no such luxuries to help him.

The bone-setter had come to attend his wound, and had with dubious authority pronounced that the bone was back in proper alignment. He had given Orfeo a sling for his arm and had firmly instructed him not to make much use of it – though he was well aware that the left hand could not stand in for the right when others were there to see.

If I had only ducked the other way, Orfeo thought, or gracefully accepted upon the crown of my head the first of those cudgel-blows which were aimed to knock me down, instead of striving to draw more blood while I awaited the second, I would have been a wiser man.

He seemed to hear another voice then, chiding him as it often had in his youth: *Headstrong Orfeo. All-too-human in thy recklessness, as though thine heartbeat were a petty wardrum.*

He had bathed himself, and dressed himself in a black leathern suit of his own, from the pack which had been sent to him. All his possessions were there, save only for his rapier. They were prepared to trust him with the knife which he used in eating, but not yet with an instrument whose only purpose was to carve human meat.

His lute was undamaged, and though Alkadi Nasreen's magicians had surely copied the devices from the scroll which he carried they had taken care to preserve the original from any tear or mark. Maro's possessions had come too, but they were poor in kind and their hosts had added to them a cotton shirt and a pair of loose trousers in the Arab style, which the boy was unashamed to wear. They were both well fed, but Orfeo could not yet be comfortable because his head still throbbed with the echo of the blow which had stunned him.

He had expected a summons before now, but the business of a pirate caliph clearly had more duty in it than he might have supposed, and he was beginning to wonder whether his story might have to wait for the morrow. But when the sun had slipped so far below the horizon that only a thin arc of fiery red was left above the darkling hills he heard the bolts withdrawn again, and turned to see the person who entered.

It was a female house-servant, veiled after the fashion of her race – save that this veil was flimsy and transparent, revealing instead of hiding the features which it overlaid.

'Your pardon, sire,' she said, 'but you must come with me.'

Orfeo bowed politely, and passed through the door which she held for him.

The corridors of Arjijil's citadel wound round its walls in complex fashion; their walls were sometimes brick and sometimes stone, sometimes whited and sometimes decorated with rugs and hangings, lit by huge candles nestling in their alcoves. They passed a dozen scurrying servants and a few men-at-arms, such as might have been seen in any castle of the Old World, made so alike to Oldworlders by the shadowy light that only their turbans accurately betrayed their true location.

Eventually, the woman brought Orfeo to his destination. It was a small chamber, and not as sumptuous as he might have expected of the humblest of a Caliph's private apartments. To his surprise, Orfeo found that it had a high table and upholstered chairs, sturdy enough for the home of an Imperial man of business. Furthermore, there was a jug of wine upon the table, and goblets of crystal. Between them stood a candelabra of Bretonnian manufacture, with three long candles only just alight. In taking the turban, it seemed, the man who now called himself Alkadi Nasreen had not forsworn entirely the habits of his former life.

'Sit down,' said the Caliph, when the servant had gone. 'I have seen to it that we will not be disturbed. The night is the proper time for men to talk, and I have cloaks in case it should grow cold when the sun is too long gone. And if your tale should be so long in the telling that it exhausts the dark hours... well then, I trust that you will leave it at a proper point, so that we may take it up again when the night frees us yet again from the burdens of my kingship.'

Orfeo sat down, and the other poured wine into his cup. 'If it is not good,' he said, 'you must blame the captain whose generosity you repaid with your swordplay. It was his own, reserved for his private use. He cannot use it now, for our wise priests have banished wine from the land, saying that the will of the One True God is such that men may only lighten their heads with hasheesh and opium. I agree entirely with their discretion, for bad wine is not fit for any man to drink, and the good is far too precious to be wasted. Your health, Master Minstrel!'

Orfeo drank from the cup, fearing not in these surroundings to use his left hand to lift it. He found the wine altogether agreeable, though by no means of the very best.

'Thank you, my lord,' he said. 'The desert wind dries a man's throat, if he is not used to its bite. But I wish you would not call me minstrel.'

'I had forgotten,' said the Caliph, though Orfeo did not believe him. 'I judge from your niceness in labelling that you have had close dealings with elves.'

'I was raised as a foundling by wood elves in the deep Bretonnian forest,' Orfeo explained. 'But as soon as I grew old enough to fend for myself I left them – it was all too plain that I was not of their company. My foster father taught me the lute and gave me my name – to have taken the title of minstrel also would have seemed a kind of theft, for I had heard and seen the real minstrels... more of them, perhaps, than any margrave of the Empire.'

'I have heard it said that the wood elves are fearsome warriors and clever magicians,' said the pirate lord, casually.

'Then you have heard mistaken rumours,' Orfeo countered. 'The folk I knew were more peaceful by far than the men among whom I have moved in recent times. They reserved their bows for hunting game, and such magic as they had was to conceal them within the forest, and to help the forest bear such fruit as it could. They had better lives than the warlike, and they made me a lover of peace as well as freedom.'

'And a lover of their quiet magic, too?'

'Their magic was their own, my lord,' Orfeo told him, with some impatience at being so artlessly tried, 'and not such as to be trusted to a human foundling. They kept me for a while; they never sought to make me one of their kind.'

'A pity,' said the Caliph, levelly. 'But let us not talk of your youth. It is your sojourn in Zaragoz which interests me. Many years have passed since I saw a man who had been in Zaragoz, and though I thought I had laid its memory to rest, I find that my curiosity waited only for the spark to set it afire – for what reason I may explain to you when I have heard what you have to tell. I beg you to leave out nothing, for I would know all that you know, in the richness of its every detail.'

'And so you shall,' said Orfeo, signing with his right hand that the other should take his seat.

When the Caliph lifted his cup again, and drank from it, Orfeo cleared his throat and began. 'Orfeo,' he said, 'had walked beneath the hot sun for many an hour, along the north shore of the river Eboro...'

'You tell the story as if it had happened to another,' said the Caliph, uneasily, 'although the name which you use is your own. Why do you not say "I had walked" as any other man would?'

'It is not the proper way to make a story,' said Orfeo, gently. 'And the fact that a story is true does not mean that it should cease to be a story. When a man says "I did this" and proceeds to tell you about the bravo whom he bested in a fight, or the fish which he landed from the stream, does he not often lose the truth in self-aggrandizement? If I am to tell you most precisely what happened, then I must look at this man who was myself with a dispassionate eye, to weigh what he did and why as though his lack of hero-ism and cleverness were neither here nor there. Otherwise, the temptation to remake him in a finer image might prove too strong. I beg you, my lord of Mahabbah and the Twin Seas, to let me do this in the proper way.'

'Very well,' said the Caliph, though he sounded a fraction unsure. 'I will not interrupt again.'

'Well and good, my lord,' said Orfeo, placidly. 'And so: Orfeo had walked beneath the hot sun for many an hour...'

Part One
A WEB OF INTRIGUE

One

ORFEO HAD WALKED beneath the hot sun for many an hour,
along the north shore of the River Eboro. It was a lonely
place, without a proper path. There were no ferrymen's sta-
tions on this reach of the river, for there were few travellers
who passed this way. The paths which he had earlier followed through the forest were used only by woodcutters
and hunters, who had little reason to cross the miles of
barer land which separated them from the river's course.

The Eboro was still fast-flowing here, not far from the
foot of its descent from the eastern reaches of the Irrana
Mountains. It would slow in its paces as it described a long
and lazy loop across the Estalian Plain before quickening
again into the gorges by which it navigated an unlikely path
through the Abasko Hills to reach the sea beyond Tobaro.

He had left the forest behind a little while ago, and was
now in open pasturelands where sheep and goats were
grazing. There were farms on the higher ground in the
north, with orange groves and vineyards, from whose

fields the animals could be driven down to the river to drink their fill. Where he walked the soil had been scoured away by floodwater to leave a dry and sandy reach where thorny bushes and tall grasses grew in ragged clumps.

Ahead of him, he could see a road which descended from the farmland to meet the river at a place where it became calmer in its flow, and wider. The road and the river continued together, side by side, and Orfeo knew that it would bring him to a more populous land, and eventually to a town of some size.

Although the land to the south of the river stretched away very flatly to a far horizon Orfeo's view of the land on the north shore of the river was still blocked by trees and low hills. He was surprised therefore, when he followed the road and the river around a leisurely bend, to see a single conical crag, which had not been visible to him before, loom upon that part of the horizon in a manner both striking and incongruous.

With low-lying land all around it this lone crag seemed not to belong to the landscape at all. It was as though some god carrying mountains to a place where they belonged had suffered an accident which chipped the peak from one of them, and had carelessly let it fall. Perched atop the crag was a citadel, but the rocky slopes beneath were too sheer to allow more than thirty or forty houses to cling there; thus, the town over which the castle stood was arranged in a tight ring about its base, confined by a low wall. The farms which fed it formed a greater circle, cut across one side by the river's course.

Orfeo was glad to see the town, because he had slept in the open for three nights, and had exhausted his supplies of food. This was the first time he had come into the sprawling land called Estalia, and this was the first of its petty kingdoms and principalities whose people would have the pleasure of receiving him.

He had been told by the hillmen of Irrana that he could expect a proper welcome in Estalia, for its folk had the conceit to think themselves the eldest and most civilized

race of all the men of the Old World, and were fond of
music and tale-telling. The new dances which had recently
become the fashion in the best cities of Bretonnia had
been unknown in the strongholds of Irrana, but he knew
that they would be popular in Estalia because he had met
a northward-bound traveller of his own kind not three
weeks since, who had listed a dozen kingdoms and duke-
doms where the nobility were ever avid to make this new
display of their gentility. That same man had told him that
an important Estalian festival would soon fall due, called
the Night of Masks, and had urged him to make what
speed he could to reach a city of the plain before that day,
when there would be a chance to earn a healthy wage with
his lute and his voice.

When he first saw the lonely crag it did not seem so far to
the town, but distances were deceptive in this level terrain
and the lonely crag with its pale fortress seemed to grow no
larger as he walked on. He never lost sight of the peak
again, but the rest of the crag was often hidden from him
by the crowns of trees which, though they grew in no great
profusion, were aggregated in his line of sight by the flat-
ness of the land.

While the town was still some miles away Orfeo came to
a junction, where the river road met another which came
from the north-east. Although it was not a proper crossroads, there being no southward extension, the place was
marked by two things which were often placed at crossroads in that region: a signpost and a scaffold. The one was
a guide for honest travellers, the other a macabre warning
to the highway robbers who all too often outnumbered
them.

The signpost had only one arm, upon which was written
only one name: ZARAGOZ. It pointed towards the invisible town and the all-too-obvious castle on the crag.

The scaffold, on the other hand, had two arms, and both
bore messages, though neither had been written in the
recent past. The corpses which hung there had been dried
by the sun so that the flesh was shrivelled and leathery, the

bones within barely connected by the rotting sinews. The legs were missing, having been stolen by scavenging beasts, but the wolves of the region plainly could not leap high enough to pull down all they might have desired.

There were two black carrion-birds sitting on one arm of the scaffold, and they watched Orfeo approach without apparent interest or alarm.

The scaffold was a sad and sorry sight, and as Orfeo came closer to it whatever life was left in his tired legs seemed to ebb away. He looked steadily into the black eyes of one of the ravens, which met his gaze with a morbid stare, as though to say: The day might come when you are here beneath me, and I will come to tease what morsels I can from your pitiful human flesh.

'Not yet, my friend,' said Orfeo, aloud. 'Not yet.'

Caw, replied the raven, hoarsely, as it condescended at last to leave its station.

Tiredly, Orfeo looked about for a place to rest, where he might hide from the sun and the scaffold for a while, until he could cheerfully continue his journey to the citadel of Zaragoz.

He saw a cluster of a dozen thin trees beside the road which came from the north-east. There was just enough shade within the stand to make a pleasant place to rest, and so he found a spot where he could lay down his pack, took a few frugal sips from his water-skin, and set his head against the bole of a tree.

He intended only to close his eyes for a few minutes, and not actually to sleep, but he had underestimated the extent of his fatigue. He drifted off into a dream.

HE WAS AWAKENED by the sound of voices, and came to himself with something of a start, realizing immediately that more time had passed than he had planned.

He sat up quickly, and looked for the angle of the sun to see how late it was. The day had perhaps less than an hour remaining before the sun would set, and he cursed silently – silently because there was something in the tenor of the voices he could hear which counselled caution. He came cautiously to his feet and looked out from the shelter of the trees to see what was happening.

There was a lone man backed up against the signpost which bore the name of Zaragoz. He was dressed in the habit of a priest – not a lightly-coloured costume such as most of the priests of these warm lowlands wore, but a darker one, such as priests in more northerly lands adopted. The hood was over his head, concealing his face. In his right hand he had a staff, which was plainer than the staffs which most spellcasters carried, rather resembling the kind of quarterstaff which was used as a weapon by the foresters of the north. The priest's other hand clutched the strap of the pack he bore upon his back, which he seemed to be trying to shield from the attentions of a group of five men.

The men must have come upon him quickly, and three had already moved to block all the ways by which he might seek to make an escape. The fourth was moving cautiously forward to face the priest while the fifth hung back, close to the trees where Orfeo hid. All five of the bandits were armed – one with an axe, two with long knives and two with cudgels – but they were in no hurry to get to grips with the man they were threatening, and seemed to be a little in awe of him.

Orfeo was not surprised by this reluctance; even five-to-one might be unfavourable odds when common brigands sought to make victim of a spellcaster. Priests were usually frugal men, whose magical powers were limited, but this was presumably no local priest whose abilities were fully known, and there was no way by which his talents could be reliably estimated. In all probability, he was harmless, but there was a possibility that he was not – and without even knowing which god he served, the boldest and most desperate of robbers would be inclined to hesitate when the moment came to challenge him.

Orfeo drew the slender sword which was scabbarded at his belt.

He wanted only to have the weapon ready, and had no firm intention of rushing immediately to the aid of the fellow under siege, but the shiny blade caught the light of the lowering sun, and the man who stood close by picked up the gleam in the corner of his eye. He turned promptly, calling a warning to his fellows and lunging forward with the blade which he held. Orfeo had no difficulty turning the blow aside, and parried a second lunge with ease before thrusting with his own sword. The robber stumbled backwards hurriedly, realizing that he had a real swordsman to face – one who could kill him easily in fair combat.

The others had turned now, and as their companion hurried to place himself alongside the man with the axe Orfeo could see the profound unease in their faces. Their minds were already clouded by doubt, and now that they faced two strangers instead of one they were even less certain of themselves. They did not know what to do.

Orfeo knew that it was safer to help them make up their minds than trust to their discretion, for these were reckless men, whose very foolishness might make them dangerous. He did not doubt that he could out-fence them all, but in a melee even an expert fighter might be hurt by an unskilled thrust.

He stepped quickly from his hiding-place, and said: 'You are surely tempting fate when you choose to descend upon your prey beneath such a sign as this.'

With the tip of his sword he pointed to the broken corpses on the scaffold. His voice was light, its tone expressing amusement, though in truth his heart had begun to race.

The man with the axe took one step towards him, and Orfeo smiled. 'I fear that I have no practice-sword,' he said. 'I must engage you with my blade, if you will it, and I think you have no more chance against its sting than you have against that man's magic. No doubt there are many sign-posts to Zaragoz, as there seem to be so many silly fellows on its roads, so eager to dress the scaffolds that they let fat merchants pass, descending instead on men too dangerous to rob and too poor to be worth the robbing. Still, 'tis a cleaner death to be cut than to be hanged, so come to me and I'll make a neater end of you than any other you could hope to meet today.'

While he spoke, he stared full into the eyes of the brigand who had taken a step towards him, and was heartily glad to see the fragile courage melt from the other's gaze.

It only needed one of the five to turn from his purpose to give the others what they sorely needed – advice to run away. The man with the axe was easily convinced that he would be all kinds of a fool if he elected to face Orfeo's blade, and so he reversed the step which he had taken, and then turned on his heel to run along the road to the north, as fast as he could go.

His four companions did their very best to overtake him, but while Orfeo watched them, they did not manage to achieve that goal.

When they were out of sight, Orfeo returned to the trees to pick up his pack. Then he came back along the road to the place where the priest still waited, holding on to his pack. It was impossible to tell, now, whether he had been frightened, or whether he had needed Orfeo's help.

'Highwaymen without horses,' said Orfeo, drily. 'I doubt they will make much progress in the art of theft.'

'This is as poor a realm for thieves,' replied the priest, in a voice equally dry, 'as it is for aught else. The sun-dried land offers poor sustenance to those who must break their backs to till and plant it. Zaragoz might be reckoned the least of all the kingdoms in Estalia – and the richness of robbers' prey must in the end be determined by the richness of the soil.'

Orfeo tried to look more closely at the other man's face, but the hood's shadow was too deep. He caught a glimpse of bronzed skin and a remarkably hooked nose, but could not yet see the priest's eyes or mouth. Nor did the other make any effort to show himself, seemingly content to hide from all the world. He was a big man, though –

almost as tall as Orfeo, whose height was unusual, and more sturdily built than the player.

Orfeo sheathed his sword, and told the other his name. He did not say anything about what manner of man he was, or where he was bound, but he knew that the lute which was strapped to his pack would identify him as an itinerant entertainer.

'Are you bound for Zaragoz?' asked the priest, without immediately revealing his own name.

'I believe that I am,' answered Orfeo. 'There is certainly no other town which I could reach before sunset, and its name was included in a list which was read to me by another man of my profession. They know the new dances there, I think, but have no expert players of their own to lead them. Perhaps the king will be glad to see me.'

'Zaragoz has no king,' said the priest, 'but only a duke. I am not sure that the present duke is the sort of man to give liberal welcome to a travelling musician, but it is not for me to judge. His castle is a dour place which would certainly gain from a measure of your art.'

'Then you know the town?' said Orfeo, courteously. 'You are bound for its temple, perhaps – or one of its shrines?'

'I do not think that there are shrines of the Gods of Law in that town,' replied the other. 'But I own that I have not been there for many years. My name is Arcangelo, and I would be honoured if we could walk the road together.'

Orfeo was mildly puzzled by this speech, but did not let his doubt show in his face. He knew little enough of the Gods of Law and their followers, and could not easily judge what mission such a one might have, though he had heard of the exploits of servants of Solkan, holy master of witchfinders.

Solkan's priests were wrathful men, ever eager to take arms against the viler kinds of sorcery, and if this Arcangelo was of their company he might not be the most comfortable of companions. But he seemed mild enough for the moment, and the road was clearly unsafe for lone travellers.

'I would be glad if you could tell me a little of Zaragoz,' said Orfeo, as the two moved off together. 'My road will eventually take me to the southern lands, but I do not know how quickly I should hurry on my way. I have heard that there is a feast-day called the Night of Masks, and I wonder whether I should wait in Zaragoz until it comes, or pass through to a richer realm.'

The priest did not answer immediately, but seemed lost in thought. In the end, though, he said: 'It is too late to cross the river tonight. As you have said, you must spend this night at least in the town. If what happened just now is a true indication of the safety of the road, we must look for a secure lodging within its walls. But as to the matter of your staying beyond tomorrow, I am reluctant to give you advice.'

Orfeo thought this reluctance something of a calculated mystery, but did not want to press the man.

'You are right about the road,' he said. 'Stupid thieves are, alas, more to be feared than clever ones, who would easily have judged that our packs are not worth taking.'

Arcangelo made no answer to this, but when they had walked on a little way he said: 'You are Bretonnian, are you not?'

Orfeo did not mind that the other was suspicious of him, and hastened to put him at his ease. 'I am,' he said. 'But I have spent time in the Empire too, and these last few months I have been in the highlands of Irrana. Of the ways of Estalia I know little or nothing.'

'I know more of them than most,' replied the priest, with a slight bitterness in his voice, 'but I have not been in this realm for many years. I wish that I could hope to find it changed, but the rumours which reach other realms give no encouragement to such a hope.

'I too have been in the mountains of Irrana; even there the people had heard of Marsilio diAvila and his reputation for cruelty. He is the duke now, having succeeded his father six or seven years ago. The father, whose name was Ruffino, was a hard enough man who took a savage way with his enemies – of which he had not a few – but the son, they say, is worse.'

'It is the way of common men to complain about those who rule over them,' said Orfeo, in a colourless manner. 'Every man is a tyrant to his enemies.'

'Perhaps,' said Arcangelo. 'But Zaragoz has ever been a troubled realm. The dukedom is the object of a dispute, and has been for centuries. The diAvilas argue that the right to rule has always been theirs, but some claim that the rightful rulers come from a family named Quixana, whose members sometimes sat upon its throne. This means that those who come to dislike the man who rules have a ready-made cause with which to ally themselves, and it means that those who rule are always fearful of pretenders who may take arms against them. It is a situation which breeds fear, and that fear has sometimes erupted in violence.'

'I have heard of such disputes,' said Orfeo. 'They play a sad part in some of the stories which I know.'

'A sad part indeed,' agreed the priest. 'Such arguments are running sores which fester while they are passed from generation to generation. The lineages of the feuding families of Zaragoz have been intricately tangled by complex patterns of intermarriage, and in the time of the old duke many who were innocent of any intention to challenge his rule suffered by virtue of the names which they bore. If there are Quixanas in the realm today they go by other names, and are careful to choose substitutes which will not give them away. How anxious Marsilio may be about these hidden enemies I do not know, but if you stay in Zaragoz and play in the castle, you must be careful to guard your tongue.'

'Still,' said Orfeo, 'feuds or no, these Estalian princes are civilized men, are they not? I can amuse them with a tale or two, I have no doubt. And if a holy man has come to the town, it will surely become a safer place for honest men than it was before.'

This was only a jest, but it induced the priest to turn and face him, briefly. The movement made his hood slip back a little, so that Orfeo saw the man's features clearly for the first time. He was only a little older than Orfeo – perhaps forty-five years old – and what hair he had was still black, though it was reduced to a thin fringe around a great bald pate. His thin nose was rather crudely-shaped, and his brow-ridges, still thick with black hair, were very pronounced. His eyes were as black as coals, and he seemed altogether the sternest man that Orfeo had ever seen.

'There are no shrines to the gods of order in Zaragoz,' he said. 'But there may be good men there who will give me welcome, for there is a sore need of order in the realm. As to whether my coming will make it a safer place, I must say that I cannot promise it.'

'Perhaps my coming will help to calm the town,' said Orfeo, though he felt that his jesting was not being received in the proper spirit. 'Music is a soothing art, and when men invest their energies in dancing, they have a little less to spare for quarrelsome pursuits. Even the noisy hillmen of Irrana were more cheerful when I left them than when I found them.'

'I hope you are right,' said the priest, 'but I fear that you must have received less thanks than you deserved for the gifts of good cheer which you brought to the mountain men. There is litle enough coin in Irrana to be spared for men like you – you must have sung for meagre suppers these last few weeks.'

'Aye,' said Orfeo, cheerfully. 'But the hillmen in their little forts are as hungry for tales of mischief and derring-do as any men in the world, and I amused them. They were good enough hosts, by my reckoning. If the Duke of Zaragoz is as generous within his limits as they were within theirs, I will be pleased to meet him.'

The other looked away, then, to look at a raven which swooped low across their path and disappeared between two thorny bushes which grew beside the road. As the dark man turned he said one thing more, voiced so low that Orfeo could not have heard it had his ears not been exceptionally keen.

'You little know what his limits are,' the priest had murmured to himself, 'and I think that he does not know them himself.'

But when he looked at Orfeo again, what he said aloud was quite different. He said: 'I wish you good fortune in Zaragoz, my friend – but I say again, beware. Its noblemen have more to hide than most when they don their carnival masks, and that night when they put them on might be far less joyous than they intend it to be.'

Two

THEY REACHED THE western gate of Zaragoz soon after sunset, with the twilight fading quickly from the sky. The two guardsmen at the gate watched them go through, but offered no challenge – they seemed too lazy even to be curious.

Orfeo allowed his new acquaintance to lead him through the streets, looking about him as they went. They had the customary stink of town streets everywhere, but they were not badly made, being adequately levelled and having solid pavements. Even the smaller streets had central ditches which served as sewers, though the water which was supposed to carry away the rubbish and other excrement was very sluggish in its flow.

The fact that the sewers were there at all was a mark of civilization, for many towns of this size relied on muck-carts to collect the nightsoil and the animal-droppings, and carry them away to the distant fields. The streets were narrow, but not too crowded – only on feast-days and market-days, when the labourers descended in a swarm from the surrounding farmlands, would the town fill up to the real limit of its capacity.

Arcangelo led his companion into the inner courtyard of a tavern, saying: 'This will serve our purpose for tonight. Tomorrow, if you wish it, there will be an opportunity for you to advertise your skills at one of the houses on the hill – perhaps at the castle itself.'

Orfeo was content to let the other be his guide, and they hired a room with two beds, with no third party to share. Having deposited their loads, they descended again to the main room of the inn, where the priest asked for a loaf of bread, a half-cheese and a jug of wine. He asked Orfeo to share the meal with him, and Orfeo agreed. No mention was made of this being payment for the assistance which Orfeo had offered on the road, though the cleric appeared to feel that his was the obligation.

They took a table in the corner, and put their knives to work in cutting the bread and the cheese. While they ate, Orfeo took stock of the surroundings. The room was cramped, the innkeeper having crowded in far more furniture than his present custom required. The only other customers as yet were five townsmen, three of whom were huddled about one table, engrossed in gambling with dice, while the other two sat together at another. These two made little pretence of conversation, and no secret of their curiosity regarding the two strangers, at whom they stared in a rude manner. Orfeo did not mind that – his way of life was to be looked at and listened to.

The innkeeper was sparing with his candles and the room was ill-lit. The black wooden beams which supported the ceiling seemed huge because of the shadows they cast in the spaces between them, and whenever a candle-flame flickered in a draught those shadows would move in a sluggish fashion which seemed oddly ominous. Though the room was quiet and the customers very ordinary, Orfeo could not help but feel that there was some tension just beneath the surface of things.

While they were still at their meal three newcomers arrived – men dressed in a uniform livery which Orfeo took to be that of the Duke's militia. They were plainly off-duty, but were wearing their swords nevertheless. They called for wine, and set to drinking it with the avidity of men whose sole intention was to become intoxicated, though one of them quickly deserted his comrades to join in the game of dice.

Two street-women came in then, and promptly joined the soldiers, accepting a meagre ration of their wine as a token fee in anticipation of negotiations to be later taken up. The women had spared the two strangers but a single glance, apparently losing interest when they saw that one was a priest, but Orfeo noticed that one of them cast several covert glances in his direction, measuring him carefully. He did not mind that – women usually liked him, and he loved to be liked by them – but he made no gesture of encouragement.

Arcangelo sipped his wine slowly. He had put his knife away when he finished his meal, and whenever he put his tankard down he knitted his bony fingers together and sat quite still – he was clearly no man for fidgeting.

The priest was in no hurry to go up to his bed, and though he seemed to be lost in private thought Orfeo observed that he was watching very carefully all that was happening in the room. Orfeo sat quite still also, with his hands in his lap, wondering what it was that his companion might be waiting for.

The shadows overhead moved languidly, as though they too were waiting.

Everything seemed dull and orderly, but Orfeo could feel something simmering behind the facade. Even so, he was most surprised when the change did come, by the rapidity with which two tiny seeds of dissent grew into an outburst of violence.

The soldier who was dicing had begun a losing streak the minute he sat down to join the game, and was cursing the dice as men often do in such circumstances, complaining that they had been bewitched to rob him. In the meantime the street-women, dissatisfied with the portion of the wine which had been given to them, were hinting that necessity might drive them to seek entertainment elsewhere. The one who had earlier studied Orfeo in a secret manner now began to do so more openly, in order to make an argument of her interest, but the soldiers did not take kindly to this gambit, and made resentful remarks about the relative worth of regular customers and fly-by-nights.

When these two arguments began to flare up, Arcangelo – who had let his hood fall back upon his shoulders – became much stiffer in his seat. It seemed to Orfeo that the priest was keenly interested to see how the quarrels would go.

They went badly. The soldier at the game turned his curses from the dice to the townsmen, who retaliated by suggesting that if he could not win he ought to search his own soul for evidence of the sin which had lost him all favour with the gods. Meanwhile the girl, impatient with the other guardsman, stood up in order to make good her threat to seek entertainment elsewhere, and was promptly pulled back with more than necessary violence.

Then the soldier at the game struck one of his fellow players with his fist, and the girl upturned a wine-jug on the head of her oppressor.

The dice-players moved hurriedly away from the table, clutching at coins and dice as the table was knocked over. The soldier dampened by the dregs of the wine – who was more insulted than soaked – changed his mind about pulling the girl towards him, and threw her away instead, with such force that she was catapulted across the room, tripping over one of the stools of which the room was overfull. She would have fallen heavily had not Orfeo risen swiftly to his feet and stepped forward to catch her.

Seeing this, the soldier who had thrown her reached for his sword. It was an instinctive action, and he probably did not intend to draw it, but one of the gamblers chose that moment to chase a rolling coin between the legs of a nearby stool, and pitched it over so that the seat caught the soldier a painful blow on the knee.

The man howled, and plainly felt that the sum of his indignities had now become too much to bear. He hauled the sword from its sheath and let out a loud cry of mingled anguish and anger, which was presumably intended to call his companions to arms.

Orfeo quickly placed the woman behind him, but did not reach for his own weapon; he had no wish to start a fight with servants of the Duke of Zaragoz. Instead he raised his hands in a placatory gesture. The enraged soldier took one step forward, but seeing that Orfeo was not disposed to fight he did not attempt to thrust at him with the sword, merely holding it in a threatening manner.

Arcangelo picked up his staff from the place where he had rested it and held it in front of him – not at all aggressively, but as if he sought to erect a symbolic barrier against the possibility of violence. The soldier's angry gaze flickered from Orfeo to Arcangelo, and then back again, and he said: 'Give the woman to me, or I'll take the pair of you into custody.'

This statement was loudly delivered in order to be heard above the din, but as it was pronounced the noise stopped, and the last few words fell into a deathly silence. The soldier turned, to see what had happened to still the hubbub.

The door of the tavern was wide open, and in the doorway were two gentlemen. Both were young, about nineteen or twenty years of age. Their dress was not sumptuous but there was no mistaking their quality. Each wore a rapier at his side. They looked around the room with affected disdain, their eyebrows deftly raised to signify surprise.

'A call to arms,' said one, icily, 'should not be raised in the course of a common brawl. Had it reached the ears of the officer of the watch, I believe there might be some here who would learn that lesson painfully.'

The gamblers who were scrambling about on the floor came slowly to their feet. The soldier sheathed his sword,

and mopped with his sleeve at the wine which was trickling down his forehead.

'Well and good,' said the youth. He lifted his hand, and
put out his forefinger. With the gentle pressure of that single finger he pushed the soldier out of the way, stepping
past him to confront Orfeo and the priest.

'I judge by your fair hair, sir,' he said to Orfeo, 'that you
are far from your homeland. No doubt you have been
lonely on the road, but you should not start a brawl in
Zaragoz over the favours of some common whore. Her like
is not in short supply, at this season.'

'I could not agree more, my lord,' said Orfeo, easily. 'I
did not seek to steal the pretty girl – she was hurled in my
direction. I was merely anxious that she should not hurt
herself by her fall. My name, sir, is Orfeo – I am a storyteller, and have some little skill with the lute, especially as
a player for the dance. I dance far better than I fence, and
would never seek to make a quarrel with such a sturdy
fighting-man as this one here.'

The sturdy fighting-man in question had the grace to
seem flattered by the compliment, and could not have sus-
pected how very insincere it was.

'I am glad to hear it,' said the gentleman. 'I am Don
Rodrigo Cordova, and my friend is Don Theo Calvi. If
what you say is true, then we are pleased to make your
acquaintance, for we have no dancing-masters among our
own poor players, and the Night of Masks approaches. I
see that you do not have your lute about you, or I would
ask that you play a song for us, to calm the heated tempers
here – but there is no room for dancing in any case.

'If you will come to my house tomorrow, I will give you
a better lodging than this, and a chance to show what you
can do.'

Orfeo bowed. 'You are very kind. I trust that I will be
able to find the way.'

'You will have no difficulty,' Cordova promised. 'I am
well-known in the town, and anyone will direct you.' He
looked then at the quarterstaff, which was still placed as a

barrier before the dark-cloaked priest. 'It is not often,' he observed, 'that we see a walking-stick as heavy as that one.'

'It is a Staff of Law,' said Arcangelo, coolly. 'I dare say that you have not seen its like before.'

Cordova raised his eyebrow again. 'I have heard of the Gods of Law,' he said. 'But in Zaragoz, our noble Duke is the law, and we look to our gods to guide our hearts. We have shrines dedicated to Verena, though – perhaps her clerics will give you a welcome, if you wish to seek your lost goddess within the confines of our humble realm. That is the mission which the priests of Law follow as they wander through the world, is it not?'

'There is a goddess named Arianka, whose prison is sought by some of my kind,' said Arcangelo. 'But we have other gods too, who inspire us in other ways.'

When he said this, Cordova's eyes narrowed slightly, and not in the same calculated way that his brow had been carefully raised. Orfeo was surprised by that, for he had not thought to find this kind of Estalian gentleman sufficiently familiar with the Gods of Law to take an inference from this remark.

It appeared that Cordova, like Orfeo himself, had jumped to the conclusion that the priest was a servant of Solkan, patron of witchfinders.

But the young man said nothing further on this matter, turning away instead to look at the townsmen and the soldiers, who had collected themselves by now and were watching closely.

'It is sad,' said Cordova, 'that those who are appointed to keep the Duke's peace should be so anxious to break it. If I hear of any more trouble in this quarter of the town, I will be forced to discuss it with the officer of the watch.'

Then he turned on his heel and went to the door, with Calvi following.

He glanced back only briefly, to meet Orfeo's gaze and favour him with the most unobtrusive of nods, to confirm that the storyteller should come to him on the morrow, and would be expected.

When the two noblemen had gone, the stools and tables which had been overturned were all set to rights. Orfeo heard resentful murmurs from some of the townsmen, who clearly had not liked Rodrigo Cordova's manner, but nothing was said aloud – which may have signified that there was more than the usual risk in expressing open resentment of the aristocracy of Zaragoz.

The three soldiers left abruptly, taking their custom else-where. One of the women went after them, but the one who had landed in Orfeo's arms would not follow her. Instead, she drew up a stool to sit at the table with the story-teller and the priest.

'I might have hurt myself,' she said, 'if you had not caught me.'

'So you might,' replied Orfeo. 'And we might all have taken a bruise or two, had it not been for that young man. Who is he?'

'A distant kinsman of the Duke, and friend of the Duke's son. He is said to be a favourite, and might one day marry Veronique, the Duke's daughter.'

'A fortunate prospect, no doubt,' said Orfeo.

'Oh yes,' she replied, 'Veronique is a great beauty. But some say that the Duke would do well to look further afield for a suitor, to make an alliance with another city.'

Orfeo thought it undiplomatic to enquire whether rumour said that the Duke might need alliance with another city in order to quell a rebellious spirit among his own people. Instead, he asked a safer question: 'And is this Cordova a lover of song and the dance? I hope I may look to him to treat me generously, for I am in sore need of a little coin.'

He saw that she took the hint, but he saw also that she did not really care about the state of his pocket.

'If you play well, sir,' she said, 'I am sure that there are those in Zaragoz who will take pleasure in your playing.'

And this was a prediction which seemed to be borne out, during that night at least.

* * *

NEXT MORNING, WHEN the sun had attained a comfortable height in the sky, Orfeo gathered his belongings together before setting out in search of Rodrigo Cordova's house.

He bid Arcangelo a pleasant goodbye, and apologized lest he should have kept the priest awake during the night. Arcangelo assured Orfeo that he had slept very well and wished him luck in his dealings with Cordova. It seemed, in fact, that the priest liked his new acquaintance, for his manner seemed more open than it had been while they walked along the road together, and he asked if he might offer a word of advice. Orfeo said that he would be glad to receive it.

'Zaragoz is a troubled kingdom,' said Arcangelo. 'That hill which you intend to climb is enmeshed by a web of intrigue whose complications you cannot begin to guess. Go carefully, my friend, and do not get caught by that web.'

'I thank you,' replied Orfeo, gravely. 'It happens that I have had some experience in the noble houses of Bretonnia, where webs of intrigue gather dust in every corner and corridor. I hope that I am adept in avoiding them.'

'I am glad to hear it,' said the man of Law, 'and I will be sorry if the trick of fate which brought us together on the road makes it difficult for you to follow my advice and exercise that skill.'

What the priest meant by this, Orfeo could not tell, but it caused him little anxiety as he set forth on his journey, because he did not expect to see the priest again.

Orfeo was not surprised to find that in order to reach the house where Cordova lived he had to carry his pack more than half way up the crag which loomed above the circlet of the city walls. Zaragoz was clearly a town where a family's standing in society was closely correlated with its elevation above the level of the plain. In noticing this, however, he could not help but observe that some of the houses which perched high upon the rock seemed precarious by comparison with those which were set below on baser ground. One or two, in fact, had fallen into ruins, and the wrecked towers had been given for nesting-sites to jackdaws, which clustered about them in noisy flocks, and to ravens, which soared above them in more solitary fashion.

The road by which he climbed the mount was a narrow one, scarcely wide enough in some places to take a tradesman's cart, and though it had a wooden rail erected on the outer edge it seemed less safe than it might have been made. A man who tried to ride a horse full-tilt from top to toe would certainly be hazarding his life, and a drunkard with his senses fuddled might easily find a way to fall to his death. But Orfeo was very sober, and the horses which passed him as he walked were picking their way most carefully, whether they were headed up or down.

There had been a moment when he waked after dawn when he had asked himself whether he really wanted to remain within the walls of Zaragoz, or whether he might better set himself on the road again – but having seen a little of the realm he had fallen prey, as he often did, to a certain curiosity about its people. He was, after all, a collector of stories, and in what he had so far been told of the city and its dour ruler he could sense the seeds of a tale. In any case, he had greatly admired the way in which Rodrigo Cordova, despite his tender years, had quelled the brawling in the tavern. In that youth, he felt, there was the promise of a brave and clever man.

The person in question received Orfeo most courteously, and did not trouble to put his playing to any test, but immediately offered him the hospitality of his house for the day and the night, on condition that he would sing for his supper and play for the dance thereafter. To this Orfeo readily agreed, and Cordova asked his steward to see him safely lodged in the servants' sleeping-quarters, which were the attics beneath the roof.

The room where he was placed was very tiny, but it had a real bed with legs instead of a straw pallet, and clean linen on it. A maid brought him warm water to wash himself, and when he had used it he put away the drab clothes in which it was his habit to travel, and put on brighter ones, more suited to the role which would be his that evening. Then – the steward having told him that he had the freedom of the kitchens and the narrow gardens around the house – he went downstairs again. He did not put on his sword, and kept his knife hidden beneath his tunic.

He ate a hearty breakfast, with better bread than he had tasted for many days – the grain imported to the mountain strongholds of Irrana was usually of disappointing quality, and the best of it had been reserved for men of better quality than he. Then he sat for a while and amused the kitchen boys with a joke or two, while keeping an appraising eye on the prettiest of the maids.

In the afternoon, Cordova sent for him. The steward, whose name was Cristoforo, took him up to the room where he would play in the evening.

The young nobleman was waiting for him, with three companions. One was a man of middle age, who wore his years better than most. Though plain of dress he was a man of some dignity and station, and though he wore no weapon he had the carriage of a warrior and the sharp eye of a predator. The others were women, though one might as well have been called a girl, as she seemed no more than eighteen years of age. She was very beautiful, especially her hair, which was a most remarkable dark red colour – a hue which he had never seen before, even in the north, where ruddy hair was far commoner than it was among the darker folk of Estalia. The other lady, who was much older, must have been equally handsome in her youth, though in the ordinary mould of Estalian folk.

'May I present the minstrel Orfeo,' said Cordova to the three, with a certain pride. 'I believe that I was fortunate to discover him, for he says that he is practised in playing for the dance.' To Orfeo he said: 'May I present the lady Veronique, daughter of the Duke of Zaragoz; the lady Marguerite Cordova, my mother; and Don Estevan Sceberra, a minister of the realm. The lady Veronique is enthusiastic to hear you play tonight – she has promised that her brother will come, and that she will do what she can to persuade her father the Duke to attend. We shall have a good company, and a fine evening.'

Orfeo bowed to the lady.

'You are a man of Bretonnia, I believe,' said Sceberra. 'Which town is your own?'

'I have been for some time in Bretonnia,' agreed Orfeo, 'but I do not belong to any particular town. Indeed, I was twelve or thirteen years old before I ever saw the wall of a town. Nor am I, begging your pardon Master Cordova, a minstrel. I could not presume to the skill of an elf, though my art serves well enough for the accompaniment of such songs as humans sing, and for the better forms of dancing, too.'

The lady Veronique smiled at this, but the man who had asked the question leaned forward with seeming impatience.

'How well do you know the spellcaster in whose company you entered the town?' he asked.

Orfeo made some display of his astonishment, though he was not entirely surprised to be asked the question, in view of what the priest had said to him when they parted.

'Why, not at all,' he said, glibly. 'I met him on the road by a signpost to the east of the city. He had come from another direction, and was being chased by rude fellows who had some silly notion of robbing him. Though they ran away, we thought it safer to stay together until we were within the shelter of the city wall. Even here, we may have been in difficulties, had the young lord not come to our rescue.'

The dark man frowned, and said: 'You have had a poorer welcome in our realm than we should like to give. We do what we can to discourage robbers and brawlers alike.'

'I know it,' replied Orfeo, smoothly. 'The measure of your discouragement was plain to see on the scaffold beside the signpost, on the very spot where the bandits tried their luck.'

The frown changed briefly to a scowl, but that expression was wiped away within an instant as the man controlled himself.

'I will have inquiries made,' he promised. 'I am entrusted by the Duke to maintain order in this realm, and the lady Veronique will think me a poor minister if I cannot do something in this matter.'

'Don Estevan,' said Rodrigo Cordova, mischievously, 'is the master of our secret police.'

Sceberra did not seem pleased with the description, but did not dispute it directly.

'It is my duty to discover the enemies of the realm,' he said, 'and to see that its bounds are secure. If a witchfinder comes to the town, the Duke is naturally interested to know his purpose, for he has his own wizards to preserve his people from such evil.'

'I do not know that Arcangelo is a witchfinder,' said Orfeo. 'He said nothing to me of serving Solkan, though I believe that Solkan is the most widely-followed of the Gods of Law.'

'Then you know something of this worship?' said Sceberra, his voice like the crack of a whip.

'I am a traveller,' said Orfeo, evenly. 'I meet many people, who worship many different gods. I know something of the gods of order, just as I know something of the Old Faith. I even know the names of such as Grungni and Liadrel, who are gods to other folk than human. Perhaps the priest is a servant of Solkan, but if he is, then good and honest men have no need to fear him. Perhaps he is in quest of Arianka's prison, despite what he said last night. I do not think he is a violent man – although he may have been ready to use his staff on the road and in the tavern, it was only in his defence, and he did not attempt to repel his enemies with magic, as some priests might have done.'

The minister was no more impressed by this than by anything else that Orfeo had said.

'Did he tell you where he came from?' he asked, coldly. 'Or whether he had been in Zaragoz before?'

'He did not tell me his birthplace,' Orfeo replied, 'but he did say that he had been in this city before, though not for many years.'

Having received this information, Sceberra straightened up, and then turned on his heel to walk away. He nodded briefly in the direction of the ladies, but did not favour Rodrigo Cordova with any such politeness.

'My apologies,' said Marguerite Cordova to Orfeo. 'He is only serving the Duke in the best way he can. Ours is a quiet realm, where the order of things changes very little. There is always anxiety when an unknown spellcaster comes here, especially when he serves a god we do not know. I am pleased to receive you in my son's house, and bid you welcome. Go now and occupy yourself until it is time for you to play, and we will have such a merry time this evening that even Don Estevan will be brought to smile.'

Orfeo bowed deeply and left the chamber. He was not dismayed by what had happened, but he was not entirely sure that the lady Marguerite's prediction was as safe as the last one he had heard. Don Estevan did not seem to be a man much given to smiling.

But when they dance, he reminded himself, even the sternest men may forget themselves for a little while – and whatever it is that Arcangelo has come to Zaragoz to do, I have only come to illuminate dull lives with music and excitement.

Three

WHILE RODRIGO CORDOVA'S guests ate their evening meal Orfeo sang to them, alternating ballads of courtly love with more lively songs whose narratives were a little bawdier, though he was careful to maintain the standard of politeness which was required of him.

While they ate and talked Cordova's friends did not really listen to his playing or his songs, and for the most part they seemed almost oblivious to his presence, but he did not mind – while they did not deign to notice him it was easier for him to observe them, which he did with intense interest.

Young Cordova sat at the head of the table, with his widowed mother at his right hand. The place at his left had been given to the Duke's son, Tomas, while the lady Veronique sat beside the lady Marguerite. Had the Duke himself been present he would have taken the head of the table, but if Veronique had actually made good her promise to ask him to come, her plea had not been heard.

Estevan Sceberra, on the other hand, was not only present but seemed to constitute such a powerful presence that he drew occasional anxious glances from almost everyone present. Master of secret spies he might be, but his own status was certainly no secret, and there were evidently many there who wondered whether he knew *their* secrets, whatever they might be.

The only other person Orfeo recognized was Theo Calvi, who had a lower place at the table – but Orfeo was glad to note that of those present Calvi seemed to be paying more attention to the music than almost any other, and actually seemed to be straining his ears to catch the words. At least three times while Orfeo watched him he bid the chattering girl at his side to be silent, and cease distracting him.

It was a compliment of sorts, and Orfeo was glad of it, for the only other person who was paying as much attention to his performance seemed not to be much interested in his tunes or his words, but only in his person. This was a lady seated close to Sceberra – above Calvi – whose considering stare had as much naked lust in it as Orfeo had seen in a woman of such quality. This too, he supposed, was a compliment for which he should be glad, though the lady was almost twice as old as Veronique diAvila, and not quite as comely in his eyes as the stately lady Marguerite.

There was a change of manner when they moved from the dining room to the ballroom. Eating was something which noblemen and peasants alike had done for centuries, in much the same fashion, but dancing was different. There had been dancing in olden times, of course, and the peasants had their jigs and reels, but the dancing of noblemen was very much a matter of fashion, and hence a measure of civilization.

Though Zaragoz might be reckoned by outsiders the least of all the principalities of Estalia, its haughty folk had this way to prove that they were as fine as the courtly gentlemen and ladies of Bilbali and Magritta: they could dance like the richest lords and the very highest kings, and hold their heads as proud as any while they trod the paces of brarle and the farandole. The meanness of their duchy was rooted in the meanness of its soil, but the pride of its rulers was elevated by their very modern ability to know a *ballo* from a *danza*, and to cope with its complicated changes.

Alas for Zaragoz, its native players – who were not travelling men – had far less opportunity than their masters to learn new tunes and dance-steps. No doubt the best of them could play well enough to guide the dancers in their paces, but there was none among them who could lead the company in line-dances, or take possession of the company by means of the seductive magic of fine music.

Now was the playing of Orfeo to be properly put to the test, and he knew it. As a measure of true artistry the test was nonsense, for he knew that there was more opportunity to show subtlety in the playing of sweet and plaintive lyrics than there was in twanging the rhythm of a dance, but it was his danceplay that these people cared about, and it was in this way he must serve them to the very best of his abilities.

So Orfeo played merrily and loudly, and led the parade in the steps of the line-dances, which he alternated with the couple-dances in which gentlemen and ladies aped the rigmaroles of courting birds.

It was a great success, and Orfeo watched Rodrigo Cordova shine with triumph at his discovery of this player who – though he was too modest to call himself minstrel – was very probably the best to be heard in Zaragoz for thirty years or more.

But there were two things that Orfeo noted which gave him cause for some anxiety.

One was the attitude of the lady who had watched him throughout the meal, who watched him now more eagerly still, her bright eyes like the eyes of a carrion crow perched upon the scaffold while the stink of the hanging was still upon the air. There was more than honest lust in that stare, and though there was admiration of a kind in it, his own preference was for soft but unbesotted faces, such as had been worn by the street-girl he had taken to his bed the night before.

The other cause which he had for mild alarm was the very different attitude of Estevan Sceberra, who seemed determined that he would not fulfil the promise made on his behalf by his amiable hostess. There was not a flicker of a smile upon his face, and though he was as careful in his steps as any other dancer on the floor he was not in the least committed to the dance, for its pleasure or its display.

Oh yes, Orfeo thought, this is a civilized court in a contented land, which bathes in the best of the sun's gold light – but there is something beneath this surface which is not so very civilized, nor so very contented, and I am as curious to know what it is as I am fearful to invoke it.

THE DANCING CAME to an end when the lady Veronique finally signalled to her dutiful host that she was tired. The company, seemingly well-pleased, applauded Orfeo for his confident play. He was confirmed in his opinion that he had done well when Tomas diAvila came to him and told him that the Night of Masks would be celebrated at the castle within the week, and asked him whether he would be content to join the musicians who would play there. Orfeo, suitably proud of himself, agreed that he would.

Rodrigo Cordova, equally pleased with the success of his discovery, asked Orfeo to continue the entertainment by telling a story. The footmen hurried back and forth with the chairs which they had earlier removed, bringing enough to seat the whole company. The large doors which led from the ballroom to the terrace were thrown open to let in the air of the night to cool the ruddy faces of the dancers.

Orfeo laid down his lute, and after a moment's thought he launched into a wild and fantastic tale, which he set for convenience in his native Bretonnia. It featured three magical objects, each of which seemed able to give great opportunities to its owner, but each of which carried a secret curse.

The first object was a mirror of truth, which would show the person who looked into it a true scene from his future. The curse on this mirror was that on the first two occasions when it was used by a new owner it would show a scene calculated to inspire hope and generate profit, but on the third it would discover a scene which would imply damnation and bring despair.

The second object was a magical sword which would make its owner powerful in battle. The curse on this sword was that on the first two occasions when it was drawn by a new owner it would protect him from harm and make a hero of him, but on the third it would be so bloodthirsty as to make him a reckless murderer, destroyer of all that he loved.

The third object was a pipe which summoned a daemon-slave who would perform miracles to instruction. The curse of this pipe was that on the first two occasions when it was used by a new owner the captive daemon would work to his advantage, but on the third, the daemon would possess the body of the hapless piper, and use it to wreak havoc in the world.

In Orfeo's story these objects came into the hands of a woman and her two suitors; one of the suitors used his gift greedily, and the other altruistically, so as to reveal the falseness of the first and the worthiness of the second. Orfeo so contrived his plot that as the climax of the story approached, and the three characters moved towards their third uses of the objects in their possession, it must seem certain to the listeners that all three were doomed and could not possibly be saved.

But then, by a paradoxical combination of the working of the three unfortunate gifts he managed to bring good out of evil, so that the false suitor's perfidy was revealed and the two lovers were united, to enjoy future happiness without magical aid.

It was, Orfeo admitted to his hearers, a very improbable story – but he reminded them that the great world, taken as a whole, was a very improbable place, and he was sure

that many stranger things happened there than the ones
which he had described.

At least some of those who had listened were prepared
to agree with him, and there were those who applauded
the story vigorously. Among those who did not – whose
amusement was mingled with contempt – were Estevan
Sceberra and the woman whose name he did not know.
However, the fact that the lady had not liked his story overmuch had not served to lessen the lustful admiration in
her stare, and when he had finished she walked towards
him, evidently bent on conversation.

Before the woman had a chance to speak, though, there
was an interruption. A sharp voice cut through the chatter
of the company like an icy knife, compelling silence.

'That was a very fair story, my friend – but it has little to
say to the people of Zaragoz, and there are those here who
could not take kindly to its lesson.'

Before the unknown woman turned away from him to
see whose voice this was Orfeo saw a strange expression
cross her face: an expression of shock and disbelief which
struck the colour from her cheeks in an instant. He was
certain that the woman had recognized the voice.

The speaker was standing before the doors which had
been opened to admit the dry night air. It was Arcangelo,
the priest of Law, with his hood thrown back to reveal his
bony face and his bald head. In his hand he gripped his
plain staff, holding it vertically beside him.

Sceberra started up from his chair with a curse, his hand
on the hilt of his sword, but Rodrigo Cordova had stood
up beside him, and quickly put out a hand to keep him
back.

'No, Don Estevan,' he said, mildly. 'This is a cheerful
evening, and I would not like it to be spoiled. If we are to
have one more guest, then let us make him welcome. In a
louder voice he called to the priest: 'Enter my house, friend
– and if you have a better story to tell us, whose lesson has
more to teach us, pray tell it. I am sure we can all be grateful for good instruction.'

Arcangelo came forward, but only a few paces. He stood on the carpet where the company had danced, five yards from any gentleman or servant, and did not seem inclined to come too close. Orfeo watched Sceberra, and saw him make a clandestine signal after glancing upwards. Following the direction of the minister's glance, Orfeo saw that there was a small balcony at one end of the room, curtained behind. Though he was not quick enough to see who had stood there he could see the curtains still astir, and knew that someone had gone out through a doorway – presumably to fetch assistance. Sceberra, it seemed, was not prepared to deal with the spellcaster with only such help as he had ready to hand.

'I can tell you a tale,' Arcangelo said, in a voice which was now less chilling. 'A tale of Zaragoz. A tale in which this very house is featured – aye, and others you will know. A tale of betrayal, which happened long ago, but whose tangled threads extend, as the threads of treason always do, across the years and the centuries to the present day. Will you hear it, my lord Cordova?'

'Aye,' said Cordova. 'Why not?' But his tone, though light, had a note of threat in it, which said that although he had offered hospitality to this enigmatic visitor, he would tolerate no abuse of his invited guests.

'Once,' said Arcangelo, gravely, 'there was a duke of this realm who ruled it well – better than any before or after him. His justice extended beyond the ordinary business of punishing the guilty, and much that he did was reckoned to improve the lot of the poorest people of the land. I call this justice because that is what he called it, for he would not have it called charity that he tried to better the condition of the worst of his subjects; instead he owned that when any man suffered in his realms, the whole realm was poorer for it, and that when any was hurt, the whole was injured.

'Alas for the poor, and alas for the realm itself, the work which he did to raise up the poor was seen by the wealthy as a thing which threatened their own position, and to this end they plotted to be rid of their duke.

'This was not an easy thing to do, for there never was a duke who had such loyalty and devotion from his servants, and from those of his soldiers who were of common birth. In addition to these advantages the duke had good magicians by his side, whose powers of divination were considerable, and who brought him warning whenever evil stirred upon the slopes of the mount.

'Nevertheless, the plot was brought to fruition, with the aid of foul magic and fouler treachery. The duke was toppled, and his most loyal followers slain by the score.

'This end was achieved, in part, by the treachery of one that the duke thought was his trusted friend – a learned man, who discovered more about the history of this peculiar mountain than had formerly been suspected by those who built a castle here and called it Zaragoz. Those who leagued themselves against his wizards and diviners could only hide themselves by making pacts with daemons and pleading for the favour of forbidden gods, but those who hated the duke and his justice were not ashamed to do it.

'The castle of Zaragoz was legendary then as now, as a citadel which could never be taken, by virtue of its high position and the sheerness of the rock on which it stood. It was said in the land that once justice reigned within that fortress then its rule would be absolute and unassailable, but to the great misfortune of the land, it was not so. This rock which seems so solid is rotten at the core, full of caves and hollows, and there was a secret way into the castle – not from the plain, where the common folk live, but from one of the noble houses which cling to the slopes.

'From *this* house the castle could be reached – aye, and breached as well, by a creeping army which did not mind the darkness and need not fear the dire things which haunted that darkness. An army which had the favour of evil things came treacherously from below, to seize the castle and depose the duke. Though the battle was short and easily won, much bloodshed followed as the usurpers murdered all who seemed to pose a threat to their rule... but they could not murder everyone who had loved the rightful duke, the man of justice, because there would scarce have been a kingdom left for them to rule. They killed the strongest, and the bravest, and the most virtuous, but sought only to cow the rest by taking away their hope, by proving to them that justice never could return, and that where right had once been indomitable, might was now unconquerable in its place.

'So swift had been their victory that none could strike back at the traitors – not even the virtuous wizards who had taken the good duke's cause. But even as those wizards died or fled, they cursed the evil which had overwhelmed them. They cursed this house, that its secret ways should never again be used in the cause of evil, and that should dark magic ever be worked inside its walls, the walls themselves must awake and rally to the cause of justice. And they cursed the house of diAvila with a promise that one day that house would be brought to the wretched fate which it had earned by its deceit.

'All this happened a long time ago, and many generations of noblemen and commoners have come and gone. It might seem that the one-time reign of justice has been forgotten, and that the hope of its return has been eclipsed. But this is not the whole truth; for there are two things we must remember in considering this history. One is that a citadel once captured can never again be reckoned truly unassailable; the other is that hope for the future can never truly die, for when men think themselves robbed of it, it really remains imprisoned in their hearts, waiting for the key which can unlock it.

'In Zaragoz, that key is but a single word, and when the time is ripe for that word to be cried aloud it will leap from mouth to mouth in an instant, and raise such a hue and cry that the rock itself will shake, and the houses which cling to it will crumble, and the castle itself will fall into ruins, only to rise again when the hand of justice is put to the work of its rebuilding.

'That word which is the key I would speak now, but there is no need – for the time which is not yet come will come soon enough, and there can be none here who does not know, in his heart of hearts, what that word is.'

As he said 'none here' Arcangelo's eyes met Orfeo's, for the briefest of moments, as if to say that even he, the stranger, knew what word he meant. And Orfeo, remembering what Arcangelo had said to him on the road, realized that he did indeed know what word it was.

When Arcangelo had finished speaking, there was a long moment of silence. It was broken by Estevan Sceberra, who said with a sneer: 'Not a priest, after all, but a prophet. I have heard of such, who cry woe to the world and are forever threatening destruction. Madmen all!'

'If I am mad,' said Arcangelo, 'then madness is come among you, and will tear your world apart. I come to warn you all that the choice is soon to be made, and that those who side with diAvila against the claims of justice will die as the friends of justice once died. Only those who will let the word undo the lock which is in their hearts can possibly be saved. If justice cannot come again to Zaragoz, then I promise you that Zaragoz is doomed!'

'Enough of this treason!' said Sceberra, hotly and contemptuously. He turned then to Rodrigo Cordova, and said: 'Have I your permission to seize the rogue?'

The question was put in such a way as to imply no possibility of refusal, and Cordova, whose face was drained of its colour, nodded – though with no great relish.

Sceberra drew his sword at last, and so did three others of the company, while six armed men in the livery of the Duke came through the open doors behind the priest. But as they reached out to seize their quarry, what had seemed a simple task dissolved into confusion.

Arcangelo lifted his plain staff into his two hands, as a man does when using such a weapon in a fight, and lashed out forward and behind with its two ends.

Orfeo knew that a heavy blow from such a rod could knock a man down, but he also knew that a man who sought to use it in a crowd would quickly find it seized and rendered harmless. He expected to see one or two of the

swordsmen take a tumble, but thought that the rest would
soon disarm their enemy.

Alas for the swordsmen, it was not so – they seemed as
they tried to close in to have become uncommonly clumsy,
and fell about before the passes of the staff in a fashion
that was almost clownish. The odds were ten to one, and
yet the dancing staff wove such a pattern about the priest
that none could lay a hand on him – and those assailants
who did not trip over their own feet were sure to trip over
another's. As fast as they rose they were put down again,
and Orfeo was not the only onlooker who burst into
laughter at the sight.

Only Sceberra kept his feet during the first bout of tumbling, but when he tried a thrust with his sword it was
effortlessly parried, and though he tried to fence and draw
the staff into single combat he could not do it, and was
sent dizzily staggering away.

The melee was so tightly packed that the tumbling men-
at-arms blocked any possible attempt at escape which
Arcangelo might have made, but Orfeo quickly saw that
the priest had no intention of trying to make for the door,
being quite content to stand his ground and make fools of
those who sought to arrest him.

Orfeo realized also that there was more in this comedy
of errors than immediately met the eye. As it extended he
became quite certain that it was no mere silliness on the
part of the attackers which condemned them to play the
buffoon. Here, for the first time, the spellcaster had put his
magic on display, and though it was a petty spell laid at no
great cost it was nonetheless a demonstration of considerable cleverness. Most magicians, so far as Orfeo had had
the chance to observe them, were content for their magic
to have its effect, and used it relatively brutally; Arcangelo
possessed a delicacy of deployment which he had rarely
encountered.

Sceberra too must have realized that there was artistry at
work, for he showed no anxiety to hurl himself back into
the fray when he had once been spun out of it. Instead he

paused, touching his head as if to check for a bleeding wound, and then looked up at the gallery. Orfeo looked up too, and saw that a man was standing there, patiently watching the farce which was playing upon the dance-floor.

As soon as he caught sight of the man Orfeo knew that this was a magician, and a very dangerous one. He was as tall as Orfeo, but even thinner (though Orfeo was himself a slender man). He seemed far older, his face being very dark and wizened, the features subtly warped into a dreadful living mask. His hair was very thin, and quite white.

Sceberra, having made certain that the wizard was there, called out to his men, telling them to fall back.

This order was by no means an easy one to obey, for Arcangelo continued to ply his staff, tripping and tumbling the swordsmen as they attempted to retreat in disarray, but the circle around him gradually widened, until none was any longer within his reach, and when that moment came he put up his staff. A subtle smile played upon his lips, but Orfeo could see that he did not overestimate his triumph.

Arcangelo raised his head to look at the magician in the gallery, staring insolently, as though to taunt this new opponent.

The other was not disposed to give Arcangelo any chance to amuse his audience further – without any preliminary he stretched forth a hand and unleashed the power of his will in a blast whose force was felt throughout the room.

Arcangelo moved like lightning to lift his staff, holding it two-handed before him, above the level of his head. If this was intended to make the staff take the full force of the blast it succeeded, but if Arcangelo hoped that the staff would then prove an efficient shield, he had overestimated his own resources. The blast shattered the staff into a dozen pieces, hurling the shards to the four corners of the room with such velocity that several ladies screamed and almost everyone turned away, shielding their faces with their arms. Only Sceberra, Orfeo and Rodrigo Cordova resisted the impulse to flinch and turn.

Orfeo had seen magical contests before, but never had he witnessed such a violent outburst of power calculated solely to destroy. He knew enough of magic to understand what enormous effort went into the production of such blasts, and he felt sure that this one could easily have drained sufficient power from its sender to render him insensible, if not to kill him. Yet when he looked up at the balcony, he saw that the magician was still standing straight and tall, holding his expression as rigid as his bones and sinews. Only his eyes moved, and though the distance between them made it difficult to be sure, Orfeo thought that there was a hint of anxiety in the moving gaze.

Orfeo remembered what Arcangelo had said about the effects of working evil magic within the walls of this house, but when he looked about him he could see no difference. He looked back at Arcangelo, thinking to see him burned and broken, but although the priest had been knocked flat his limbs were stirring feebly, and he emitted a faint groan.

No one else moved, so Orfeo went quickly to the stricken man, and picked up his heavy head in his own hand, turning him on to his side so that he would not choke. Within a minute, he was sure that the priest would live, but he was equally sure that the man had been sorely hurt and that all the inner strength had been blasted out of him. Clever spellcaster he might be, but he would be casting no spells at all for some considerable time.

While he still knelt by the injured priest Orfeo felt the point of Sceberra's blade come to rest upon his back, between his shoulder-blades.

'Now, my lanky popinjay,' said the minister. 'I think the time has come when we must make more urgent enquiries about your acquaintance with this man, and your involvement with his treason.'

Orfeo looked up. 'I told you that I did not know him,' he said, calmly. 'It is still true.' Then he looked at Rodrigo Cordova, hoping for support.

The youth seemed uncertain, and was clearly shocked by what had taken place. After a pause for thought he shook

his head. 'You may question him if you think you must,' he
said to Sceberra, 'but not brutally. I believe that he is innocent, and I would not have any needless injury done to
such skilful hands. If the truth of what he says must be
properly tested, then Semjaza must use *his* art to do it.'

Orfeo felt a thrill of relief when he heard these words,
but when he looked again at Sceberra, he saw that the man
was not entirely displeased – and then he knew that whoever Semjaza might be, the attentions of his art were not so
very much less to be feared than cruder tortures.

Perhaps, he thought, sourly, it will not be as easy to
avoid the sticky clutches of this web of intrigue as I supposed.

Four

ORFEO WAS TAKEN to the castle of Zaragoz as a prisoner, but
he was not treated roughly, nor were his hands bound.

The approach to the gate of the fortress wound about the
crag, but was not quite as steep as the lowest part of the
road. The fortress was laid out in the conventional rectangular fashion, with a tower at each corner, but the manner
of its building had been constrained by the contours of the
crag on which it was perched. For this reason, the walls
were not at all straight, meandering in both the vertical
and the horizontal dimension. The north tower – which
one of the men-at-arms in charge of him referred to as the
High Tower – loomed above its counterparts, while the
one which faced south had by far the lowest elevation.

When the party passed through the gate Orfeo saw that
the space within the walls was no more level nor evenly
sloped than the ramparts; where conventional design
placed a courtyard there was instead a series of giant irregular steps, each one having two or three flights of stairs

sculpted into it, and two of the larger vertical faces having
doorways which gave access to chambers hollowed out
within the stone.

The living quarters erected within the castle – including
the stables – were extended from the east and west towers.
These two towers were on much the same level, connected
by the widest of the natural ledges. Orfeo had little chance
to study the scene in detail, though, because he was
quickly taken to the door of the High Tower, and guided
up a narrow stair to a doorway with a small barred window. Beyond this door was a guard, posted in a narrow
corridor where two doors faced one another, each one
with a sturdy bolt and a small hinged square cut at eye-
height so that the guard could look in if he so wished.

This place was certainly a prison, but it was not the lowly
kind of dungeon in which a common man might be
shackled. When Orfeo was taken into the room where he
was to be kept he saw that it was a cell designed for one
above his own station, with a chair and table as well as a
bed, a good supply of candles and a chamber pot.

The men-at-arms who had brought him there left him to
his own devices, but those who were coming to put him to
the question were not long delayed, and Orfeo was not
surprised to find that Sceberra was accompanied by the
magician who had felled Arcangelo.

Seen at close quarters, the wizard was a more fearful
sight than he had seemed from a distance. The colour of
his flesh was very odd, having about it far more redness
than one would expect to find in a man of such dark hue.
His eyes, which gaped so wide at all times that a rim of
bloodshot white was always visible about the iris, were
likewise dark and red in colour. His nose was thin and the
nostrils were reduced to tiny slits, and his mouth was per-
petually crooked. But that was not the whole of it, for it
was as if he came with a kind of aura – a radiance given off
by some unearthly inner fire. When he breathed there was
a strange scent on his exhalation, which seemed to Orfeo
a graveyard odour.

Here, thought Orfeo, is a man who is corrupted, and not by any ordinary sin. There is something of the daemon in his deeper being.

He saw that the man sensed his dismay, and was pleased by it, for it confirmed his power – but he also saw that the sorcerer was tired, and that the blast which he had hurled at Arcangelo had taken more out of him than he would have wished.

Sceberra ordered a liveried servant to bring more chairs, so that he and the magician could sit by the table with their captive guest, facing him with all the fierceness and determination which they could muster for his intimidation.

'I am Semjaza,' said the magician, 'the Duke's friend and chief adviser. I think you can tell well enough what manner of man I am?'

Orfeo nodded his head, but only a little. It signified agreement, not respect for the other's station.

'Loyal Don Estevan would like to try another way to make you speak,' the wizard continued, 'but we would not like to offend Don Rodrigo, and we have assured the lady Veronique that should you prove to be our ally and not our enemy, then you will play for us on the Night of Masks, which is some few days hence. In view of these considerations, I have agreed to test you in my own way. Will you give me your hand?'

Orfeo hesitated, but then reached out to offer his right hand, palm upwards.

The magician took it in his own, which was claw-like and nearly black. The fingers felt like snakeskin, and had the same surprising warmth about them. Then, with his other hand – the left – Semjaza made a few slow passes over the upturned palm, describing symbols whose meaning Orfeo did not know.

After a moment's contemplation, Semjaza reached out that same left hand to touch Orfeo lightly on the forehead. The reptilian fingers rested there for some two minutes before the magician removed them.

'You are no dolt,' said Semjaza, evenly, 'but we expected a man with some strength of mind. I do not think you have any magic, unless you have learned a few petty tricks which do not matter, but you have a strong will which has been schooled to some degree of resistance. Have you lived among elves, perchance?'

Orfeo started in surprise, and said: 'I was taken in by wood elves as a child, when they found me in such condition that I would otherwise have died.'

Semjaza nodded. 'Of course,' he said, as though it had been so obvious to his touch that he had not really needed to ask.

'They must have taught you a little of the art of the minstrel – I regret now that I did not hear you play, but I will surely have a second chance. Do you believe that I will know if you lie to me?'

The last question was asked abruptly, fired like a missile into what had been a laconic speech. The sorcerer was fatigued, and would perhaps have preferred not to use his talents further until he had recovered his strength, but he was determined that Orfeo should not be let off lightly on that account.

'I do not believe that you can read my mind,' said Orfeo, 'but I think you would sense it if I tried you with outright deceit.'

'A wise reply,' said Semjaza, with apparent sincerity. 'No one can overhear the thoughts in another man's head, save perhaps the god to whom he prays, but a man of power can weigh the feelings in another man's heart, if he has the wit. Now, when did you first meet the one who calls himself Arcangelo?'

'Yesterday, when my route met his, within sight of this citadel.'

'Good. I am glad to hear it. What did he tell you of his plans?'

'Nothing at all – until I listened with Don Estevan to the speech which he made in Don Rodrigo's ballroom.'

'Are you a servant of the Gods of Law?'

'I am not – though I am not entirely out of sympathy with their cause.'

This answer made Semjaza smile a little, but he did not seem wholly displeased by it.

He touched the player again upon the forehead, and Orfeo was convinced that he could feel the power in those fingertips.

'And how much do you know of those whose cause the Gods of Law oppose?' asked the wizard. Orfeo was surprised by the whimsicality of that question, which seemed rhetorical, and certainly was not conducive to the rendering of an exact answer.

'Very little,' he answered, 'and that uncertain. In the Empire, they have a saying: *Those who know do not speak; those who speak do not know.* I am a story-teller, and have listened to many stories. I do not believe the ones I tell, let alone the ones I hear.'

The interlude was brief, for the magician's next question was rapped out as sharply as his first: 'Have you any reason to hate the Duke of Zaragoz, or any that are loyal to him?'

'I have not,' said Orfeo promptly. But that answer drew a sharper look from his interlocutor, and he quickly elaborated: 'I know nothing of the Duke or his realm save what I have seen these last two days. Nor am I the kind of man who quarrels with the people of the lands through which he must pass. But I must in honesty say this – that if I were told the story which Arcangelo told tonight, wherever I might be in the world, then my sympathies would be with the just lord who was deposed, not with the others who displaced him. For all I can tell, the story was only a story, but I judged from the reaction of one or two who were present at its telling that there is truth in it. Nevertheless, the man of Law advised me not to involve myself with the intrigues of the men of Zaragoz, and that is advice which I certainly intend to take.'

Semjaza still held Orfeo's right hand in his own, and now he touched it again with the fingers of his left. Then he released it, and sat back. He looked sideways at Sceberra.

'An honest man,' he said. 'He would have told your tor-
turers no more, and they would never have known
whether a word of it was true.'

Sceberra scowled. 'I suppose I must be satisfied,' he said,
'if you tell me so.'

Semjaza looked back at Orfeo again. 'May I ask one
more question? I ask permission now, because now that I
have judged you honest you are a guest again, and not a
prisoner – the Duke's son has invited you to the castle, and
I understand that you have agreed to his proposal.'

'Ask your question,' said Orfeo, gruffly.

'The man of Law referred to a word – a word which
might unlock false hope in the hearts of those men of
Zaragoz who do not love their Duke as they should. Do
you know what that word is?'

'Not for certain,' said Orfeo, truthfully. 'But there was a
name which he used in idle conversation while we walked
the road together. I suspect that may be the word he
meant.'

Semjaza leaned forward suddenly, so that his foul
breath was very noxious in Orfeo's nostrils. 'Do not use
that word!' he said. 'If you value your life, do not let it
pass your lips. If you hear it whispered, turn away, and
put it from your mind. In Zaragoz we welcome honest
men, but while you are in this realm you must recognize
its lawful duke, who is Marsilio diAvila. Through no fault
of your own, you know more than is good for you, and
must now be careful. When the Night of Masks comes,
play your lute with all the skill which your elven tutors
could impart, and lead our courtiers in a happy dance –
but do not meddle in matters which do not concern you.'

'A wise traveller does not meddle,' Orfeo told him, quietly. 'A wise traveller learns what he can, and goes on his
way, raising his hand against no man unless that man
raises a hand against him.'

Semjaza stood up, and just for a moment there was a
hint of unsteadiness in his manner, as though his old
bones were aching.

'Wise man,' he said. 'Wise, and honest. I think that something might be made of a man like you, my friend, and so I will say one thing more to you: do not be tempted to confuse law and justice. The man of Law who claims to stand for justice is a cheat. If you would serve justice, take Verena for your patroness, and shun the champions of Solkan, who are bitter and uncaring men.'

With that parting shot, Semjaza left the room, but Estevan Sceberra did not immediately follow him. Instead, the minister waited in his seat until the sound of the magician's footsteps had completely died away. Then he stood up himself, and leaned forward to emphasize his words.

'You are a man of wit,' he said, thinly, 'to win the favour even of that monster. Everyone loves you, it seems. Well, pretty player, I do not – and I feel it in my stony heart that I may yet have the chance to tease your tender flesh after all. Should that time come, I promise that you'll pay for all your wit and prettiness.'

Orfeo leaned back, casually, but did not lower his eyes before the minister's hostile stare.

'Poor Don Estevan!' he said. 'You should not be so resentful of your failings. There is many a man of your station who is deaf to a lovely tune and cannot dance a lissome step. I would try to teach you, but I fear you are too tense in mind and limb.'

For a second, Orfeo thought that Sceberra might lose control so completely as to strike him – but this was not a reckless man, however ugly his temper might be. In the end, the minister tried to smile instead.

'You may have no reason to hate the rulers of Zaragoz,' he said, 'but you must still beware of giving them cause to hate you.'

'I think the wizard has told me that already,' replied Orfeo, 'and I am certain that I would be very foolish to make an enemy of him.'

Sceberra conceded him that last word, but put a punctuation mark to the dialogue by slotting the bolt on the further side of the door. Orfeo did not care about that,

though it could surely be reckoned an insult to one who
was once again a guest, but when he thought over what he
had said, he regretted being so wounding with his words.
He had gained nothing by his churlishness, and had
inflamed a hostility which he might have calmed had he
made his words more soothing.

Reckless Orfeo, he said to himself, as though using the
voice of another. *Poor headstrong human boy. What can possibly be done with him?*

That reminded him of what the sorcerer had said, about
there being 'something that might be made of him,' and he
shuddered. He had little enough knowledge of the gods
and demi-gods which that man served, but he knew
enough to have a sensible idea of what those gods and
demi-gods made of their worshippers. He hoped, in his
heart, that nothing ever would be made of him by such as
they, because he had reason to believe that they were very
treacherous servants, and the cruellest masters imaginable.

HE LAID HIMSELF down upon the bed, eventually, though he
did not immediately try to go to sleep. He lay on his back,
alone with his own thoughts, assessing the story of his
own life and finding it somewhat lacking in pace and plot,
despite that it was not devoid of action and suspense.

He sat up again, abruptly, when he heard the bolts of his
prison drawn back.

He had to shield his eyes for a moment against the light
which came in. It was an unnatural light created by petty
magic, but it burned no brighter than an ordinary lantern,
and he could not admire a person who made magic when
ordinary means would do, merely to display his skill – or,
in this case, her skill.

It was the unknown woman who had cast such covetous
eyes upon him while he played and danced.

She looked down at him now, with the same avidity in
her gaze.

'We were rudely interrupted,' she said, 'when I came to
speak to you before. But we will not be interrupted now.'

Orfeo studied her carefully. She was handsome in her way, though no longer young. It was not easy to guess her age, because he had a strong suspicion that she might be older than she seemed. There were no crow's-feet by her eyes or wrinkles in her neck, but there was something in her manner which gave her away. Her full lips were carried slightly forward, as in a perpetual slight pout, or as though she were about to lick them in anticipation of some tasty sweetmeat.

He judged that she was a sensualist through and through, and though she shared something of Semjaza's dark artistry it was plain that she employed her magic to different ends.

'My name is Morella d'Arlette,' she told him, while she still stood over him. 'It is a Bretonnian name, as you will doubtless know, but my mother married for a second time, to a nobleman of Zaragoz. I was afraid to come here when I was a child, for the journey was so long and the hills so steep, but I love it now, and am proud to have adopted it as my home.'

She knelt down then, and put out her hand to touch his forehead, almost as Semjaza had done. He felt the warmth of her fingers, and something else, which made him pull away.

'You have little faith in your charms, my lady,' he said, 'if you think you need your sorcery on a mission such as this.'

She laughed. 'Oh no,' she said, 'it was not a bewitchment of *that* sort. I can see in your eyes and your arms that nothing lacks in your enthusiasam for love. But I doubt that you have ever had a sorceress before, and I suppose you do not know what a little art can add to the experience.'

He hesitated just a little, but she *was* handsome in her way, and he was not usually a man to refuse what was freely offered. Even the thought of her magic, and its possible source, did not inspire such fear that it dampened his desire entirely, now that he could smell her hair and see the curve of her breast.

He was still afraid of her, but he was curious too.

'Do you seek to spoil me for other women, then?' he whispered, as she placed her body closer to his. 'Is it your intention that no other night of my life will ever compare with this one?'

'Of course,' she said. 'It is too long since I had a fair-haired man, and for all that I love this place, it becomes tedious to visit the same beds too often. Let me enchant you, just a little, and *I* promise you *no* disappointment. I will teach you the true meaning of luxury, without detracting at all from your strength.'

She took his hand then, and placed it inside her blouse, as if to tempt him with the beating of her hungry heart. He felt the curve of her breast, which encouraged his own desire.

The touch took his fear away, and the uneasy feeling which had come over him when first he saw her watching him seemed foolish now. She was only a woman, after all.

'I need no magic,' he whispered to her, as his fingers began to tease her flesh. 'I suppose that you have grown so used to these moody Estalians, that you have forgotten what the men of our own nation are like. Bretonnians, my lady, have always known the meaning of luxury in love. Let us play our tunes with ordinary skills, and I promise you no disappointment.'

At that she laughed, and seemed to agree, but when she climbed on top of him and he relaxed his wits, she brought her magic to bear after all, and when he felt the ecstatic thrills which she set to running through his body, he was not sorry that she had defied him.

He was consumed by fierce sensation, whose intoxications drew him to extraordinary efforts. The taste of her sweat was sweet upon his tongue, and her caresses were empowered by her magic to reach into the very core of his being. She shuddered and shrieked with the pleasure of it. In that long moment, while he struggled to hold her, he longed for magic of his own which might allow him access to such ecstasy.

Indeed, when at last they lay still together, he wondered in the contentment of his satiation whether he might not have spoken truer than he knew, and that this might be a memory to make many future nights seem dull. But the excitement ebbed away, and the sweetness upon his tongue turned to a bitter aftertaste.

He had always thought of love making as a kind of music, better when it was played as a duet than as a game of soloist and instrument. The girl who had lain with him the previous night made a living by offering herself as paid instrument, but she had come to him freely as a player, and though she had had no magic to thrill her as the lady Morella had thrilled, there had been artistry as well as honesty in her enthusiasm. Tonight, *he* had taken the instrumental part while his lover merely used him – and all her magic would not serve now to make him glad that he had been used.

He knew, furthermore, that with the morning light his memory would fade, and that when passion came to take hold of him again, even if it were inspired by a tired street-girl seeking comfort in his arms, that moment would drive all others from his mind. The present would always drown out the past: that was what gave lust its privileged place in human affairs. He was tempted to languish in the fullness of his feeling, but the opportunity to be inquisitive seemed too good to miss, and he thought that this lady Morella might be in a better mood now to feed his curiosity than any other he was likely to meet.

So he said to her: 'What have they done with the priest?'

She stirred in his arms, and gave a little laugh. 'They have not killed him yet,' she said. 'They will save him for a while, to make a pleasant morsel for one who will not care that his meat is less than tender.'

She said it warmly, almost lasciviously, but the meaning of the words struck a chill into Orfeo's heart.

He resolved that he must hide his disgust, though, for he thought that she would tell him more if he followed the tide of her feeling.

'He will be food for daemons, then?' he said, as though it were a light matter. 'I had thought that their kind would not like the taste of a man of Law.'

'Oh no,' she said, with a liquid chuckle, 'that is the taste they love best of all. To feast upon the flesh of an enemy is e'er to make a satisfying meal.'

'It had not occurred to me,' he admitted. 'Perhaps there are luxuries of life which I have not tasted yet.'

'Oh yes, there are,' she said, wallowing in her contentment. 'A man like you could make so *much* of them, if only you cared. There is a god of luxury, you know – I cannot tell you what a joy it was to find that out. You are a clever lover, I concede, but a novice in the true art of ecstasy. I have given you a taste tonight, but I swear to you that you cannot imagine the harvest of pleasure which an adept may reap, if only he has the will, and knows the way.'

'I have heard of the way,' said Orfeo, in a small and distant voice. 'But it is one I have not cared to follow. You knew the priest of Law, did you not, when you saw him come into the hall? I saw that you recognized his voice.'

She was a little surprised by this, but not discomfited.

'I met him once in Gualcazar,' she said, 'when I undertook a small mission on the Duke's behalf. I did not think that he would care to face Semjaza a second time, but it seems that I was wrong.'

There was much left unsaid in this speech, but Orfeo did not dare to become too precise in his questions, because whatever he said to the sorceress would surely be reported to Sceberra, and to Semjaza as well. He had spoken the truth when he said that it was not his intention to involve himself in this affair.

'Semjaza told me you had travelled far, and were not born blind, so to speak,' said the lady Morella, when she saw that he did not mean to ask another question. 'And you have that appetite for love in you that a wanderer should have. A commoner by birth you are, but not so very common in mind and soul. I knew when I heard you play that you were no man of Law, and I knew that when we made love the pleasure would carry you away. Law is all hard discipline and sullen strength, and you were not made for such a life as that!'

'But I was not made for Chaos, either,' he said, softly.

'You know that name! You are as clever as I had supposed. But you do not know what lies behind the name, nor can you. I dare say that you heard it from the lips of some disdainful elf, who spoke of it as though it were something dwarfish, not fit for those who know the meaning of beauty and sublimity. But did you not sometimes hear your vainglorious woodsmen say the word human in much the same way, as though spitting it out from their mouths like a vile taste? You are not an elf, my love, as I know to my reward. You are one who might gain much from the powers which I command – and should know that without some spirit of disorder the world would be dead and dull, and humans little more than halfling dimwits. There is a touch of Chaos in all men, my darling Orfeo, and were you to cut it out of a soul like yours it would be as if you had severed the hand which plucks the strings of your lute.'

'You are right to say that I know little of Chaos but that which is contained in fearful stories which men tell to frighten one another,' he said, 'but I have known those who would call you daemon-led, and seek to sentence you to death by fire.'

He said it grimly, careless as to whether she took offence, but she only laughed with apparent good humour.

'All men die by fire, dear Orfeo,' she said. 'Some burn more quickly than they like, on a witchfinder's pyre, but all are in the end consumed. Life is fire, my lover, and we begin to die in its subtle flames before we are even born. Those who know how to live must learn the secrets of the fire which they are, and the ember which they must become. Our bodies are filled with mordant fluids which sear our flesh as we move, and use us up while the clocks tick away our litle measure of existence. There is no fate but fire, my love, but the luckiest and the best of us can learn to fan that fire into better kind of life, to burn more brightly than is given to us by our destined span.'

As she said this, her own eyes seemed lit from within, and he saw how red they were. Suddenly the thought came to him that perhaps this was not Morella d'Arlette who spoke to him at all, but another who had placed these words upon her tongue – and then the idea came to him that while he lay with her there may have been others sharing in the pleasure of his body, and in the magic which had enlivened it.

The thought that he had lain, somehow, with the monstrous Semjaza he quickly put out of his mind. That it was Semjaza's voice which spoke to him now, though, he could not doubt. The lady Morella was not *entirely* herself, but had been made an instrument for his temptation.

Something might be made of a man like you, Semjaza had said. Orfeo repeated those words to himself again, and for a second time he shied away from the notion.

He resolved then, with a stubborn spirit of rebellion, that if it should transpire that he might somehow find Arcangelo, and could reach out a hand to help him, perhaps he would do it after all, in spite of all the warnings he had heard. It might serve as a kind of penance, offered in return for that guilty pleasure which he had recently enjoyed with Morella d'Arlette – who was, he had no doubt, a toy of daemons.

Five

ORFEO WAS RUDELY awakened shortly after first light when the door of his cell was thrown open with a bang. His own start of surprise was quickly controlled, but the lady Morella was clearly unused to such entrances in the places where she normally slept, and the discomfort of her abrupt arousal was more than redoubled by the anger she felt at being discovered here. It was probable that she had intended to leave before dawn, but had slept too soundly, in which case it was no one's fault but her own that she was found here – but as she came quickly to her feet, hugging a blanket in order to hide her nakedness, she was by no means intent on blaming herself for the unfortunate situation.

In the open doorway there stood a man-at-arms with a naked sword, and there walked into the cell before him a servant boy, no more than ten or eleven years of age. The boy was carrying two trays, each loaded with a wooden dish, a loaf of bread on a plate, and a jug of water. He was such a small boy that the task of balancing the two heavy trays was not an easy one in any case, and when he caught sight of the furious woman leaping up before him, that balance became instantly precarious.

'How dare you!' screeched the lady Morella.

Inertia carried the boy forward one more hesitant step, and then the fear of dropping his burden made him stagger forward even further.

The lady raised her arm, and caught the boy a tremendous blow about the head, which he could not duck because of his problem with the trays. The blow, of course, settled the matter, and the contents of the trays flew everywhere, while the boy was hurled across the cell. He crashed into the wall, and struck his head hard, falling limply to the ground on the instant.

The man-at-arms tried feebly to make some excuse, but could only produce half of some garbled statement about the prisoner's breakfast before Morella – further enraged by the fact that her protective blanket had been drenched – shouted him down.

'Imbecile!' she cried. 'This is no prisoner! He has been examined by Semjaza and found innocent – did no one tell you that he is to be moved today to a proper apartment? Has no one taught you that servants do not come to a sleeping guest slamming doors and hurling slops, but wait to be called? You will learn that lesson now, that I swear!'

Orfeo, meanwhile, had gone to the stricken boy, and found him nearly unconscious. There was blood in his mouth where he had bitten his tongue, and more in his hair where the collision with the wall had split his scalp.

'My lady,' he said, 'the child is hurt.'

'And so he should be,' she said, still speaking very angrily. 'And he will certainly be whipped for his stupidity.'

'My lady,' said Orfeo, very soothingly, 'it is plain that no one *did* tell these people that I was no longer to be reckoned a prisoner, and they were only doing their duty as they saw it. The fault is not theirs, and the boy is hurt far worse than he could possibly deserve. Let me take him back to the servants' quarters, where I will see what can be done for him – this man must guide me.'

There were two ideas in his mind while he said this – first, that the boy was indeed hurt, and did need attention; second, that it would leave the lady alone in the room, to put her clothes on and take herself away before the commotion attracted more attention.

If she did not care about the first matter, she certainly cared about the second, and she was quick enough to agree. The man-at-arms began some protest, but Orfeo stilled his tongue with a fierce look as he picked up the stricken servant-boy and immediately handed him over. The soldier looked surprised, having no time even to sheath his sword, but accepted the burden and allowed himself to be pushed away from the door. The boy moaned faintly, but suffered himself to be carried out.

Orfeo then took up his own clothes – as many of them, at any rate, as would serve the purposes of decency, and brought them outside the cell, closing the door behind him before he put them on. He found that he had left his shoes, but he decided that his stockings would have to do, even though the stone floor was cold. When he had dressed himself he took the boy back from the arms of the other man, and said: 'Show me where the kitchens are!'

The unfortunate man-at-arms was desperately confused. Here, it seemed, was a prisoner (or perhaps, his slow mind had now realized, a man who was not a prisoner) walking out of his cell, leaving a lady of the court behind him, and demanding to be taken to the kitchens bearing a bleeding servant in his arms. It was an occurrence for which no possible precedent could offer him guidance.

'The other prisoner...' he protested, feebly. 'Food for the lady Serafima...'

'Whatever food and drink there was has been spilled,' said Orfeo firmly. 'If you have a prisoner to be fed, then we must first go to the kitchens. Now go!'

The man-at-arms went reluctantly, leading the way downwards through the cold corridors. They had to go outside, and then came inside again to pass through a huge room which must have been the Great Hall, but the hour was very early and they met no one en route save for sleepy men-at-arms who did not challenge them. Orfeo was certain that the lady Morella would be able to make her way back to her own quarters without attracting any more attention.

'What is your name?' asked Orfeo, sharply, as they passed through a door in the further wall of the hall and began to descend into the bowels of the castle.

'Fernand Arrigo,' replied the man-at-arms, after an unhappy pause. He had apparently decided that having gone so far as he had, there was nothing left to do but take the orders given to him by this person who was not a prisoner.

'Well, Fernand,' said Orfeo, 'I will tell you something now which you must remember, as a fact which you know beyond a shadow of a doubt, so that you may tell it to anyone who demands the truth from you. When you came to my cell this morning, I was alone. The boy tripped over his own clumsy feet and hit his head against the wall. You permitted me to bring him to the kitchens because you had been told that I was not to be treated as a prisoner, though you had not been told that my breakfast should not be brought until I asked for it. Is that clear? I was alone, and the boy fell over his own feet.'

'But...' began Fernand Arrigo.

Orfeo looked down at the boy, to see if he had heard, but the child was too dazed and confused to listen properly. 'When the boy is better,' he said, 'you must remind him of everything I have said. You must make him understand. Do you hear me, Fernand? *You must remind him.*'

'Yes sire,' said the man-at-arms, sullenly.

'You need not address me as sire,' Orfeo informed him, drily. 'I am but a common man, like yourself, and you may call me "Master Orfeo", or simply "Orfeo" if you prefer.'

They soon reached the kitchens, where many other servants were busy with their duties. Half a dozen of them gathered around while Orfeo laid his burden on a table.

'Poor boy!' said Orfeo, having explained his own version of what had happened. 'I fear that he may be badly hurt.' He examined the child again, but he was no healer, and could not say for certain whether the skull was cracked or not, though by now the boy seemed to have come to his senses again, and had never been unconscious. Fernand, meanwhile, was saying something to the cook about the lady Serafima's ruined breakfast.

All was confusion until a senior manservant came in, demanding to know what was afoot. Orfeo explained yet again, and though the man seemed suspicious he did not challenge the story.

Orfeo guessed that this was due at least in part to the other's realization that whoever *had* been informed of Orfeo's altered status had made a bad mistake in omitting to make sure that the news was passed on to the likes of Fernand Arrigo and the boy.

'I thank you, sir,' said the manservant – his careful 'sir' being far less a term of respect than Arrigo's 'sire'. 'I will take care of the boy now.'

Orfeo shot a warning glance at Fernand Arrigo, reminding him to hold his tongue regarding Morella d'Arlette, but he left without saying any more to anyone.

Orfeo fully intended to make his way straight back to the cell where he had been placed, which would by now be empty of any other persons. There he planned to wait, until a servant came to bring him to better quarters. It did cross his mind, though, that he might peep into the other cell which was across the corridor from his own, to see if he could catch a glimpse of the other prisoner who was lodged there – it intrigued him to discover that there was someone there whose quality properly required such a prison, all the more because it was a lady.

Unfortunately, Orfeo had been so preoccupied with the task of pressing upon Fernand Arrigo's dull mind the

necessity of giving a diplomatic account of what had happened in the cell that he had not efficiently memorized the
route by which he had been brought to the kitchens. He
quickly found himself confronted with a series of archways
which he certainly had not come through before, and
could not then find an upward-leading stair which would
take him in the direction he wanted to go. The corridors
were ill-lit in the extreme, having only single candles
placed at intervals of six or seven paces, and one or two of
these had gone out. There were no windows in this low
part of the fortress, which was let into the crag itself.

Orfeo was annoyed with himself when he found that he
was lost, but by no means anxious. He knew that if he only
kept walking, turning corners at random, then he would
be sure eventually to meet some servant who could give
him directions. But when he finally heard voices, and went
towards them, he found himself in a very gloomy place
indeed.

Two men were talking together in a covert which had no
light in it, and which had presumably been chosen
because of that fact. Because he was in his stockinged feet
Orfeo made no noise as he approached, even though he
was not at first disposed to conceal himself. As he drew
nearer, he became very glad of this, because he caught several words of conversation which converted his intenton to
ask for directions into a determination to wait and hear
what else was said.

Alas, he had come too late to hear the greater part of the
exchange, and there was little more to be discovered. But
there was a final instruction given by one man to the other
which he heard quite clearly, and which worried him
intensely.

'Remember,' said that man, in a voice which was as hard
as stone, though not unmusical. 'You must kill Calvi, but
take Cordova alive if you can. He may be more useful in
that condition, and his disappearance will suffice for our
effect. Remember how to write the word, and inscribe it as
I showed you, in Calvi's blood.'

'It will be done,' said the other, and immediately began to walk away. He came directly towards the place where Orfeo had halted, but Orfeo was able to step back into an alcove which was utterly dark, so that the other passed by without suspecting that he was there. He carried no candle, plainly knowing his way well enough to find it even in near-darkness, and Orfeo could not see his face.

The other man had turned away too, and had gone in the opposite direction. Orfeo had not seen *his* face either, nor had he recognized the voice – both of which facts he regretted, in view of what he had heard. He had, apparently, discovered a plot against the one man in Zaragoz he could confidently reckon a good one, and yet he had no idea at all who might be involved in the plot, or how it was to be put ito execution, or when.

After a moment's pause, he continued on his way, trying to retrace his steps to more brightly-lit corridors.

He went more carefully now, because he was anxious not to be found too near the place where he had overheard the end of the conversation – but he need not have worried, for it was fully ten minutes before he found an upward stair and a way into the part of the castle where the floors were carpeted with wooden tiles and the walls decked with hangings. Once there he had no difficulty in finding a maidservant, who took him back to the place where he had been lodged for the night.

There, to his astonishment – waiting for him amid the mess of spilled food – was Tomas diAvila, the son of the Duke.

'It APPEARS,' SAID Tomas, 'that there has been an accident.'

'The boy who was bringing the food was unfortunate enough to slip, my lord,' said Orfeo. 'He was hurt when he fell against the wall, and the man-at-arms permitted me to carry him to the kitchen.'

'You did not need his permission,' said Tomas. 'You are no prisoner here, though it was so late when Sceberra left you last night that he thought it best not to have you moved to another room.'

'The man did not know that, my lord,' Orfeo told him, mildly, 'and therefore I begged his permission. I am sorry that your other... guest... should have lost her breakfast.'

Tomas frowned, but only replied: 'The lady will not go without.'

There was a pause then, while the Duke's son cast about for something else to say, and Orfeo realized that Tomas had not come to these quarters in order to see him, but on some other errand – perhaps to visit the mysterious lady Serafima. Seeing that this offered him an opportunity, he said: 'May I ask a favour, my lord?'

After a moment's hesitation, Tomas said: 'By all means.'

'I understand that the steward has been asked to find other accommodation for me within the castle, but my belongings are still in the servants' quarters at Rodrigo Cordova's house. I am well content with those lodgings, and if your lordship does not require my presence here until the Night of Masks, perhaps it might be simpler if I returned there.'

The youth was slightly surprised by the request, but by no means dismayed. From his point of view, at least, Orfeo's continued presence in the castle was obviously to be reckoned at best an irrelevance – and in view of the morning's events, perhaps something of a minor nuisance.

'You are not a prisoner,' he said, as though repeating the words to remind himself. 'You may certainly return to Don Rodrigo's house, if that is your wish.'

'Thank you, my lord,' said Orfeo, with a bow. He paused only to collect the garments which he had left off in his hurry to be dressed, and to put on his shoes. Tomas diAvila waited while he did so, but seemed relieved when he bowed again and took himself off.

He was stopped at the gatehouse of the castle, and the officer of the watch seemed inclined to hold him there while his story was checked, until there appeared – still about the business of delivering breakfasts, to judge by the leather bucket which he carried, containing loaves of bread and a corked jug of wine – none other than Fernand

Arrigo. Arrigo confirmed that to his certain knowledge the player was a free man, and he was allowed to leave.

As he descended the path which spiralled around the crag Orfeo was overtaken by a detachment of eight soldiers, who were urging their horses down the hill at what seemed to him a precipitate speed. No doubt the beasts had taken the path at a canter a hundred times before, but he nevertheless formed the impression that they were being taken along in haste. He immediately became anxious lest they have the same destination as he, and he looked down the rock to see whether they came full circle around it, and if so, how many times.

He was glad to see that they eventually appeared on a part of the path below Don Rodrigo's house, and had obviously not paused there, but he did not let relief slow him down. If what Arcangelo had said was true, there was another path connecting the castle to Don Rodrigo's house, inside the mountain. That route could presumably be trod in either direction by those bent on treachery and assassination.

Even though his road was downhill all the way Orfeo did not find it comfortable. His excursion in stockinged feet had not hurt his feet at all, but some of the water which the unfortunate boy had spilled had splashed into his shoes, and the dampness soon soaked through his stockings. But this was only a further encouragement to hurry, and by the time he arrived at Rodrigo Cordova's house he felt that he was not a moment too soon.

He quickly found, though, that he was by no means soon enough, for when he inquired at the lodge whether the owner of the house was at home, he was informed that Rodrigo Cordova had ridden out immediately after dawn, having business in his vineyards, which lay to the north of the town.

Orfeo was more dismayed by this news than he showed, and asked to be allowed to go to the room where his things were. The gatekeeper, knowing that he had been taken away on the previous night by Sceberra's men, was apprehensive, but was persuaded to go with him to the house to find Don Rodrigo's steward.

The steward Cristoforo accepted his account without question, and let him go to the room where his pack was. There Orfeo changed into his travelling clothes, and buckled on his sword.

He considered, briefly, telling Cristoforo what he had heard, and asking that a group of Cordova's own men should ride after him with a warning, but he dared not do it. For one thing, he had not the slightest idea who might or might not be involved in the conspiracy. For another, he did not want the word spread around that he knew anything of it, lest he be imperilled himself – he was now prepared, despite what he had told Semjaza, to involve himself in this tangled affair so far as to give a warning to a man he liked, but he was not prepared to have it broadcast to all and sundry that he had taken it into his head to meddle in a matter which plainly did not concern him.

Accordingly, he begged Don Rodrigo's steward for the loan of a horse, on the grounds that as he must stay in Zaragoz for a few days waiting for the Night of Masks, he would like to see something of the realm. The steward, presuming that his master's order to see to Orfeo's needs had not been cancelled by the previous night's events, reluctantly agreed, and took him to the stables. There the loyal and careful Cristoforo conscientiously picked out a horse so old and sad of eye that its loss would be no grave matter.

It was not the steed which Orfeo needed, but he held his tongue, feeling that it would be for the best to get on his way as quickly as possible. He knew, in any case, that if the riders from the castle were upon the errand which he had heard discussed, he would need a horse with wings to catch them. He could only hope that the difference betwen a fast steed and a slow one would not be vital.

He obtained directions from the steward regarding the location of the Cordova estates, and found them simple enough to cause no difficulty. The main north road from

the town went directly through those lands on its way to
the foothills of the Irrana, from which he had lately come
by a nearly-parallel route. He rode down the hill as fast as
he dared, cursing the indirectness of the road. No one
stopped him at the town gate, for which he was very grateful, considering how much time he had already lost.

He pressed the old horse as hard as he could, and was
pleased by the way that it responded now that its path was
straight. Though no one now would choose to ride it into
battle it must have been a warhorse in its day, for it had a
proud step and a good heart. Slow it might be, but unwill-
ing it was not.

He passed several groups of men upon the road, making
their way to the town with handcarts and donkey-trains.
Once he believed that he saw one of the men who had
attacked Arcangelo near the crossroads to the east, but the
man hardly glanced at him as he rode by, being intent on
some heated discussion with his fellows. There seemed to
be a good deal of discussion going on, and Orfeo wondered whether news of the remarkable happenings at
Cordova's house had already flown so far as to feed the
gossips of the whole realm.

Twice he paused to ask how near he was to Rodrigo
Cordova's land, but the men he asked were as vague as
peasants everywhere in judging distances, and had not the
imagination or the calculative power to tell him how long
an ordinary horse might take to go there at a tired trot.

As it turned out, the sun was past its zenith when the
road began to wind through valleys whose slopes were terraced for the growing of vines, and where countless little
streams and rivulets carried the water which was the
lifebood of the region towards their confluence with the
Eboro.

At last the labourers in the fields were able to confirm
that he was now on Cordova land, but when he asked
where he should look for Don Rodrigo they merely
shrugged their shoulders and pointed vaguely in one direction or another, entirely without conviction.

Although he was impatient, he could do no more than follow the road, rarely able now that he had left the plain to see more than a hundred yards ahead of him.

So it was that he came upon a crossroads rather abruptly, and saw the crowd gathered there only a minute or two before he joined it.

He leaped from the saddle in order to shove his way through the throng, whose numbers were still being swelled by people running from neighbouring fields. He did not know until he had got past them exactly what he would find.

When he did manage to see what it was that was the centre of attraction, he could not judge how utter his failure had been, for Rodrigo Cordova was nowhere to be seen.

There was only poor Theo Calvi, who had listened to his songs with such keen attention. The youth would listen to music no more, for he had been injured beyond all possibility of recovery. His hacked and battered body had been propped up against the empty scaffold which stood by the crossroads.

Beside him, on a boulder, there was written in blood – in a curiously childish hand – the single word: QUIXANA.

Six

ORFEO ROUNDED ON the crowd, and began to shout at them: 'Who saw this done? Who saw the ones who brought him here?'

No one replied, and they began to fall back, as if regretting that they had come at all.

They did not know Orfeo, but he had come on horseback, and he wore a sword; they were afraid of him, and afraid to say whatever they knew – if, indeed, they knew anything at all.

'Where is Don Rodrigo?' said Orfeo, angrily. 'Which way did they take him?'

Still no one replied, and now he saw that some of them were whispering, and that one or two looked darkly at him. They had no reason to think that he was their enemy, but he saw how very frightened they were. There was none among them who would know how to read, but still they knew what name it was which had been written in Theo Calvi's blood – and they knew, too, what reprisals the writing of that name might bring down upon the innocent and the guilty alike.

Orfeo realized that when this news spread it would send a wave of panic across the whole realm. If this really was the first blow in a campaign of terror to be waged by the enemies of the Duke then it was surely a foolish one – especially if those enemies had men within the castle who could easily strike a deadlier one. On the other hand, perhaps its real purpose was to spread alarm among the Duke's supporters, and give a licence to the Duke's soldiers and Sceberra's secret police to ride boldly where they would, over any man's estates, in search of treason and resentment. If Rodrigo Cordova were to be held for ransom, what would that ransom be, and to whom must it be paid?

Orfeo saw that the web of intrigue which he had been advised to avoid might well be more complicated than he had earlier suspected – and that he was now dangerously close to an entanglement from which it would be very difficult to escape.

But Rodrigo Cordova was a man he liked, who had made every effort to befriend him. And Theo Calvi had liked his playing.

He heard words sounding in his head, which said: *Reckless man, beware!* It was a chorus in which many voices seemed to join.

He looked wildly about, seething with frustration. The crowd was already breaking up, its members running to their homes to make what preparation they could for the dark time which was to come. None would say a word to him. But then he heard from behind him a strange whisper, which said: 'Orfeo!'

He whirled around, and saw that Calvi still had breath in him, and had opened his eyes.

Quickly, he knelt beside the stricken man, wondering whether his wounds might possibly let him live. But Calvi was very nearly gone, and even the effort of speaking seemed likely to destroy him; nevertheless, the youth was trying desperately to speak, and Orfeo bent his head to make sure that he did not miss a word, however faintly pronounced.

'Go west,' whispered the dying man. 'Killed one... wounded others... slow them down... dare not leave them to be found... West... Watch for... blood...'

Though he fought hard to keep his eyes open, Calvi could not do it. Unconsciousness claimed him again, and though Orfeo knew that the wounded man was not yet dead, he also knew that he would probably never wake again.

Furiously, he rounded on the remaining onlookers again. He pointed at the nearest man, and said: 'Do what you can! If he lives, there is gold in it for those who help him.'

Then he pushed his way between them, and caught the rein of his waiting steed. The animal was tired and thirsty, but there was no time to lose. Even though the other company was slowed by a prisoner, and its members further inconvenienced by their own dead and wounded, it would not be easy to catch up with them.

As he urged the ancient warhorse along the road to the west he wondered what he could do if he did catch up, now that his original mission – to deliver a warning – had come to naught, but he did not pause to debate the matter with himself. He was in the affair now, and his wrath had been roused by the sight of poor Calvi, murdered to lend emphasis to a word scrawled by an illiterate – a mere move in some vicious game of trickery and treachery.

Orfeo had seen men killed before, some of them for reasons no better and no worse, but that did not make it easier to bear that he had ridden hard to try to save this boy, and had failed by a matter of minutes to reach him in time to warn him of impending ambush. If there was a chance of saving Rodrigo Cordova, then he intended to take it, no matter what the risk.

This road was like the one which had brought him into the realm only two days before – it was a meagre thing of ruts and animal-tracks, connecting paths which led to out-lying farms and hamlets. Though there were grapevines growing on the hillside terraces there were also reaches of clustered thorn-bushes, and scree-slopes which were use-less for any kind of cultivation.

His eyes searched the road ahead for splashes of blood, but he could see none. He knew that Calvi had not been killed at the crossroads, but simply taken there to be aban-doned. The men appointed to that job must have been uninjured, and though they had come this way they had left no obvious sign. If they had left the road in order to meet their companions, he would not be able to tell which way they had gone.

After a while, though, he did catch sight of a smear of blood upon a rounded stone by the roadside, and guessed that either someone with a wound had sat on it for a while, waiting for friends, or that a body wrapped in a blood-soaked cloak had rested there a while.

He dismounted and stood beside the stone, looking this way and that, hoping to see which way the company had gone when they left the spot. He could see no other blood-stains, but the ground on the slope below the road, which led down into a wooded valley, had been recently dis-turbed, and he reckoned that the men who had captured Cordova had gone that way. He followed, picking his way carefully. When he reached the stream he let his mount pause to drink, but then pulled the animal's head about, and forced it onwards. The horse, remembering its train-ing, obeyed him without protest – but now they were among the trees they could only proceed at a walk in any case.

Orfeo followed the course of the stream as it wound along the valley floor, going against the direction of its flow. About a mile further on he saw from a distance that there was a hut not far ahead, and he promptly dis-mounted.

After tethering the horse he approached the hut on foot, creeping along very carefully. When he came close, he saw

that there were four more horses loosely secured beside
the hut, on a long rein so that they could graze and go
down to drink from the stream. The fact that there were
only four immediately gave him hope that the other party
had split into two, with some of the number returning to
the town while others remained here – including, he
assumed, those who were hurt.

But had the ones who had left taken Rodrigo Cordova
with them?

The hut was a crude one, with no windows, and its condition was so poor that part of the ill-thatched roof had
fallen in. It could be no more than a temporary hiding-
place, to which the other men must intend to return –
possibly with a healer, or with the man who had dis-
patched them on their violent mission.

Orfeo moved around the hut to a tall tree which over-
looked it at the rear. He climbed up into its branches,
continuing until he was high enough to see through the
hole in the injured roof. Through the gap he could see a
pallet of straw, with someone lying on it, but the interior
of the hut was too deeply shadowed to allow him to see
whether it was a bound prisoner or a corpse. Nor could he
judge with any conviction how many other men might be
waiting inside the hut.

There was a hollow where the branch on which he
perched met the trunk of the tree. Moss grew upon the
debris which clung there. He took up a handful of the
moss, and crushed it in his hand until it was a compact
ball. Then he threw it over the hut, aiming for a bush near
to the door.

It rattled the leaves loudly enough to attract attention,
and he saw two men rush out, swords at the ready, looking
quickly around, though they did not think to look behind
and upwards. One of them had his left arm bound, though
his sword-arm was uninjured.

Orfeo felt certain that these two must have been in the
company of guardsmen which had passed him on the road
from the castle that morning, but they were not in the

Duke's livery now; they were dressed as anonymously as
he was himself.

Someone called to them from within the hut, petulantly,
and they replied, saying that there was no one to be seen.

Orfeo came down to the ground again, as soundlessly as
he could. He drew his sword from its scabbard. Then he
made his way to the back wall of the hut, treading very
carefully.

He would have liked to get up on to the roof, but there
was no way he could do it without betraying his presence,
so he worked his way slowly around to a position just outside the door. Then he picked up a handful of earth, and
threw it at the same bush. Once again the armed men
popped out, staring hard at the spot from which the noise
had come. Orfeo had his sword already raised above his
head, and brought the hilt down hard on the back of the
nearest man's head.

The soldier cursed as he fell, and Orfeo knew that he had
failed to knock the man out, but as he sprawled in the dust
Orfeo was able to deliver a hard kick to the outside of his
knee before bounding into the open space to face the
other swordsman – the man whose left arm was already
bandaged.

His opponent had a heavy sword which was designed
for slashing rather than thrusting, and he swung at Orfeo
with all the artlessness of a peasant wielding a pitchfork.
Orfeo dodged the blow with ease, and was able to thrust
from a safe distance while the other was off balance. The
point of his rapier pinked the other's sword-arm, and
though the wound was by no means a crippling one it
must have hurt a good deal, all the more because it was
one of a pair.

The man Orfeo had kicked was staggering to his feet
now, but with his head ringing and his leg unsure whether
it could bear his weight he was in no condition to balance
himself for a proper blow. Orfeo danced around so that he
was equidistant from both opponents. He was at least
three inches taller than either of the men he faced, and his

uncommonly long arms gave him a further advantage in terms of reach.

The point of the rapier licked out – once, twice, thrice – with the speed of a striking serpent. One thrust caught the staggering man in the throat, and sent him down choking on his own blood; the second cut the other man in the breast and made him lurch backwards, while the weight of his weapon dragged his arm down to leave him no defence at all; the third took advantage of this conspicuous open- ing by driving into his belly just below the rib cage.

A third man had appeared in the doorway of the hut, but he was already hurt too, much worse than his companion with the bandaged arm – his right leg was so badly cut and patched that he could only stand by supporting himself against the doorway. He had a sword in his hand, but no obvious determination to use it now that he had seen what Orfeo could do with *his* blade. The man lowered the blade to signal his disinterest before Orfeo could thrust at him.

'Who in the name of all the gods are *you*?' he demanded, resentfully. 'What business have you here?'

'I might ask the same of you,' replied Orfeo, lightly. 'I think you have taken off your colours, in order to hide your own identity, and make a secret of your own busi- ness.'

The man whose arm and belly he had cut was writhing on the ground, moaning.

'You must see to your friend,' said Orfeo to the man in the doorway, as he pulled the stricken man's weapon away with his foot, and took it into his own hand. 'But throw your sword into that bush before you move a step, and go carefully.'

The man with the hurt leg did as he was told, throwing his weapon away and lurching forward to kneel beside his companion. The man who had been cut in the throat did not move – he was dead.

Orfeo moved to the doorway and looked quickly into the hut, while keeping one eye on the injured soldiers. Inside there was a body lying on the floor, apparently dead. The man on the pallet whose form he had glimpsed through the roof was tightly bound, but not gagged, and he exclaimed with surprise when he saw who it was that stood there.

'Master Orfeo!' said Don Rodrigo Cordova. Then, when he had had a moment to recover his wits, he said: 'I must be living in one of your stories, my friend, for I could never have expected when I rode forth this morning that I would first be seized by highwaymen, then rescued within the hour!'

'Do you know who these men are, my lord?' asked Orfeo.

'I believe I do,' said Rodrigo, as Orfeo moved into the hut, stepping over the corpse, 'though they have taken off their uniforms.'

Orfeo cut away the prisoner's bonds with the captured weapon, then gave it to him for his future use. They went outside together, to see what had become of their enemies. The two wounded men were still together, in evident distress.

'Should we kill them?' asked Orfeo. 'There may be a slender chance of keeping the secret of my coming here – though I was seen by half a hundred men on the road, and at least a dozen by the crossroads where they left poor Calvi.'

'Dead?' asked Don Rodrigo.

'Not quite. He lived long enough to send me after you. But I do not think he could have lived long thereafter. I told your field-workers to summon help, but I had no hope.'

For a moment or two, Cordova seemed half-inclined to butcher the injured men in reprisal for what had been done to him and to his friend.

But he took no more than half a step towards them before relenting of this decision.

He paused for a moment, then said to Orfeo: 'Better let them tell their story to someone who might help them. I hope they tell it to so many that the story is broadcast throughout the town, for I would like to have it generally known what work they came to do. My men will carry poor Calvi to his own house, where his mother will see to him, whether he be alive or dead.'

Orfeo nodded. He had no appetite for the cold-blooded slaughter of men who had laid down their arms, and was glad to hear Cordova's decision. 'Should we question them?' he asked.

'It would waste time,' said Rodrigo, sourly, 'and I dare say they are practiced liars. We both know whose colours they wore, but whether they were traitors to those colours is a question which might be better answered by the course of events than by their crafty lips.'

Then he turned from Orfeo to address the stricken men, saying: 'If you can, you should quit this place, for I think that your master will not be quite as kind as I have been. He will want to seal your lips, now that his scheme is gone awry.'

Orfeo saw from the expression in their eyes that they believed it – and perhaps the fear of what might yet be done to them wiped out what gratitude they might otherwise have felt, because they did not thank Rodrigo Cordova for the mercy which he showed.

'Come,' said Orfeo. 'We must take the best of their horses, and lead the one which brought me here. I hope that you will know where to go, for I do not know what whirlpool of intrigue it is in which I have immersed myself, and must trust myself now to your care.'

RODRIGO CORDOVA TOOK the lead when they had mounted up, and Orfeo followed him. First of all they went back to the road where Orfeo had found the tell-tale bloodstain, but then the youth hesitated, and when he set off again he left the road to lead his companion across country. Orfeo had expected him to head north-east towards his own estate, but in fact he went south, towards Zaragoz. While they rode at a careful pace, with Orfeo's former mount behind them on a long rein, Orfeo told Cordova about the words he had overheard which had sent him forth on his errand, and what he had seen en route.

'Did you recognize the voice?' asked Cordova, anxiously.

'I could not,' Orfeo replied. 'Of all the voices in the castle I had heard but two – Sceberra's and Semjaza's. I am sure that it was not Sceberra who gave the order, and would be certain that it was not Semjaza either, save that I am ever wary of wizards and their tricks.'

'Can you swear also that it was not your friend Arcangelo?'

'He too is a spellcaster,' Orfeo pointed out, 'but it was not like any speech of his that I have heard – and besides, I think Arcangelo is a prisoner beneath the castle, held in a secret cell far worse than the one where I was lodged.'

'If only you had seen the man!' exclaimed the young man, in exasperation.

'Only be thankful that he did not see me!' replied Orfeo. 'But there is another way to approach the question, is there not? What enemy have you who might gain from this? Remember that they were prepared to kill you if they had to, but preferred to take you alive – was that for ransom, or some other purpose?'

'In Zaragoz,' said Rodrigo, bitterly, 'a man may have many enemies, and never know them all. There is hatred and mistrust in the blood of every man, engraved there by centuries of dispute and betrayal. The Cordovas have been loyal to the diAvilas for many generations, and that would be enough to earn the enmity of the Quixanas. As you heard last night, there is a special rancour to add to that, for rumour says that a secret passage extends from the Cordova house into the caves which are the bowels of the castle, and that it was such a secret route which the assassins used when they toppled that last Quixana duke in the time of my great-grandfather.'

'Is it only rumour, my lord?' asked Orfeo, with gentle scepticism.

'Do not call me that, Orfeo,' said the young aristocrat. 'You are my friend, and I would not have you address me as servant to master. I give you my hand, and beg you to call me Rodrigo.'

So saying, the young man held out his hand so that Orfeo was able to reach across and take it, briefly. It was not the first time that a nobleman had offered him friendship, but he knew that such condescension was rare in tiny realms like Zaragoz, where every man had an exaggerated consciousness of his station.

'I do not mean to doubt you, Rodrigo,' said Orfeo, 'but if we are to unravel this mystery then we must acknowledge what is true.

'*Is* there a passage within the crag which connects your house to the castle? *Was* it used in the coup of which Arcangelo spoke?'

'I honestly do not know,' replied Rodrigo. 'As I have said, the Cordovas have long been loyal to the diAvilas, and if my ancestor could have served the cause he would have done so – but if there was such a passage, the new duke would certainly have closed it once he had used it. I know nothing, either, of any curse placed upon my house.'

'And what of the rest of Arcangelo's story? *Was* the Quixana duke a man of justice, slain by a tyrant?'

Rodrigo Cordova laughed. 'Justice is a relative thing,' he replied. 'In every dispute at law the winner claims that the end of justice has been served, while the loser cries cheat! All those who resent the strong hand of a ruler call him tyrant, and wherever they can find a pretender to his position, that pretender becomes in their eyes a paragon of all the political virtues. You are a much-travelled man, Orfeo, and you must have seen that these are the ways of the world.'

'Perhaps,' replied Orfeo, without enthusiasm. 'But I have known men who were certainly tyrants, and others who held to better principles. For now, we must confine our attention to the present case. Is it your belief that there *is* some traitor within the walls of the castle, who was spurred to action by the prophecies which Arcangelo uttered in your house last night, and that Calvi's murder and your seizure were the first blows in a campaign against the Duke?'

'It would be better if that were so,' answered Rodrigo, with a sigh. 'For if it is not, then I must look for enemies among the Duke's loyal servants. If those men were sent by Sceberra or Semjaza – or by Marsilio himself – then my escape can hardly be reckoned to end the matter. Yet I cannot see what any of them would gain by hurting me. I had thought myself a friend to them all.'

'I cannot see much sense in it, either,' admitted Orfeo. 'Nor can I begin to understand what happened last night. If Arcangelo came here to spark a rebellion in the name of Quixana, it must have been foolish in the extreme for him to declare his aim so publicly. Did he come to your house for a different reason? And if so, was it his speech which has attracted the attention of unknown enemies to you?'

'I do not know,' replied the youth. 'I cannot begin to understand. Perhaps we should have put those scoundrels to the question after all.'

'Perhaps,' said Orfeo, uneasily. 'But I doubt that they know any more than we do about the reasoning behind their orders. I am, as you say, a much-travelled man, and I have heard many tales of treason and rebellion. If there is one point on which history and romance seem to be agreed, it is that when melodramatic messages are written in blood they are likely to be lies and libels. The men who killed your friend and made you captive were the Duke's men, and the simplest conclusion is that they were about *his* business. Perhaps he simply needed to contrive an atrocity, to prove that any who are sympathetic to the cause of Quixana are murderers and terrorists, and to quell any opposition to the methods he will use to root them out. You must ask yourself, Rodrigo, whether men like Marsilio diAvila and Estevan Sceberra would hesitate to sacrifice a pawn like Theo Calvi – or even a scrupulous friend like yourself – if they thought that a greater game must be played. Perhaps it is your very innocence and goodness which made them choose you as a target.'

When Orfeo looked to see what effect his words had had, he saw that Rodrigo Cordova was frowning very deeply. If the younger man was not convinced, he was certainly reduced to perplexity. But this was a story which he did not want to believe.

'You must remember that I am an outsider here,' said Orfeo. 'I see with a more distanced eye. But I am also ignorant of the true situation. When Arcangelo mentioned the name Quixana while we walked together on the road he implied that the Quixanas had been all but destroyed when their last duke was overturned. Who, then, would be the champion of any revolt?'

Rodrigo sighed again. 'This is a small nation,' he said, 'but it has a long history. Marriages across the centuries make complicated patterns of relationship, which are sometimes in dispute. The scribes in the castle use their records to prove all claims of inheritance, but the records do not always speak as clearly as they might. Among the nobility, some younger sons and daughters always leave the realm to make lives elsewhere, and their descendants are often unrecorded here. There are probably lines of descent different from those which are presently recognized, which might be traced by a scribe who looked at the records with an eye which favoured Quixana against diAvila; there are certainly lines of descent which might be invented by those with sufficient imagination to do it. But the one person who is universally acknowledged as a blood descendant of the last Quixana duke, and bears his name, is the lady Serafima Quixana.'

'Who is a prisoner in the castle!' Orfeo exclaimed.

'She is in the castle, to be sure,' said Rodrigo. 'But whether she is a prisoner is a different matter. Marsilio has become anxious for the stability of his realm since he succeeded his father, and I think that he would like to erase the legacy of hatred which the name Quixana carries by another means than wholesale slaughter. He sent his emissaries to Gualcazar some years ago, when the lady was but a child, in order to arrange her betrothal to his son. It is believed throughout the realm that the marriage will take place when the lady Serafima comes of age, but there have been rumours that she is not altogether happy with the prospect.'

Orfeo remembered what the lady Morella had said to him, about having seen Arcangelo some years before in Gualcazar. 'When does the lady Serafima come of age?' he asked.

'Soon, I think. I do not know the exact day, but this will certainly be the year.'

'In that case,' said Orfeo, 'we have a ready explanation for the timing of this wretched affair. That must surely be what brought Arcangelo here to try his art against Semjaza's – but if he has already failed, it is difficult to see how anyone else could make a serious attempt to release the lady from her prison. The sorcerer seemed ready enough to believe that I knew nothing of any wider conspiracy, but I suppose he may be anxious lest Arcangelo has not come here alone, and may be waiting for a more powerful magician to take Arcangelo's place.'

'I know nothing of this,' said Cordova tiredly. 'And I do not see what it has to do with me. I am loyal to the Duke, and I cannot believe that Marsilio could be so foolish as to conclude that because Arcangelo came to my house, I must be in league with the Quixanas.'

'No,' said Orfeo, grimly, 'I do not think it is as simple as that. But my friend, we must decide in spite of our ignorance exactly what we should do next. I think we must decide now, for we are coming close to Zaragoz again, and we will certainly be seen and recognized if we go through the gate of the town. This adventure did not end with your release; it has hardly begun. Your enemies – whoever they may be – will surely strike again.'

'I know that,' answered Cordova, in a tone which was equally dour. 'But I cannot go into hiding. Were I to ride back to my estates, I could be no more certain of having men I can trust about me than if I were in my house on the hill, and I would be no less vulnerable to an assassin's dagger. My enemies, whoever they are, have tried to act treacherously against me, but I am not that kind of man. I would rather bring them out into the open if I can, where I can confront them face to face. I intend to return to Zaragoz, openly and boldly. You need not come with me if you are afraid – this is not your affair, and I can make sure that you have safe conduct to the border.'

Orfeo considered this for a few seconds, but he quickly saw that just as Rodrigo could not be certain of his safety wherever he was, so he could not be certain of his own, even though he left the borders of the realm. In any case, the fact that there was so much he did not understand made him reluctant to let the puzzle alone.

'No, my lord,' he said, forgetting for a moment the equality of friendship which had been offered to him, 'I will not do that just yet. After all, my lute is in your house, and how am I to live without it? And I have promised, have I not, to play for the lady Veronique on that Night of Masks to which you Estalians look forward with such enthusiasm?'

Rodrigo Cordova turned in his saddle to look into his companion's eyes, and Orfeo knew that the young man was staring straight through the mask of his irony, into his very heart.

'Thank you, my friend,' said Rodrigo. 'I will be proud to have you by my side. And if my enemies prove too strong for me, I swear that I will do all in my power to see that they do not harm you.'

Orfeo was grateful for this promise, though he knew well enough how difficult it might be to keep. Well, he thought, I am in the web now, and will not escape until its strands are ripped apart, to reveal whatever monsters are lurking at its heart. And if Chaos has Zaragoz in its grip, let us pray that the forces of Law may yet prevail against it!

Seven

As THEY RODE through the streets of the town Orfeo looked about him all the while, wondering whether any who saw them would be surprised or alarmed, and whether news of Rodrigo Cordova's homecoming might already be winging its way to the heights of the crag by mysterious means. But he saw nothing untoward in the way that any man looked up at them as they passed by, and there was no sign that rumour of the murder of Theo Calvi had yet been broadcast in the streets. They had come through the gate unchallenged, and as their horses mounted the narrow road to Cordova's house they were saluted most politely by all those whom custom forced to acknowledge their presence.

While their horses were being stabled Cristoforo came out to meet them, and Rodrigo immediately instructed him to send a messenger to the castle, to summon Estevan Sceberra.

Privately, Orfeo wondered whether this was altogether a wise thing to do; although he had declared his certainty

111

that the man who gave the instruction for Calvi's murder had not been Sceberra, he was by no means convinced that Sceberra was not behind the scheme. Still, if young Cordova was determined to take the bull by the horns, then the minister was certainly the man he must first confront.

Rodrigo led Orfeo into the house by the same door which had admitted Arcangelo the night before. It gave direct entry into the hall which had been used as a dining-room and ballroom. As they passed the spot where Arcangelo had been struck down Orfeo looked up at the balcony from which the magical blast had been fired, and was suddenly disposed to wonder about the exact circumstances of that event.

'Rodrigo,' he said, ignoring the start of surprise which the steward Cristoforo gave when he heard the familiar mode of address, 'last night I saw Sceberra signal to the man who fetched the sorcerer. He could not have come from the castle even if there is a secret way. He was already in the house, was he not?'

'Yes he was,' answered Rodrigo. 'He came with the party from the castle, as he often does.'

'But not to dance?'

Rodrigo smiled, but mirthlessly. 'Semjaza does not care for dancing,' he said, 'and if he did, I think he might spoil the pleasure which the others took. He is not a handsome man, and you have seen that he can hurt with the power of his will.'

'Why, then, does he come here?'

'He likes to look at the books and scrolls which my ancestors gathered here. Many were once owned by wizards, though my family has not kept a wizard of its own for three generations now. Were it not for Semjaza the books would remain unread, and I think that even he can only read a few of them, for they are written in many different languages. Cristoforo, who has sufficient skill in the literary arts to keep account of all my business affairs, cannot make head nor tail of any but a few of them.'

The steward gave a sad nod to confirm this judgment of his relative incompetence.

'May I see these books?' asked Orfeo.

'Of course – can you read, then?'

'Like your steward,' said Orfeo, 'I can read both Estalianand the Imperial tongue which we speak, and write it after a clumsy fashion, but little more than that. Nevertheless, I have a certain interest in books.'

Shrugging his shoulders – for it was obviously not an interest which he shared – Rodrigo led Orfeo up the principal staircase of the house, and then along a carpeted corridor which led to a wing beyond the rooms which were commonly used. There he unlocked the door of a small room, using a key which he took from one of the recesses where candles would be set after dark.

The room had a glazed window, but the diamond-shaped pieces of glass were heavily begrimed, and the room seemed a dark and dingy place. It was narrow, with wide shelves to either side, on which books were stored in untidy heaps. There was a table in the centre of the room, with two chairs at either end, and the table-top was littered with candle-trays and the stubs of candles, as well as several scrolls, three inkwells and an assortment of quills.

There was a good deal of dust on the table-top, too, but its pattern was irregular, sitting much deeper here than there, occasionally having been wiped away from a little area before one or other of the chairs. There was an unpleasant odour in the air, which Orfeo immediately connected to the noxious stink of the sorcerer's breath. Though it was in Rodrigo Cordova's house, this room was Semjaza's if it was anyone's. And yet the house, if what Arcangelo had said was true, had been bewitched by some Quixana spellcaster to work against the cause of the diAvilas.

Then he remembered that Arcangelo had not said that, but had actually said instead that the house had been charged to serve the cause of justice, and to react against any who dared to work 'dark magic' within its walls.

Was that, he wondered, why Arcangelo had come here – to provoke the working of 'dark magic'? And had Semjaza often come to study here in the hope of discovering a way to set aside the curse which had been set upon the house?

Orfeo ran his finger along the binding of a nearby book, and found it black with dust and fungus. The parchments were literally rotting on the shelves. It was not that the room was damp, for it was as dry as a bone – but that dryness had not kept decay at bay.

'After all,' said Rodrigo, as he read disapproval in Orfeo's roaming eye, 'parchment is but a kind of flesh, and it is the destiny of all flesh that it should return to dust in the end. What does it matter, when no one can read them?'

'The men who wrote them intended that they should be read,' murmured Orfeo. 'And it seems that Semjaza has tried to penetrate their mysteries. Arcangelo spoke, you will recall, of a learned man among the traitors who betrayed the Quixana duke, who learned more about the history of this mountain than had been known before. Perhaps the book from which he learned it is here.'

'I do not know,' said Rodrigo. 'I have kept the books, because they belonged to my father and my father's father – they are part and parcel of the House of Cordova, which I hold in trust for my son, and my son's son – but my father never cared for them and nor do I. I saw no reason to hide them from Semjaza.'

When he heard Rodrigo use the phrase 'House of Cordova' Orfeo saw what he should have seen all along – which was that the word 'house' had more than one meaning. Arcangelo had said of the defeated wizards who had helped Quixana rule that they had 'cursed this house', and then had gone on to imply that he meant the building itself by talking about its walls. But Estevan Sceberra may not have understood the words that way, and may have thought that the curse was upon the family of Cordova and not the walls of the house in which they lived. Was that why the Duke's men had been sent against his loyal servant?

'I am not sure that Semjaza's curiosity is a harmless thing,' said Orfeo, cautiously. 'Do you know what kind of wizardry he practises?'

'Kind?' replied Rodrigo. 'I hardly know what kinds there are – all wizardry is alike to those who have no magic, though I think that the greater part of it is mere trickery. I know that the common folk dislike him, and call him an evil man who has daemons to command, but evil is like justice: where the unfortunate see evil, the fortunate see only good, and the common folk see daemons in every peculiar shadow. Semjaza likes to be feared, like all his kind, and is pleased when others call him sorcerer and suspect him of acquaintance with vile gods and demi-gods. I do not say that he is a good man, but I do not think him half so black as he is painted.'

'I wish I could agree with you, my friend,' said Orfeo, quietly. 'I know well enough how rumour sees daemons where there is naught but darkness, and I have known many spellcasters who have taken great delight in seeming more powerful than they are, encouraging false belief in their ability to command dark powers. Anyone who believes every story which is told of men who deal with daemons is a fool – but I think that is to the great advantage of those who really do make pacts with Chaos, and I know that some peculiar shadows do indeed mark the work of daemons.

'I cannot believe in all the wonders which are spoken of in travellers' tales, and have certainly never seen such things as dragons or manticores, but there is something in the wisdom of lore and legend which I trust, and I know that there are powers in the world which men do well to fear.'

'Perhaps there are,' answered Rodrigo, 'in distant and savage lands near the World's Edge. But this is Estalia, which is a civilized place.'

'You are a good man, Rodrigo,' said Orfeo. 'And I wish that those to whom you owe fealty were as good as you. But Semjaza and Morella d'Arlette belong to a different kind, and I suspect that they have brought others into the morass of their corruption.'

When he looked carefully to see what effect this statement had on Rodrigo Cordova, Orfeo saw that the other was not disposed to believe him. He was not entirely surprised, given that the young man was reputed to be enamoured of Veronique diAvila, and given also that he must have known Semjaza all his life, and grown up thinking of him as a friend no matter how repulsive his face might be.

'Would you have me destroy these books?' asked Cordova. 'I would not like to do it, despite that I do not care for them at all.'

Orfeo shook his head. Though he did not like to think that a man like Semjaza might find the means here to increase his power, nor did he like to think of knowledge being destroyed – and he believed that there might indeed be knowledge here which could be put to use by those who could learn to decipher it. He had been in university towns in the Empire, and had seen much larger libraries than this one, and which seemed infinitely better kept – but he knew that they consisted mostly of the routine produce of copyists and paid scriveners. Never before had he seen such an accumulation of very old books as this room contained, and he knew they would be reckoned a fine treasure by any honest scholar of the Empire or Bretonnia, all the more so because most were written in languages forgotten and arcane.

Orfeo sighed, and said: 'How many secrets are buried in this room, not needing lock and key to keep them in? Words by the thousand, written by those whose main purpose was to keep them for a few privileged eyes. What a world it would be, Don Rodrigo, if those who had knowledge were to write it plainly for every man to read – for then it would be in the interest of the many rather than the few to learn their letters and be privy to the accumulated wisdom of the generations. How then might men make progress!

'Instead, the knowledge which men have is hoarded thus, condemned to die and rot and crumble as their own frail bodies die and rot and crumble. No wonder we are naked to corrosions of the soul, my lord, when we consign our best thoughts and our worst to such tombs as this, where only such necromancers as Semjaza can bear to come in quest of their resurrection. Even so, my friend, I beg you not to destroy what you have. It is too precious.'

Orfeo came out of the room, wiping grime from his fingers on to the hem of his tunic.

'I wonder....' he said, and then hesitated.

'What do you wonder?' asked Rodrigo.

'I wonder whether Arcangelo knew that Semjaza would be here last night, and whether what happened was part of his plan. I think Semjaza and Sceberra might be wondering about that too. They may be anxious that their victory was too easy.'

'I do not think so,' said the younger man. 'Is it not more likely that he intended to deliver his dire prophecy and disappear into the night?'

'Perhaps,' said Orfeo, 'but he did not seem surprised when Semjaza struck him down.'

They reached the head of the stairway again, and descended in a calm manner. When they had nearly reached the bottom they heard the sound of hooves clattering in the narow courtyard, and within a minute the main door of the house was opened by the guard which Rodrigo had set there, admitting Estevan Sceberra, with two men-at-arms of his own.

As Rodrigo Cordova strode forward to meet the minister Orfeo hung back, and watched the two men come together. While they looked at each other Sceberra's expression was all friendship and concern, but when they clasped hands in greeting they came so close that Sceberra was able to look over Cordova's shoulder, at the spot where Orfeo stood. In that brief moment, Orfeo saw the expression change – and it was as though the hostility of it emitted a brief cold blast which struck him in the face.

That Sceberra did not like him, he already knew – but he could not help but feel that there was far more in that foul glance than mere dislike. And when the other looked away, Orfeo formed the distinct impression from the way his gaze flickered right and left, then up and down, that Estevan Sceberra was a worried and uneasy man, who felt that the course of events had perversely turned to his own disadvantage.

'I SWEAR,' SAID Estevan Sceberra, 'that when I find these men – and I do not say *if* I find them – then I will make them talk. I have a way with men's tongues, as you know.'

Sceberra was sitting in an armchair, sipping from a goblet of wine. Rodrigo Cordova sat opposite, apparently at ease, though Orfeo – who sat nearby – knew that the young man's mind was very active.

The lady Marguerite was also present, having been informed of all that had happened to her son, and she seemed every bit as uneasy as the minister, perhaps for very different reasons.

'I know how you treat your prisoners, Estevan,' said Cordova, gently, 'but I know only too well that a man in pain will confess to anything which is put into his head. I could have questioned the two we left alive, but I would never have been sure that what they told me was the truth.'

'Semjaza can judge the truth of what men say,' said Sceberra confidently, turning his stare to Orfeo.

'Semjaza undoubtedly has many ways of discovering the truth,' replied Rodrigo. 'And I have no doubt that he is making most urgent enquiries on the Duke's behalf at this very moment. If there is a plot against the Duke which involves men in his own service, then Semjaza will surely discover it – unless, of course, Semjaza is with the plotters.'

Sceberra scowled at the suggestion and shook his head. 'No,' he said, firmly. 'I could doubt any other man in the realm, but not Semjaza.'

'I cannot see why not,' said Rodrigo, who was intent on making Sceberra more uncomfortable than he already was.

'He is a very powerful wizard, is he not? I have often wondered why it is that wizards do not use the power of their
will to seize the crowns from the heads of common men.
I cannot believe that they have no ambition, when they
sacrifice so much to their learning, and take such terrible
risks in their dealings with daemons and the legions of the
undead.'

'The ambition of wizards is not towards temporal
power,' Sceberra told him. 'It takes them in another direction. Semjaza is as loyal a friend to the diAvilas as you are
yourself, Don Rodrigo.'

'There is another way to look at it,' said Orfeo, mildly.

Sceberra looked at him with affected contempt, imply-
ing by his disdain that a common man ought not to
interrupt his betters in such a fashion, but Cordova said:
'What way?'

'I have heard it argued,' Orfeo continued, in the same
mild tone, 'that wizards are already the true rulers of most
earthly realms, and that the men who actually sit on
thrones are mere instruments of their power, whose duty it
is to deflect and bear for them the burden of hatred and
mistrust which naturally accumulates to the debit of
oppressors.'

'If a man were to believe one tenth of all that he heard
argued,' Sceberra opined, 'he would be not a man at all,
but a radish. There is nothing more absurd than the resentful arguments of the envious and the stupid.'

'Oh, you are right,' said Orfeo, with little evident trace of
irony. 'You are undoubtedly right, my lord, to argue thus.'

Sceberra looked at Rodrigo Cordova, his stare quite
stony. 'If there is one man in the realm I could *not* trust,
Don Rodrigo,' he said, 'it is the one who sits at your elbow
and pretends to be your friend. Semjaza examined him last
night and pronounced him honest, but the spellcaster was
tired and may have been more easily misled than on
another occasion. I have heard that the player hurt a child
this morning, by striking him about the head and making
him fall, and I cannot help but wonder whether his tale of

a mysterious conversation overheard in darkness might not
be a malicious invention.'

'You think this player is a wizard, then?' said Rodrigo,
mockingly. 'Wizard enough to make a fool of Semjaza?'

Sceberra merely scowled, and made no reply.

'How is the child?' asked Orfeo.

'He recovered from the blow,' replied Sceberra, ungra-
ciously.

'And did he say that someone hit him?' Orfeo riposted,
with the tiniest emphasis on the word *someone*.

'No,' said Sceberra. 'He said that he stumbled and fell.
But I do not think that he was telling the truth.'

'Then you must send him to Semjaza,' said Orfeo, 'and
let the sorcerer make sure – though I do not think he can
possibly be the mastermind in this plot to murder the
Duke's loyal subjects.'

Sceberra stood up then, and placed the goblet of wine,
unfinished, on the table nearby. 'I must be about my business,' he said, gruffly. 'There is treason in the realm, and I
must root it out. I do not need to tell you, Don Rodrigo,
that you must be on your guard at all times. Trust no one,
I beg of you – including myself, if you will. Wherever we
may choose to point our accusing fingers, one thing
remains certain: a plot which extends into the castle itself
can extend into every house in Zaragoz. No man should
sleep too soundly until this affair is finished, lest he fail to
awake.'

Rodrigo Cordova stood too, and went to the door with
his guest. Orfeo remained in the room until his host
returned.

He looked at the lady, to see what her reaction might
be to the guarded hostility of the conversation, but she
did not say anything to him. Nor did Rodrigo Cordova
say anything about the minister's attitude when he
returned – though it had been plain all along that he did
not like it.

'We still do not know the source of the danger which
threatens you, Don Rodrigo,' said Orfeo, softly. 'And while

that is the case, the minister's advice is good. Be on your guard against everyone.'

'I have not yet asked Cristoforo to move your belongings to a better room,' Cordova said, deliberately passing over what Orfeo had said. 'Would you like me to do it now?'

'No,' Orfeo replied. 'I shall be quite comfortable there.' He knew that the remark about his room was a hint that he should go, though the hour was not so very late, and so he stood up. No doubt young Cordova had a great deal to think about, and felt that he could do it better in solitude. But the lady Marguerite came to her feet also, and spoke to him.

'You have saved my son's life today,' she said, 'and we owe you a greater debt than we can easily repay. May this house protect you as it has always protected me.'

She spoke, of course, as one who had married into the House of Cordova, and so had come under its 'protection'. Orfeo wondered, privately, how much benefit that protection had really been to her, and how much benefit it could continue to be, now that some secret curse might have been awakened in Cordovan walls or Cordovan blood.

There was a sword-bearing servant waiting in the corridor when he came out – which did not surprise him, given that the staff had been called to arms and placed to keep a watch upon their master. Orfeo acknowledged the man's presence, then went up the main staircase.

There was another man on guard on the upper floor, who watched Orfeo as he went to the foot of the smaller stairway which led to the servants' attics. The upper floors were dimly lit, by candles which were poorer than those used downstairs and fewer in number. They cast strange shadows in the alcoves and the doorways.

It was easy to believe, as Orfeo looked about him here, that the ancient walls might somehow be alive, ready to awaken from their stillness. Whether there were daemons hiding in the pools of darkness he could not tell, but he had cause enough to feel uneasy as he searched for the little stairway which would take him up to his room.

As he climbed that gloomy flight he reflected that he was, in fact, very tired. That was only to be expected, given that he had had such an active day in hot pursuit of a more than usually active night. He felt in dire need of a period of quiet solitude, safe from all threats, when he could put aside the mysteries which troubled him in favour of healing sleep.

As he opened the door of his room and passed through it, though, he was promptly clubbed from behind, with sufficient force and precision to rob him instantly of his senses.

Eight

ORFEO WAS BROUGHT rudely back to consciousness by a
bucketful of icy water which was poured over his head as
he lay on a cold stone floor.

His head felt very thick and heavy, and he could not
immediately raise it from its uncomfortable resting-place,
but as soon as he stirred his shoulders were grabbed and
he was hauled unceremoniously to his feet. Held erect
from behind, by hands which felt as though they must be
unnaturally large, he had to fight hard to keep his head
from lolling sideways, but he managed in the end to hold
it up.

He blinked hard and his vision gradually cleared. Then
he saw that he was looking into the face of Estevan
Sceberra.

Sceberra, seeing that he was recognized, smiled.

Orfeo looked down at the hands which gripped his
arms, which were indeed the largest he had ever seen. Then
he looked from side to side. He was in a gloomy cellar,

whose air was dank and damp. It had no windows, and he
guessed that it must be in the deepest regions of the castle.
There was a big stone slab which served as a table – though
it seemed more suited to be an altar – and laid out on the
slab in neat rows were various iron instruments, including
pincers, broad-headed irons, knives and crushing vices.
His sword was also there, and the knife which he used
when he cut meat or cheese.

He tried, rather feebly, to return Sceberra's smile.

'No rack?' he said, faintly. 'I had thought that Zaragoz
was a *civilized* realm.'

Sceberra's smile did not alter in the least. 'Zaragoz is not
known for its carpenters,' he said, grimly. 'The trees grow
too thin and crooked in our poor soil to yield an abun-
dance of timber. My predecessors have been known to use
common ladders for stretching, but in my reckoning that
is a method best suited to the encouragement of women's
tongues. Or have you been upon the rack before, and
liked it? Perhaps that was how you came to be so tall and
thin!'

He signalled then to his huge assistant, who released
Orfeo's upper arms and grabbed his wrists instead. Orfeo
could not struggle, for the wrists were tightly bound
behind his back.

While Orfeo concentrated on retaining his balance the
man behind him threaded a long rope around the one
which bound him, knotting it around, and then threw the
other end of the rope over an iron hook embedded in the
ceiling. Then, standing back, he pulled the rope taut, so
that Orfeo's bound arms were lifted up behind him, forc-
ing his head forward. He tried to remain standing, but
could not, and was lifted clear of the ground by the giant's
tugging. The strain on his shoulders from being held aloft
in that position was very great, and the subsequent twist-
ing of his arms hurt him a good deal. He could only do his
best not to struggle, thus to minimize the agony.

His body began to rotate, but Sceberra stopped it by
putting a hand on Orfeo's shoulder.

'Are you racked enough now, my friend?' asked the minister. 'Please do not fear for my servant – he is very strong, and can hold you there as long as I ask him to. If you become bored, I will ask him to bounce you up and down a little. It is a game which he has enjoyed with several of my guests, and it never fails to amuse them. Sometimes, they laugh so hard that their arms come out of their sockets at the shoulder – oh, what tears they cry, and what songs they sing! I would wager that you would sing finer songs than most – so fine I might keep you here for ever, that I may hear your repertoire entire!'

But then Sceberra signalled again to his servant, who let his prisoner down, so that his feet could touch the floor again. Sceberra took his shoulder to help him stand erect.

'I am forgetting myself,' said the minister, with mocking concern. 'I must not damage your hands, for the lady Veronique would be hurt if you were too bruised to play the lute for her on the Night of Masks.'

Orfeo was too confused to plan what to say, and could only say what came into his head. 'Does Semjaza know that you have brought me here?' he asked.

'Semjaza!' exclaimed the other, laughing with delight. 'Do you think Semjaza would protect you? I fear that you mistook his friendly concern, and the advice which he gave you. He commanded you not to meddle in our affairs, and you repaid his kindness in discovering your innocence by promptly becoming guilty! He would be very disappointed in you, if he knew – but for what it is worth, your presence here is my own secret. You thought that I had used magic to steal you away from Don Rodrigo, did you not? You thought, no doubt, that it was a daemon who plucked you from your room and flew with you out of the window? But no, it was only a man, and not an invisible one. No one sends a daemon to perform a task which a man can do, and no one uses magic when the task can be done without. Don Rodrigo has many loyal servants, but there are some of his company who owe a higher loyalty than that.'

This speech was long enough to allow Orfeo to recover some of his presence of mind, but not quite all.

'Have you only brought me here to hurt me for your pleasure?' he asked. 'Or had you some rational purpose in mind as well?'

He was trying to appear brave, though he knew how foolhardy it was to taunt his captor.

'I have a reason for everything,' said the minister.

'What reason did you have for sending the Duke's men-at-arms to murder one of his loyal subjects and take another prisoner?'

The minister shook his head. 'You forget, my friend, that it is my turn to ask the questions now.'

'Do you really think that I lied to Semjaza?' asked Orfeo. 'Do you think that I *could* have lied to him?'

'I do not know,' said the other. 'I do not think so, but I might be wrong. Perhaps your friend, the man of Law, enchanted your tongue – I cannot tell what ways sorcerers may have of deceiving one another. But this I do know – that you are no friend of Marsilio diAvila, and must be reckoned to be leagued against him.'

'Because I saved his loyal subject from a vile plot? If I have proved myself today the friend of Rodrigo Cordova, does that not make me a friend of Marsilio diAvila too? If it does not, I would like to hear the reason why.'

'You are too clever for your own good, my friend,' hissed Sceberra, 'but your reckoning will come soon enough, now that I have you.'

'I cannot see that you need me,' said Orfeo, sourly. 'Indeed, I cannot see why you are anxious, when you have the priest of Law safe and sound.'

Even as he said the words, he realized their significance, and Sceberra could not keep his face straight enough to stop his prisoner seeing the truth.

'By all the gods,' said Orfeo, 'you do *not* have him safe and sound, do you? Despite that Semjaza knocked him down, he had strength and cunning enough to escape your clutches!'

'Aye,' growled the minister. 'He escaped from this prison last night – while Semjaza was questioning you. Had he and I not been so occupied, I do not think he could have got away – which makes me think that you served his cause, knowingly or not.'

Orfeo held his tongue then, not wanting to tell the minister what other conjectures came into his mind. But he could not help but wonder whether Arcangelo had gone into the hollow mountain, and whether Semjaza might be afraid of what he might find and do there. And he could not help wondering, either, whether Semjaza might be anxious that his enemy would find the way within the crag which led to Rodrigo Codova's house – and whether that had been the reason that the Duke's men had been sent to take Rodrigo prisoner. At last, he thought, he had begun to see the pattern which this web of intrigue had.

But what good could it possibly do him now?

'Semjaza has such faith in himself,' said the minister, 'that he still believes you innocent. For myself, I do not care whether you are innocent or not. You have done what we warned you not to do, and now you must bear the consequence of that.'

Sceberra's hand lay quietly on Orfeo's shoulder while he spoke, but when he finished he lifted it to see if Orfeo could stand alone. Then, finding that Orfeo could stand, he took the hand away, and carefully opened his prisoner's shirt by the cord which tightened the neck. Though it was not part of the player's finery it was a flimsy garment, and when Sceberra suddenly ripped at it the material tore all the way down, leaving Orfeo's left breast bare.

Sceberra touched the nipple on the breast, and said: 'How stupid the hand which shaped us was, to give to men what only women need and use – do you not agree?'

'It is no great inconvenience to have it there,' Orfeo replied.

'You do not think so?' said Sceberra with a laugh. 'You are such a disagreeable man, Master Player, that I feel a need to make you see my point of view for once.'

So saying, the minister picked up from the stone table one of the several sets of pincers which were there, and with one hand on each handle he opened the jaws wide, placing them upon Orfeo's chest. He paused for a few seconds, permitting Orfeo to contemplate the prospect, and then he closed the jaws with a convulsive thrust.

Orfeo screamed with agony, and fainted dead away. Oddly enough, though he was sure that his senses had deserted him, he could still feel the pain – not only the agony beside his heart, but also the cruel wrenching of his wrists as he fell. It was not fair, he thought, as he seemed becalmed in a world of pure pain, that he could not find release even in oblivion.

But then, mercifully, he did, and hoped that in finding it he was cheating his torturer of some small measure of his cruel satisfaction.

So EXHAUSTED WAS poor Orfeo that his oblivion ultimately gave way to sleep, which no doubt did its healing work at last – but it seemed at the time no proper release, because his sleep was full of dreams and the dreams were born of pain, which made them nightmares.

In those nightmares the luckless player was put to the question more severely than he had been in fact, racked by ropes and rent by pincers, with Sceberra's face – distorted by malice – forever thrusting itself into his to spit at him and laugh at his distress.

Semjaza's face was there too, distorted by that corruption of his being which marked him as a servant of things unknown and unnameable, but which gave him a power to hurt which was far beyond the crudity of Sceberra's tools.

Orfeo's sleep was such a hell of anguish, in fact, that it seemed a better release when he finally managed to thrust his soul back to the surface of wakefulness, where the pains which he felt were found to be ordinary after all.

His wrists were sore, but no longer bound. There was a dull fire close to his heart. His whole body had been jarred and bruised. But all of this was superficial, and it was bearable.

He opened his eyes to yellow candlelight, which would have seemed far dimmer but for the glister of the slime upon the walls of the chamber which contained him. The candle-tray was close beside him, near to his head. He was lying on a thin-laid pallet of dirty straw, which did not entirely conceal the hardness of the cold stone floor.

He lifted his head, but when he tried to move his legs he found that one was caught at the ankle, and when he sat up he saw that it was shackled, and that the shackle was chained to the wall close to the end of his makeshift bed. He could stand up and move about, but he was confined by a tether no more than half his own height.

At first the chamber seemed so large that this range seemed very meagre, but then he realized that his station was situated on a narrow ledge, no more than five feet wide, and that beyond the candle-tray there was the rim of a dark, deep pit. This pit stank horribly, and from its depths there emerged a faint sound, part rustle and part rattle, which he could not quite make out. There was something in it of trickling water, but there was something else, too – a different kind of movement.

He pushed the candle closer to the stone rim, then picked up the tray and held it out above the pit, but the light was far too feeble to illuminate its depths.

'It is the sound of rats,' said a thin, hoarse voice. 'All the wastes of the castle are hurled into pits like this one, so that they fall into a common space, where they are flushed all-too-gradually away by water hurled after them. Where they go after that, who can tell?'

Orfeo raised the candle higher then, and saw that beyond the mouth of the pit – which was only six or seven feet across – there was another ledge like his own, with another pallet of filthy straw, and another shackled prisoner, sitting on his crude bed.

The sight of that prisoner made him draw in his breath very sharply. The man must have been handsome once, and to judge by his diction he had been a gentleman, but he seemed as thin now as a starveling beggar. His skin was very white, and there were ugly sores on his face and bare arms.

His hair had grown very thin, and that too had turned white, contrasting sharply with the darkness of his shadowed eyes.

'I am sorry for my appearance, sir,' said the gentleman. 'I fear that I have not seen the light for some years now, and there is something about this dry northern bread which does not entirely agree with my southern stomach. I hope you will not be offended if I say that I am glad to see you, for if my reckoning is correct, it is three months and more since last I had a companion.

'The boy who brings my meagre rations has no time to talk nor inclination to listen, and I am not ashamed to say that loneliness has weighed upon me far more heavily than this shackle upon my leg.'

Though this speech was very carefully made its tone was undercut by anguish, and Orfeo could tell that it cost the other much to maintain such studied politeness.

'Who are you?' asked Orfeo. He spoke more abruptly than he normally would, for the shock of the place, added to the legacy of his nightmares, had taken an icy grip on his mind.

'My name is Jacomo Falquero,' said the other, speaking a little less hoarsely now. 'I am a native of Gualcazar. May I know your name?'

'It is Orfeo,' replied the player. 'I have no family name, and I have no home. I live as a travelling player and teller of tales.'

At that, the other man burst suddenly into tears – though Orfeo saw that he had all-too-little to spare in the way of actual tears, and must perforce sob rather drily.

'Oh, Orfeo,' said the miserable man, 'you cannot know how I have prayed for a companion, though I knew it was an evil thing I did. I cannot help but be glad to see you, though I hate myself for wishing such captivity as mine on another man. Forgive me, my friend, if my prayer has played a part in bringing you here. Forgive me!'

Orfeo felt a sudden lump in his throat, as if he might himself burst into tears in sympathy with the pangs of Falquero's conscience. But he swallowed hard, and said: 'Hush, man! I was brought here by an evil creature who wished me harm, and not by your prayers. And if it is my fate that I must languish here a while, I am glad that I do not find myself alone.'

He looked around, to judge more precisely the nature of his confinement. The cell was rectangular, some sixteen or seventeen feet by maybe thirteen, while the pit cut a narrower rectangle from its floor, taking six or seven feet from the longer dimension and eight from the shorter. The floor was laid out in the shape of an angular horseshoe, with a door halfway around.

'How long have you been here?' asked Orfeo, gently, when the sobbing stopped and Falquero began to win the struggle to control himself.

'Five years, as near as I can reckon,' said the other, mournfully. 'I have had other companions, but they were so broken by torture that they did not live long. None was with me for longer than a month before being tumbled into the pit – though those who keep us do not always wait until a man is dead before they give him to the rats.'

Orfeo looked down at the pit again, and could not repress a shudder.

'How did you come to this fate?' he asked his companion.

'Do you ask if I committed some crime?' replied Falquero, with a hollow laugh. 'No – I see that you do not. Nor do I ask of you how you deserved this confinement. I was sent to Zaragoz with a little girl, to be her protector, appointed by her lawful guardian. My small mistress was summoned by her relative the, Duke, in the expectation that when she came of age she might marry his son – but we did not like what we found here, and one night I tried to take her away in secret, to return her to her guardian in

Gualcazar. I have been here ever since, and do not know what became of my mistress.'

'Is her name Serafima?' asked Orfeo.

'It is,' said the other, raising his head from his hands as he spoke, in surprise and expectation.

'Then I can tell you that she is alive. She is a prisoner, but in a kinder place than this. I have not seen her, but I was near her only two nights ago. I cannot speak for the Duke, but I think his intention still is that she should marry his son, if the lady's consent can only be won. It seems that he has been patient while they were still so young – but I do not know what will happen now that her coming-of-age approaches.'

Jacomo Falquero received this news in silence, and though he was obviously grateful to know that the lady was not dead, still he could take only meagre comfort from a knowledge of her situation.

Orfeo looked again down into the pit, which drew his thoughts at every moment's pause. Was this, he asked himself, to be his end? Was he to be cast, dead or alive, into the castle's cloaca, to be devoured by the vile scavengers which wallowed in its filth?

He moved the candle closer to his bed, knowing that Sceberra had only left it for him so that he might see his eventual destination.

How long, he wondered, would Sceberra deign to let him remain in the living hell of confinement and contemplation, before tiring of his continued existence and putting an end to him? Did any other know that he was here – and would any other care, if any knew? How fiercely would Rodrigo Cordova pursue enquiries as to his whereabouts – and what effect could his efforts possibly have, given that he seemed to be surrounded by enemies of his own, and might easily be brought here himself?

'Did they hurt you much?' asked Jacomo Falquero – and Orfeo saw that the other man was staring at the ugly bloodstain on his shirt that marked the wound which Sceberra had inflicted.

'Only in anger,' he said. 'There is nothing I can tell them which they need to know, and though the minister says he doubts it, I think he knows that it is true. If he tortures me again, it will be for pleasure alone. Perhaps he will not, for he seems to have other things to occupy his mind – perhaps to do with your mistress's coming of age. The doom of Zaragoz has been cried by a strange prophet, and there is an unease in the land. If there were but a chance of diAvila's defeat–'

'My friend,' said Falquero, 'I would not deny you hope while it can still nourish your soul – but while I have been here I have found that hope, in the end, becomes one more kind of torture. In such captivity as this, one can only live from hour to hour. Once, I prayed every day for my release, but as those prayers have gone unanswered, I have forced myself to make my ambitions more modest than that.'

Orfeo stretched himself to soothe his aches, then knelt to test the strength of the shackle which bound him to the wall.

It was very strong, fixed by two thick rivets. They must have brought a smith here with him, to forge the metal while he was still unconscious – and the smith must have been a skilled man, too, for his ankle had not been seared by the heat – cold water must have quenched it in the brief interval before it spread from the rivets to the circlet.

The fact that they had sealed him thus, rather than using a lock and key, told him unequivocally that Sceberra did not plan to let him go. The minister was a man with all the necessary power and cruel inclination to turn his petulance into a sentence of slow and horrible death.

Orfeo felt a surge of righteous wrath in his guts, which screamed that this *could not be*, for he had done nothing at all to deserve it. But it plainly *was*, and all complaints that he might utter – whether he directed them at the man who had done this or at the gods themselves – would not alter it.

He considered what Falquero had said about hope becoming one more thread of torture, but put the thought from him. The time was not yet come to despair. Rodrigo Cordova lived, and was his friend. And, absurd as it might seem, the lady Veronique might still be so determined to have him play and dance at the Night of Masks as to demand that her father's minister allow him to do it.

While he knelt there, still listening to the traffic of vermin in the caves far below, the door of the cell opened. Orfeo took up the candle to see better who it was.

It was a small boy, bearing a pair of leather buckets. It was the same small boy, in fact, who had brought food to the other prison, where the lady Serafima was confined, and Orfeo realized what a sick irony it was that the boy's enforced silence had prevented him from reporting to Falquero how his mistress fared.

The boy would not break that silence even now, though he recognized Orfeo instantly. There was someone behind him in the doorway, watching to see that the rule was not broken – not Fernand Arrigo or any other man-at-arms, but the far more sinister figure of the huge man who had held Orfeo prisoner while Sceberra hurt him.

Orfeo dared not speak to the boy, lest he should cause him further trouble, but he knew that his eyes were imploring the child to spread the news of his presence here. As he tried to exert the force of his will to send that silent message he wished fervently that he had the art to work one tiny trick of magic. But he was not even sure that the boy knew who it was that had carried him unconscious to the kitchens, or would think it a debt he owed even if he did.

The boy took two small loaves from one of his buckets, and laid them carefully down, one at the end of each ledge, beside a wooden bowl already waiting there. He added a few leaves of raw cabbage. Then he poured a measure of water into each bowl.

'Thank you,' said Orfeo, in a tone as neutral as he could manage. Falquero said nothing. Then the boy left, and the giant cellkeeper closed the door behind him.

'He had a dozen loaves and more,' said Orfeo. 'There must be other dungeons like this one, each with its oubliette, a ready supply of noxious gases, and the ever-present music of the rats.'

'Sometimes,' said Falquero, 'there are other sounds. Before I was a prisoner, I was told that the caves are very extensive, and that the rats which feed on the wastes of the castle are eaten in their turn by monsters which never see the light of day.

'One of my former companions lived – for a brief while – in the terror that something whose foulness was beyond his imagining might come from that pit to devour him alive. There have been times when I would not have cared had something of that kind come for me, but nothing ever did. Whatever makes the sounds can no more fly than the rats can, and the wall of the pit must be very hard to climb.'

Orfeo could have wished for less macabre conversation as he ate his frugal meal, but he did not complain. And when the meal was over, he listened while Falquero told him more about the agonies of confinement. He felt that it was not for him to question that need which the other man had to speak his mind, and that it was a necessary act of kindness to let the thoughts spill out as they would, without interruption.

Eventually, though, Falquero's need to talk gave way to a need to listen, and he begged Orfeo to tell him a story: a story which would make no mention whatsoever of Zaragoz, or prisons, or shackles, or pits.

This Orfeo did, as bravely as he could. He wove a complicated plot out of the adventures of a Bretonnian king's three sons, each of whom fell in love with a different magical woman and was sent on a remarkable quest, which tests all would have failed save that their paths crossed and recrossed, so that they might all help one another, until in the end each one achieved his heart's desire, though only one could inherit the kingdom.

It was by nature a long story, and Orfeo made no attempt to shorten it, for he wished to be lost in its twists and turns nearly as much as his companion did, and though he knew

all along how it would end he was nevertheless carried
away by the suspenseful art of his telling.

The story helped him to forget, for a while, the many
hurts which were afflicting his body, and when he finally
reached the end of it he found that he had become very
drowsy, and was able to escape into a far gentler slumber
than the nightmare-infested sleep from which he had earlier roused himself.

WHEN HE AWOKE again, he did not know where he was at
first, and when he opened his eyes the darkness was
impenetrable, for the candle had long since burned out.
For a moment or two he struggled for recall, but then the
stench of the pit brought it all back to him, and he felt the
coldness of the stone beneath the straw.

He could still hear the sound of rats, roaming restlessly
about the depths of the pit. But there was another sound,
too, which must have played a part in waking him. It was
the sound of a creaking hinge, and he realized that the
door to the cell was being opened, very slowly.

He sat up then, and turned towards the sound – and as
the links of his own confining chain rattled quietly, so
there was a second rattle, like an echo – which was the
sound of Jacomo Falquero sitting up in his turn, having
been similarly awakened.

Having been pushed carefully open, the door was pulled
to again – and still no one spoke, for whoever was coming
in was trying to do so as quietly as he could.

Then, when all the sounds had died save for the distant
whisper of the rats, there was a little flicker of bright flame,
and there appeared from the darkness a hand, lighted as if
by a will-o'-the-wisp dancing upon the palm. By that light,
Orfeo could see a face – and no doubt Falquero could see
it too, for when they spoke it was in unison, and the name
which they pronounced was exactly the same, in its syllables and in the sheer astonishment with which they spoke.

What they said was: *'Arcangelo!'*

INTERLUDE

ORFEO PAUSED IN his narrative as one of the candles guttered and went out. It was not until he moved, and pain shot along his right arm from shoulder to elbow, that he realized how stiff he had become, entranced by the intensity of his narrative.

He was not the only one who seemed entranced. He looked across the table into the face of Alkadi Nasreen, who had been listening so intently that his features seemed carved from wood. Two or three empty seconds passed before the Caliph's concentration was broken; then he scowled.

'This is a devilish long story,' said Alkadi Nasreen, shifting an empty wine-cup and looking round. 'It has kept us here all night.'

'I am sorry,' said Orfeo. 'When I saw how interested you were, I became determined that you should not miss the slightest detail of the tale.'

'But it is all mysteries and riddles! Are all your Bretonnian tales so convoluted?'

'They tend that way,' Orfeo admitted, 'but in this case, the convolutions were not built in by me. I am simply reconstructing the pattern by which events unwound. I can promise you solutions to most of the mysteries and some of the riddles, but true stories are never as neat as the ones a player makes up for the telling. When I invent, I am like a god who knows all, and can intervene in the interests of justice to ensure that the guilty are punished and the good rewarded. When I remember, I am only a man, who sees but the smallest fraction of what occurs, and has no authority to command or understand those higher beings whose work it is to determine who shall live and who shall die.'

'If you know the answers to these mysteries now,' said the Caliph, speaking as though he had a sour taste in his mouth, 'then you need not make mysteries of them while you tell your story.'

'A story is still a story,' Orfeo replied, 'and must proceed from beginning to end. And besides, there are questions whose answers you have chosen to hide from me, in order to contrive a little drama of your own – for you have not told me precisely where your interest in my story lies, thus insisting that I risk offending you. If you would tell me what name you bore before you were Alkadi Nasreen, Caliph of Mahabbah and Lord of the Twin Seas–'

'Damn your infernal curiosity!' retorted the other. 'I want the truth, not half-truth bent to the purposes of clever flattery in the hope of securing your release. You are a slave here, Mater Orfeo, and it is I who have the sole right to make demands and ask questions. How much longer will the telling of this story take?'

'It is difficult to judge,' said Orfeo, 'as I have never told it before.'

'We have storytellers in Araby, too,' said the Caliph, coldly. 'Among the stories which they tell is the tale of a wife sentenced to execution, who obtained stay after stay by telling stories to her royal husband, each one suspended before morning in order to win another day of life by tempting curiosity, until the farce had lasted a thousand and one nights. You would not seek to treat me thus, I trust?'

'I fear that my storytelling skills would not suffice to make it last as long as that,' said Orfeo, blandly. 'I have lost track of the hours, but another session as long as this should bring the tale close to its conclusion. I assure your highness that I am no more anxious than you are to spend another thousand nights in this manner.'

'Then you must go to your room now, and sleep. Tonight, when I summon you again, you will take the tale to its conclusion. Then we will see what has become of our bargain.'

So saying, the Caliph clapped his hands loudly, and there came into the room the same female servant who had led Orfeo from his prison so many hours before. He could not believe that she had stayed awake so long, waiting outside the door, and concluded that she must have a couch nearby where she had taken her rest.

He was very tired himself, and longed to throw himself down on a soft bed. His wounded shoulder pained him, and so too did an older wound upon his breast, which he had thought quite healed.

Is this old age which creeps upon me,? he thought? Perhaps Estalia took a greater toll than I thought.

But he did not really mean 'Estalia'. He meant *Zaragoz*. The name held no particular terrors for him now, but there was much that he did not care to remember in the record of his adventures there. The memory of DiAvila's dungeons, and the things which lurked beneath them, was something which came to him now and again in nightmares, but this was the first time that he had ever undertaken to describe what had occurred there in detail. To tell the story, leaving nothing out, would be to relive the darkest and most dangerous hours of his life, and it would tax his strength and spirit. Still, it must be done.

When he was put back in the room which served as his prison the boy Maro promptly woke up, and greeted him.

'Did the Caliph like your tale?' asked the boy, fearfully.

Orfeo threw himself down upon a bed of cushions, and said: 'I cannot tell, for it is only half-told. I had hoped to see in his eyes whether he was a friend or an enemy of the men of Zaragoz who came to hate me, but I cannot. Reason tells me that if he were not their enemy, he would not have quit the town... and yet, I cannot be sure. Even if he is Quixana, there may be less in the tale to please him than I could put in, if I dared to invent an ending other than the true one.'

'Well,' said the boy, bravely, 'we have one more day to live, and I am not made a eunuch yet.'

'No,' said Orfeo, 'and I have been in too many prisons, harsher by far than this one, not to hope for release. I have been a lucky man where prisons are concerned, and have sometimes thought that the gods must like me very much as a wanderer, to set me free so often and send me on my way. I must trust in Morr and Manann, by whom he made me swear, that they will save me now.'

So saying he let his eyes fall shut – and very soon was fast asleep.

But Maro, watching him carefully, saw that he was troubled in his sleep by dreams which made him move, and sometimes make as if to cry out, though very little actual sound spilled from his lips.

He is dreaming, thought the boy, or else foul daemons are taunting him, telling him that he will soon be theirs.

Then he got up, and went to the window to watch the birth of the new and hopeful day.

Part Two
THE NIGHT OF MASKS

Nine

ARCANGELO SEEMED STARTLED himself, and it was obvious to Orfeo that he had not expected to discover two prisoners whom he knew. But the wizard recovered his composure quickly, and put a finger to his lips to ask for silence. His eyes darted first one way and then the other, as if he did not know which of them to speak to first, but after a moment's hesitation he went to his left, to that side of the pit where poor Falquero had been chained for five long years, and embraced him with one arm, while the other held his tiny light aloft.

Falquero had burst into another fit of sobbing, but he stifled the sound in Arcangelo's cloak as he pressed his face into the older man's shoulder.

The spellcaster turned then, to look across the empty space at Orfeo.

'You here?' he said, in a very low tone. 'Did I not warn you to tread carefully in Zaragoz?'

'Aye,' Orfeo replied, in a whisper. 'And so did Semjaza –

but I became entangled nevertheless, and had thought like your friend that I might never see the light of day again. Of the people I hoped might come to save me, you are the last I thought to see. But you did not come for me, did you?'

'No,' said Arcangelo. 'I came for Jacomo, who was once unwittingly betrayed by me, when I entrusted him with a mission far too dangerous for him to carry out. I should not have sent him, but I could not bear to send the child alone to Zaragoz.'

Orfeo nodded. 'So you were Serafima Quixana's guardian. Why did you send her at all, when you knew that the diAvilas could mean her no good?'

'Once they had found us, there was no other way. Had I refused, they would have taken her anyway – even if we had succeeded in gaining a fuller measure of protection from the rulers of Gualcazar, diAvila could have sent assassins to kill her. My wizardry was a poorer thing, then, and when I tested it against Semjaza and the sorceress I knew that I could not prevail. My only hope was to gain time.'

'Why did they not kill her anyway,' asked Orfeo, 'if she is the last of the Quixana line?'

'A family which has extended over centuries cannot be made extinct,' said Arcangelo. 'The bearers of the name may be destroyed, but there is always one more branch to be traced, one more chain of kinship. It is a matter of taking one more step towards the root, to find another place where the blood is leaked into the meshes of a dozen marriages. Had they killed Serafima, there would have been another heir, somewhere in Zaragoz or in the wider world. Safer, they thought, to make frail Serafima the anchor of such hope as their opponents had, and make her blood a prisoner of their own.'

'Might it not have been best to let them do it?' said Orfeo, with a hint of bitterness. 'If a marriage can put an end to centuries of hatred and violence... would that not be the preferable way?'

'Only if justice were to be forgotten... only if right were to be abandoned. You are a clever man, Orfeo, and I think that you know well enough what a dreadful kind these diAvilas have become, in the pursuit of their pleasure and ambition. I have one thing left to do with my life, and that is to save the lady Serafima – whether or not it requires my own damnation to secure that end.'

Orfeo accepted the rebuke. He did know what Arcangelo meant, perhaps better than the spellcaster knew.

Jacomo Falquero spoke for the first time. 'Can your magic break the shackle on my leg?' he whispered, in a voice tremulous with resurrected hope. 'Can you bring me safe from these loathsome walls?'

Arcangelo pushed him away, but very gently, and looked him up and down: 'Poor Jacomo,' he said, 'I had a picture of you in my mind, which was the image of a very different man. I had not imagined that they could reduce you so far, and hurt you so much. Five years has not been an easy span for me to bear, but I did not know it had been eternity for you.'

'But it is over now!' said the other, perhaps too loudly, with another sob gathering in his heart.

'No,' replied Arcangelo, in a tone which said that he wished that it were so. 'It is barely begun – and the hardest work is yet to do.'

He looked again at Orfeo, and though he said nothing Orfeo knew only too well that his help was being asked. Arcangelo had come here – by what miraculous means Orfeo could only guess – not to lead Jacomo Falquero to freedom, but to enlist his help in securing the release of another prisoner: the lady Serafima. In order to accomplish that end, Arcangelo's magic must not only claim its first victory over Semjaza's, but sow sufficient confusion to reduce a hundred men-at-arms to impotence. He had looked to have a stout swordsman of his own to help him, but he had found out now that Jacomo Falquero was ill-fitted to be that man.

'I have a score to settle with Sceberra,' said Orfeo, grimly. 'Only break this shackle, and I will do what I can. Nothing would give me more pleasure than to snatch the prize

from Sceberra's very grasp – and though I cannot see how
you hope to get her out of Zaragoz, or make her safe from
assassins if you do, I am with you to the end.'

'I have given fair warning,' said Arcangelo, gently, 'that if
justice cannot prevail, then Zaragoz is doomed. There is a
place where the lady will be safe for a while, if only we can
get her there – a place where the walls themselves will try
to hold her safe.'

Orfeo knew where those walls were, though he was not
yet convinced that the magic within them had really been
awakened by the blast which Arcangelo had tempted from
Semjaza. He was glad to think, though, that they might be
able to hold Rodrigo Cordova protectively, now that the
attempt to keep him from them had been thwarted.

'I pray that your magic will be powerful enough,' said
Orfeo, and could not help himself from adding: 'this time.'

'I let Semjaza lay me low,' said Arcangelo, 'for I had to
go to that house, before I came here. All has been planned
– as I think you now suspect, I have chosen every move
since I drew Rodrigo Cordova to the tavern where we
rested on that first night. Semjaza thought that I was helpless, but you can see that I am not, and I think that he is
anxious now that he knows how badly he mistook my
strength. I am a more powerful man by far than I was
when first I met my enemy, and I think he may be frailer.
But magic is by no means mere brute force – victory goes
to those who use their power deftly, with cleverness and
cunning.'

Orfeo remembered Semjaza's face, as it had peered into
his own while he was being questioned, and as it had
appeared again in his nightmare.

Though he had no sensible way of judging, he was not
yet prepared to agree that Semjaza was less strong than
once he had been – nor was he certain that the advantage
of cleverness and cunning lay with Arcangelo.

It was as if he heard again in his mind those words
which Semjaza had spoken to him: *Something might be
made of a man like you.*

It was Sceberra, not Semjaza, who had made him into an enemy – but it was Semjaza, not Sceberra, who made him afraid of the coming conflict.

'Well,' he said, gruffly. 'I hope that your strength will not be too severely sapped by the effort of casting off an extra shackle – and I hope too that your plan for invading that citadel above us is a very careful one. If I am destined to be food for those foul things down below, then I do not suppose it will matter whether I go to their feast tonight or another night, but I had far rather that I did not go at all.'

ORFEO WATCHED CLOSELY as Arcangelo worked on the shackles which bound their feet. Though the wizard needed no more equipment to make them loose than his own two hands it did not seem to be an easy task, and he could see the muscles in the spellcaster's neck become tense with the effort. He knew that magicians did not like to admit, even to themselves, how much their spells cost them, so he said nothing – but he had some suspicion of how much strength and skill a cunning man might have accumulated within his body during five years of preparation, and he knew how very quickly that store might be depleted, even in spells of an apparently trivial nature.

When they came out of the cell, Arcangelo led them quickly along a passage to an open door. There were five other doors in the passage, each one of which marked a cell like the one where they had been confined, but Arcangelo was not concerned with other prisoners – and Orfeo thanked the whim of fortune which had chained him alongside Falquero.

Beyond the open door there was a chair for a guard to sit, and there was indeed a fearsome guard sitting upon it – but the huge man was so deeply asleep that only the release of the spell which had put him there would let him wake. Arcangelo removed the sword from the giant's belt and gave it to Falquero. Then he picked up the candle which lit the corridor; his own magical light had gone out when they emerged from the darkness.

There was another door at the corridor's further end,
standing open like the first. Beyond it was the larger chamber where Sceberra had tortured Orfeo – and there, left
carelessly on the slab with the other instruments, was the
player's slender sword, which he picked up. There was also
a lantern, which might burn somewhat brighter than the
candle which they already had. Arcangelo picked it up and
lit it, passing the other light to Orfeo.

There was a stairway from this chamber leading up
towards the courtyard of the castle, but Arcangelo did not
take them that way yet. Instead he went to another door,
smaller than the others, which had the appearance of
being rarely used. Its two locks must have been rusted
solid for many years, but Arcangelo had broken them
already, and now he led his companions down a stair
which spiralled into the very heart of the rock.

'Remember the way!' commanded the spellcaster, as he
descended.

The passage was wide enough for comfort, but not high
enough, so that Orfeo, being a tall man, had almost to
crouch in order to make his way down.

Arcangelo saw Orfeo's difficulty when he looked back,
and said: 'There was a castle on this rock before humans
ever came to Zaragoz, and the tunnels which connect the
many caves were hollowed out by the dwarfs who were
masters of the Old World long before men began their rise
from savagery. This crag was a stronghold which the dwarfs
must have struggled long and hard to hold against their
goblin enemies before their race began its slow decline.'

Orfeo had rarely seen a dwarf, and had inherited from
his elvish one-time guardians something of their amused
contempt for that race, but while he had made his own
way in the world of men the lore of legend had told him
how much men owed to the race which had preceded
them, and how much of human civilization was raised
from the ruins of what the dwarfs had left behind.

'The sewer which collects the castle's wastes widens as it
spirals downwards,' Arcangelo continued. 'This is part of

another sequence of passages which runs always above it. There are several pits where the two conjoin, but in other times all were very carefully bridged so that a man – or a dwarf – might pass safely from the castle to any one of a dozen caves giving access to the lower slopes. Around those entrances houses were built when men first came to Zaragoz, but many of the bridges had already crumbled away. The one remaining line of connection was used to invade the castle when the last Quixana duke was deposed, but when it had been done the path was deliberately broken, and the way to the heart of the rock was sealed. Men are not like dwarfs, and they shun the inner spaces of the world, except when necessity drives them downwards into the darkness.'

They went down and around until they came to a branching of the tunnels. Arcangelo showed them a sign which he had scored on the wall with a soft white stone.

'These are the marks which you must follow when you come this way with the lady Serafima,' he said. 'You must know them, for when the alarm is raised in the castle, I must stay to counter Semjaza's tricks, while you must make all possible haste to escape.'

There were two more branches, each clearly marked. Then they came through an arch which let them through not to a further corridor but to a narrow ledge above a sheer slope.

'Take care!' said Arcangelo, urgently. 'It is not deep, but should you fall, I think you know what waits at the bottom.'

There was not the same sound of scampering which Orfeo had heard in the cell, for below him then there had been a place where the rats foraged for food, and gathered in huge numbers.

Below this sheer slope was an emptier region, where the rats went to hide and make nests – and where other things may have waited to catch them. But if a man were to fall, the rats would assemble quickly enough about his broken body.

The ledge ran along the lip of this abyss for a hundred yards and more, curving all the while, and then it came abruptly to its end. The wall of rock cut sharply away to the left, but the ledge did not follow it around – the abyss was narrow here and another rock-face could be seen by the light of Arcangelo's lantern, no more than fifteen feet ahead of them. That other face had an arch set in it, and another tunnel leading away into the depths of the crag, but here the path was broken, and the bridge which had connected the ledge to the tunnel was gone – destroyed and cast into the pit.

Arcangelo stopped, and Orfeo turned to look at Falquero, who was breathing very heavily, and whose legs semed hardly able to support him. He was moving drunkenly, and Orfeo had to catch him by the arm. Falquero looked into his face, his eyes full of pain and fear.

'I cannot,' he whispered. 'I *cannot.*'

'Wait!' commanded Arcangelo. He looked out into the gloom, then passed his lantern back to Orfeo, so that the player now held both their lights.

Suddenly, there was a flutter of wings in the darkness, and something came huriedly towards them. Orfeo raised an arm instinctively, thinking of some monstrous bat, but Arcangelo put out his other arm as though to catch a hunting falcon, and the thing came swiftly to him, grabbing his arm with its claws and steadying itself with a last few beats of its sleek black wings.

It was in fact a raven, and though it was huge enough by the standards of its kind, it was not quite the giant which Orfeo had imagined from the rushing sound of its arrival.

Orfeo had moved the brighter lantern back when he started in surprise, and Jacomo Falquero had caught his arm, so that he could not immediately lift it again to see the bird more clearly – but he could see that in its beak it held a pouch, which it surrendered to Arcangelo.

He thought that something else also passed fom the bird to the man – something like a long black thread which unwound from the bird's body like a leech or a worm, and wound itself around the spellcaster's wrist before squirming sinuously into the shadow of his sleeve. The thing was gone within a second, leaving Orfeo to doubt the evidence of his eyes, but he felt some disquiet.

The magician raised his hand again then, and seemed to throw the bird back into the empty air. There was a moment when it was reluctant to go, and it opened its beak again to emit a small *caw* of protest, but it could not retain its hold. It took wing, and was swallowed instantly by the Stygian gloom.

Arcangelo unwrapped the pouch, and emptied its contents into the palm of his other hand. He seemed very relieved to have them, and in reply to Orfeo's quizzical stare he said: 'All magic needs an instrument, and though the human body is one which plays many a miraculous tune, still there are many tricks which need the alchemist's earths or the elementalist's samples. It is said that anything imaginable might actually be achieved, if only one had the right tools, but such recipes as I have seen for spells involving the blood of dragons or ogres' teeth are very hard to try, and I suspect they have often tested the imagination of the men who wrote them down far more than their actual experience. But here are things whose virtue I know well enough. I could not carry them with me to Rodrigo Cordova's house, or they would have been taken from me, and I had other work to do when I made my way here from the cell where they thought me safely confined.'

First Arcangelo picked up a small amulet, and asked Orfeo to put it around Jacomo Falquero's neck. 'It is a special adamantine,' he said to his old friend, 'which gives resilience to the weak. Pray that it gives you all that you will need to complete the mission which has been five years interrupted.'

Then, to Orfeo, he said: 'I have but one of those, for I had not expected another companion. I need these other things for my own use. All the magical aid which I can offer you – and to Jacomo also I will give it – is to make you immune to my own illusions. It is a small thing, I know, and I cannot give you the power to see through Semjaza's illusions, should he have time and enterprise to use any, but I fear that my stock had perforce to be small enough to be carried in the raven's beak.'

'I am used to relying on my own strength,' Orfeo told him.

Then he saw the priest take something else in his hand, which looked like a tiny twig from an oak tree, bearing a single leaf and a single acorn. With this held covertly in one hand, the magician made signs with the other, murmuring some arcane incantation. There was no flash of light or crack of thunder to mark the acomplishment of the spell, but when Orfeo looked down he suddenly saw that where there had been no bridge but a moment before, now there was a solid piece of rock some five feet wide and six or seven deep.

'That is the route we must follow if we are fortunate in our task,' said the spellcaster. 'The bridge will last until morning unless I choose to make it vanish before then. If I am not here to guide you when you cross it, go carefully – and wait at the first junction until I catch up with you. If, perchance, I cannot come, then you must find your own way to safety, and may the gods to whom you pray guide you kindly and well. Now, I must use my power to discover where Serafima is to be found.'

'There is no need,' said Orfeo. 'I know the very room. It is in the High Tower, and I can guide us there from the courtyard. But there will be guards on every section of the ramparts, and there may be others about on the ledges between the east and west towers.'

'Soldiers and servants need not concern us overmuch,' Arcangelo assured him. 'I can hide us from their observation well enough, and confuse them if the alarm should be raised. If fortune favours us, I will need no more than petty magic to conceal us from beginning to end – but there may be magical alarms too, and if Semjaza awakes – and has the quickness of mind to see what is happening – then

I will need to draw on every resource which I have to keep him at bay.'

'Semjaza is not the only magician in the castle,' said Orfeo, uneasily. 'I know that you have met the sorceresss named Morella d'Arlette, and I fear there may be other followers within these walls of the one she calls the god of luxury.'

'That kind uses its magic to particular ends,' replied Arcangelo, with some measure of contempt. 'They are unlikely to add to our trouble, and insofar as their corruption has distorted and distracted the minds of those upon whom they exercise their charms, their presence here may make our task easier. Semjaza is the one we have to fear, for he has never wasted his power in licentiousness.'

Orfeo could not suppress a pang of anxiety when Arcangelo spoke of those upon whom the charms of Morella d'Arlette and her kind had been exercised, but he quelled it.

He turned to look again at Falquero, whose breathing had calmed as soon as he had donned the amulet. He was standing staighter now, and was more composed than Orfeo had seen him. The virtue of the amulet had been absorbed into his body.

'This false strength will not last indefinitely,' said Arcangelo, 'but long enough. It is time that your enemies had cause to fear what they have made of you.'

'Aye,' said Falquero – and though he said no more, there was a great enough measure of grim feeling in his voice.

Orfeo, meanwhile, was looking at the bridge which had not been there before. He knelt to touch it, to reassure himself that it was in fact solid enough to support a man.

'It will bear your weight,' said Arcangelo.

'Aye,' said Orfeo. 'Unless it vanishes as easily as it appeared.'

'It cannot do so before morning,' said the priest, 'unless I command it – or unless I am destroyed by my enemy. Even if that should happen, you must not despair, for I have tried to prepare for every eventuality in my plan, and

even my death is something which might be turned to the
advantage of the lady I serve.'

Orfeo lowered the brighter of his two lights into the
darkness beside the bridge, but could see nothing in the
gloomy depths. A thought struck him and he looked up at
the spellcaster.

'Where did you go when you escaped from your prison?'
he asked. 'You did not come this way, for you had not the
means to make a bridge until your tame bird brought it to
you.'

'No,' said Arcangelo. 'I did not come this way until I
returned in search of Jacomo. I could not leave my prison
by the door, for Semjaza took care to seal it magically
before he went about his other business. I went into
another region, where I had business of my own.'

As he spoke of 'another region' the magician glanced
downwards, and Orfeo looked down again into the
gloomy depths whose denizens were hidden by the darkness. He was not surprised that a wizard should not have
an ordinary man's fear of rats and other vermin, nor that a
wizard could go up and down faces of rock that were too
sheer to by climbed by man or beast, but he knew well
enough that it must have cost the spellcaster something to
make that descent, and to keep himself safe from harm
while he did whatever it was he had gone to do.

'I think that I would like to have your plan explained,'
said Orfeo. 'For I see that there is much in it which I do not
understand.'

'There is not time,' replied the priest, though Orfeo knew
that this was not the true reason. There was, he knew, an
essential secrecy in magic, which required that its schemes
remain covert. It may well have been the case that
Arcangelo had simply created potentials, which might be
ruined if he said aloud – or even fixed within the privacy
of his own thoughts – what patterns of development
might follow from them. It was often the strength of curses
– including the curse which had allegedly been laid upon
Rodrigo Cordova's house – that not even their creator

could determine precisely how they could and would unfold.

Nevertheless, Orfeo regretted that he could not know more about the tangled web which he had allowed to catch him. If he had to take his life in his hands to serve a cause in which he had no personal interest, at least he would have liked to know what forces were likely to be unleashed in the course of the struggle. Semjaza, he believed, was a friend to powerful daemons. If Arcangelo really had resources which were equal or superior, what could mere mortals do to protect themselves when the conflict was pushed to its limit?

'We must leave the brighter lantern at the foot of the stair,' said Arcangelo, cutting curtly through the thread of his anxious thoughts. 'You will need it when you return, if I am not with you.'

'Well,' said Orfeo, tautly. 'Let us hope that we know all that we need to know. And let us hope that your plan is as perfect as you believe it to be.'

'Trust in me,' replied Arcangelo. 'And trust, if you can, in those gods who love justice.'

Orfeo made no reply, for he knew only too well that he had no alternative but to trust in this enigmatic wizard. But he knew also that a love of justice was by no means adequate to ensure that a just result could or would be attained in any matter of practical endeavour. He knew too much of the world and its ways to trust that the gods would always act to secure its ends.

Ten

THE STONE STAIR which brought them up from the dungeons delivered them into the centre of the castle's courtyard, a little below the level of the two main towers. There were lanterns burning in the stables, and dimmer lights illuminated from within a few of the glazed windows in the main living-quarters below the eastern tower, but the place where they had emerged was in deep darkness. They waited for a little while so that their eyes could become accustomed to the starlight.

From where they were they could see a stationary sentry on each tower, and they knew that there must be two or three more hidden within the gatehouse which was in the south-east wall. A two-man patrol was walking the circuit of the walls, offering a low-voiced ritual greeting to each of the sentries as they passed him by.

Had that been all, Orfeo would have been well pleased, but it was not. Standing still upon the south-west rampart, close to the High Tower, was a solitary figure, darkly dressed but unhelmeted, who was staring out over the silent land. At first, Orfeo wondered whether it might be Sceberra, but his stature was not quite right, and when he moved Orfeo saw that the way the man carried himself was rather more graceful. When the patrol passed the man on its round the two men did not speak, but saluted him with more than ordinary reverence.

'Come now,' whispered Arcangelo, in the softest of voices. 'They will not see us.'

Orfeo touched Falquero briefly on the arm, signalling him to follow. What had been but a pale shadow of a man now seemed all sinew and strength, and Orfeo knew that Arcangelo's amulet would sustain the man through the next few hours – which ought to be more than ample time to complete their adventure.

Arcangelo moved swiftly and quietly to the next level, and then to the next, each time moving quickly up the nearest stair and across the ledge, pausing in the shadow of the vertical face. It seemed very easy to climb all the way to the High Tower without being seen.

There was an open archway at the bottom of the tower, with a door set some way within. They moved safely into the protection of the covert, and Arcangelo quickly bent to the lock on the door, letting slip a small sigh of relief – which Orfeo took to mean that there was no magic seal upon it whose breaking might disturb Semjaza.

Within a few seconds, the lock was breached and the door swung open, with only the slightest creaking as it moved upon its hinges.

There were no candles set on the stairway which led up into the tower, and the windows were unglazed slits which let in hardly any light at night.

Orfeo touched the wall with his hand, not relishing the prospect of feeling his way, but Arcangelo conjured up the same tiny flame that he had made before, and used it to light their way until they were close to the floor on which Orfeo had been confined while Semjaza questioned him.

Arcangelo extinguished his light again when they reached that point. There was certain to be a guard in the straight corridor which cut through the tower to give access to the cells, and he would be the first substantial barrier to their progress.

When they came to the door which gave access to the corridor Orfeo was able to look through the small barred window which was set at head height. There was a small table inside, with a single candle, and a chair. The guard was sitting on the chair with his feet up on the table, and though he was obviously quite relaxed he did not seem to be asleep. He had his back to the door.

Orfeo had nursed a faint hope that he might find Fernand Arrigo on duty here – which would give him the opportunity to use persuasion in pursuing his goal – but this man was far leaner in his build. Failing that, he had hoped to find this door unbolted, so that they would be able to reach the guard without difficulty – but when Arcangelo tested the door it would not yield. Orfeo expected the magician to use his art, but instead it was Falquero who eased him aside, and tested the gap between the bars with his wasted arm.

An ordinary hand would have been too well-fleshed to go through the narrow gap betwen the bars of the peep-hole, but Falquero's entire arm was so unnaturally thin that it could pass through it. By this means he could reach the bolt on the inside, and draw it back.

Orfeo and the magician stood aside. If the bolt was habitually drawn every time the door was closed then it must move easily in its track – but even the best of bolts is likely to creak as it moves. Orfeo's sword was still in its scabbard, but he drew from his belt another weapon which he had borrowed from Sceberra's torture-chamber when they had passed through it for the second time – a pair of pincers whose heavy head would make a very useful club.

Falquero drew the bolt as carefully as any man could, but still it scraped slightly as it came free. The man in the chair tried to sit upright, but because his legs were on the table there was a precious second wasted while he put them on the ground, and by the time he could turn to look at the door Falquero's arm had been withdrawn.

It could not have been obvious, in the candlelight, that the bolt had been taken back, and Orfeo hoped that the guard would simply resume his former position – but he did not. He stood up, and came towards the door. Orfeo, the priest and Falquero moved aside, so that they could not be seen through the peep-hole, and Orfeo put his hand on the handle of the door, trying to gauge the guard's position by sound alone.

When he judged that the moment was ripe Orfeo suddenly turned the handle and shoved the door with all his might. It smashed into the guard's body with a considerable thud, knocking enough wind out of him to prevent him from crying out. The unfortunate man-at-arms managed no more than a whimper of surprise before Orfeo rounded the door and brought the pincers down heavily upon his head, knocking him senseless.

He fell, but not silently – a dagger fell from his belt, clattering as it hit the stone floor, and Orfeo froze instinctively, wondering if the sound could be heard. When nothing happened, he moved along the corridor, not pausing at the cell where he had formerly been confined, but going swiftly to the other. He drew back its bolts, and then stood aside so that Falquero could precede him.

There was a candle lit within the room, but it had burned very low. The woman who lay on the bed was apparently fast asleep, her face turned towards the door so that it caught the light very well. What struck Orfeo was the odd facial resemblance between this lady and the Duke's own daughter – save that where Veronique had that remarkable flame-red hair, this lady had hair as black as a raven's wing.

The sight affected Falquero very differently, and he fell to his knees beside the bed, saying: 'My lady!' in a way that was part whisper of adoration, part cry of anguish. It was loud enough to wake her, and her eyes came open, staring at him first in confusion, then in shock, and finally in horror.

'Jacomo!' she exclaimed – far too loudly for Orfeo's liking, though it was hardly a shout. 'Oh, Jacomo, what have they done to you?'

Arcangelo still hung back in the corridor, his hand upon his forehead as though he were preoccupied with the sensing of distant events. If there was a magical alarm, it would be triggered now, and the time of their greatest danger would be fast approaching.

'There is no time,' Orfeo said to Falquero, in an urgent tone. 'Take her up, man, take her up!'

Falquero, who seemed to have lost control of himself for the moment, was slow to respond, but the woman – or girl, for now that she sat up Orfeo could see that she was younger than Veronique – put her arms around his neck to hug him. When she did that, Falquero remembered what he was about, and seized her around the waist, pulling her from her blanket. She was clad only in a loose white nightshirt, but it was capacious enough, and Falquero lifted her from the bed with an effortlessness which belied his apparent condition. She was small, and Orfeo could have carried her with ease, but that Falquero's excessively thin arms could bear any weight at all seemed incongruous.

'Now,' said Orfeo, 'we must fly. Make no sound, my lady, I beg of you.'

Arcangelo barely glanced at them as he led the way back to the stair, and Orfeo judged by his hurry that he had become very anxious, though he said nothing at all. They descended the stair as carefully as they could in the dark, knowing that a slip and a tumble might put a sorry end to their mission.

By the time they reached the bottom in safety, Orfeo was beginning to believe that they could complete what they had set out to do. He knew that it would require only the pettiest of magic to distract the attention of the unwary sentries while they fled across the open space to the stair which would let them down into the dungeons – and then into the underworld beneath the citadel. But Arcangelo peered out from the archway into the starlit terraces with obvious trepidation.

They had to pause where they were, pressing themselves into the wall behind the protective archway. The man they had seen on the ramparts, apparently taking a stroll at this most unusual hour, was no longer on the ramparts. He had come down to the courtyard, and was standing only fifteen feet away, looking down across the descending terraces in the direction of the southern tower.

There seemed to be no alternative but to wait for the man to stroll on, and so Orfeo and Falquero stayed quite still, but Arcangelo was agitated now and eager to be gone. Instead of waiting, he moved forward, approaching the man from behind very stealthily, obviously intent on striking him down by magical means. As the spellcaster came near to his target, though, the man moved on again, heading in the direction in which they must go themselves, preceding them down the first of the stairways which they must traverse.

Arcangelo looked around, as though alarmed to find himself alone and exposed beneath the weak light of the stars.

Orfeo thought for just an instant that nothing was happening, but then he saw movement in the shadows beneath the battlements, and he knew that Arcangelo had seen the movements too. What it was that was moving Orfeo could not tell, but it was nothing human – it was as if the shadows themselves were taking on substance.

Arcangelo turned, briefly, to face his two companions, and though his face should have been all-but-invisible there was a brief flicker of light which illuminated his features, and showed how tormented they had become.

'Go!' whispered Orfeo to Falquero. 'Run for your life and stop for no man!'

Half a dozen strides took them past Arcangelo, who did not try to follow them – instead the spellcaster turned to face those slow shadows which moved upon him from the looming walls. Orfeo did not look back to see what would become of him, for the only thought now in his mind was the determination to escape, if he could. While he and Falquero moved across each ledge they would be clearly visible to the sentries on the tower and the men-at-arms patrolling the ramparts – all the more so because of the lady's white gown – and now that Arcangelo's talents must be diverted to another battle his magic would no longer work subtly on the observers to make sure that their heads were turned away. In any case, there was the lone man ahead of them, who would surely turn to see them as they came upon him.

Orfeo drew his sword, keeping the pincers in his other hand, for he knew that there must now be a fight.

They rushed down the first stair, and were then within a dozen yards of the flight which was their next target, but they saw that the stroller had paused beside the head of that stair, and was already turning to see what was happening behind.

Someone else had come on to the terrace too – a manservant, hurrying from the western tower to the east with two heavy buckets, his shoes rattling on the stone above their heads. The man, confused, did not know whether to look behind him or to the side, and while he hesitated Orfeo hurled himself at his back, striking out at him with the heavy pincers.

By the light of the stars Orfeo could just make out the features of the other man, who now realized his danger and tried to bring forth his sword, but as Orfeo struck at him he turned his face away, and threw himself to the side. Orfeo took a step after him, letting Falquero overtake him and race down the stair with the girl in his arms.

'To arms!' cried the man, letting loose the cry as though a convulsive surge of air had been released, with difficulty, from his lungs. 'Stop them!' He had nearly drawn his sword by now, though he had taken another step backwards in order to gain time to do it. Orfeo, instead of chasing him further, hurled the heavy pincers at the man's broad chest. His aim was not perfect, but good enough, and as the other tried to ward off the missile with his right hand – it was his left which had plucked at his sword – he was knocked sideways, stumbling awkwardly. Orfeo ran down the stairway behind Falquero, taking the steps three at a time.

Smoke suddenly boiled out of the pavement in great quantity, in front of them and behind, but Falquero did not pause, and Orfeo was overtaken by the most curious sensation as he looked at the dark, roiling clouds and saw both that they were *there* and *not there*. He knew immediately that the smokescreen was more of Arcangelo's magic – an illusion intended to cover their retreat. He did not try to look back to see where the spellcaster was, but ran in pursuit of Falquero.

But the man he had knocked over had already come to his feet, and was bounding down the stair so quickly that he was almost at Orfeo's heels. He was too close for the smoke to hide Orfeo from him, and he was shouting: 'The dungeons! To the dungeons with all speed! *Semjaza! Semjaza!*'

As he bounded down the the next flight of stairs, touching stone only once as he leapt, Orfeo calculated that the main danger lay ahead rather than behind. The illusory smoke would slow pursuit, but if men-at-arms could be roused quickly enough by his pursuer's call to arms, which was now being relayed by many voices to every corner of the castle, they might easily find the way to the dungeons blocked.

'Fly!' he cried to Falquero, as he almost caught up with his companion. 'Stop at nothing, and I will cover your retreat as best I can!'

His sword was in his hand now, and there was a high excitement surging in his body which was part fear and part exhilaration – for he loved to be in action once his blood was up, though he had the sanity not to let his blood boil too easily.

They flew so fast that they came to the doorway to the dungeons when only two of the guardsmen had reached it – and both of those were fuddled by their rude awakening and bewildered by the smoke. Falquero pushed one aside without difficulty, and Orfeo pricked the other one in the lower leg to make him fall. Then they were through the door and descending, and it hardly mattered that a dozen men were thundering at their heels, for the passage was too narrow to let them come two abreast, and Orfeo held his blade behind him as he hurried on, ready to lash out if the leader of the pack approached too close.

In the torture chamber the massive guard was struggling to recover from the spell which had bound him. When Falquero came past him his great eyes blazed with anger, and he came slowly and awkwardly to his feet. Finding his own sword gone he snatched up one of the heavy irons which lay upon the table. A true blow from that would have knocked a man down, but even without the effects of Arcangelo's spell to trouble his movements the big man was a ponderous creature, who needed time and space aplenty to make best use of his strength.

Orfeo's thin blade licked out with furious speed as he ran past, and though the man twisted sufficiently to save his throat from being speared the point went into the side of his neck and cut the artery there, so that bright blood fountained out.

The giant howled in anguish, and tried with all his might to bring his clumsy weapon to bear, but Orfeo was too quick by far, and the rapier struck again, this time blinding the big man in one eye. Then Orfeo made shift to be gone, as other men came hurtling into the room, finding room to organize themselves for the first time.

As Orfeo went through the tiny door he turned himself around in order to go backwards down the steps. This slowed him down considerably, but it meant that his long arm and sharp blade were behind him to fend off pursuers who might otherwise have found him an easy target for a thrown dagger or any other improvised missile. Though he

was compelled to fence with his immediate pursuer that
opponent had great difficulty making enough room for
himself in the low-ceilinged passage, and though Orfeo
had not the advantage of elevation he felt that he was in
control of the duel. Furthermore, he knew that every second he used up was a further advantage to the fleeing
Falquero, who could now draw clear of him. Every pause
and clash of blades made their true mission safer, and the
cost did not seem too high in terms of peril to his own life,
for he was certain that he could defend himself even more
successfully once he reached the ledge which led to the
magical bridge.

As he danced down the first flight of stairs, and then the
second, he found no real hazard in the clumsy blade
which stabbed out at him. He was in near-darkness,
though someone behind the man-at-arms who harried
him kept trying to hold a lantern aloft so that he had light
to help him.

There were too many pursuers in the passage, and every
time the leading man tried to balance himself for a blow
he was buffeted from behind by those over-impatient for
his further progress. First one man went down, then
another – both knocked over by their friends, who then
stumbled awkwardly over the fallen bodies.

As they descended further Orfeo did not put in a single
bloody blow, but he was not worried about that, and there
seemed to him a pleasant justice in the fact that his immediate opponent was being battered, bruised and kicked by
his friends instead of his enemy. There was a clash of
swords at the second junction, where the available space
was greater, and again on the next stair as the pursuers realized what was happening and ceased to ruin the hopes of
their own vanguard – but the man whom fate had now
appointed to lead the charge was no expert with the rapier
he carried, and Orfeo quickly saw that there was an advantage to be gained by refusing to hurt the man, as he did not
want someone cleverer taking his place. By skilful parries
he kept the man's hopes alive while they passed another

junction, and came all the way to the ledge beside the abyss. There the pursuer's own clumsiness betrayed him, and he failed to make the turn, tumbling over the edge and screaming as he fell.

Orfeo heard the crashing impact below, and the shocked screeching of rats – which soon gave way to the scrabbling sound of a horde rushing to the feast.

The man's screams continued to echo from the walls, for the fall had not killed him, nor even knocked him sense-less. The horror of it made Orfeo pause, and he dropped the point of his sword momentarily – but he snatched it up again very quickly indeed, when he saw who it was that led the pursuers around the corner and on to the ledge.

It was Estevan Sceberra who faced him now.

Though the minister's features were in shadow the man behind him held a lantern – and now could get it high enough to make good use of its light. Orfeo had no diffi-culty recognizing his enemy – and his enemy, undoubtedly for the first time, realized exactly who it was he had been chasing.

'You!' he said, in a tone which mingled contempt with astonishment.

Orfeo had begun moving again, but the contempt cut him a little, and the wound in his breast suddenly began to burn again as the memory of its infliction came flood-ing back. He did not move so quickly then, but backed warily along the ledge with his blade held very carefully at the ready. The men who had faced him so far had had no conspicuous skill in swordsmanship, but he could not doubt that Sceberra would be well-schooled. When this man thrust at him, he would have to be far cleverer than he had so far been. He knew Sceberra would not need to cut him – it would be sufficient to make him lose his bal-ance, so that he followed the other man into the pit.

Thinking that attack might be the best form of defence, Orfeo lashed out, making the minister parry – but the parry was good enough to ensure that Orfeo could not fol-low his blow, even though Sceberra was crowded from

behind. The minister, in fact, called for his followers to
give him room, and they hung back, letting their leader
come forward alone. Orfeo knew that he must eventually
continue his retreat, for his only hope of attaining eventual
safety was to follow Falquero into the depths of the crag,
but Falquero had gone a long way ahead of him now, taking the lantern which Arcangelo had left for them, and
Orfeo dared not move too quickly into the darkness lest he
miss the bridge and tumble over the end of the ledge.
Sceberra, realizing that he had control of the light, followed him with greater alacrity, reaching forward as far as
he could with the point of his sword, in order to force
Orfeo back.

The minister thrust forward once, and then again, and
though Orfeo attempted a riposte his blade was very easily
caught. He suffered himself to be pushed backwards, but
went as slowly as he could while he tried to judge the distance to the other corner.

He dared not look around while facing such an opponent as Sceberra, and he was forced to keep touching the
wall with his left hand, tracking it until he reached the
turn.

The turn came, or so it seemed to him, rather too soon –
but when he was sure of his position he quickly backed on
to the bridge, going three-quarters of the way across the
abyss. Then he stopped. Sceberra had now to follow him
on to the bridge if he intended to continue the pursuit,
and he too would be exposed to the double danger, for if
either of them lost his balance now, he would be dropped
into the pit.

Orfeo stood still, saying nothing. He had assumed the
balanced position of a skilled fencer, tempting Sceberra to
follow him on to the narrow causeway and engage him in
combat.

By the light of the nearest lantern, reflected off the wall
behind him as well as the one above the ledge, he could
see Sceberra's expression much more clearly now, and
could see the wrath and hatred that were in it.

'You dare!' said the minister, in a low hiss – and Orfeo realized that his opponent was genuinely surprised by his temerity in pausing to make a duel of it. He smiled, deliberately.

'I had thought that there was not a swordsman in all Zaragoz,' he said. 'Just daggermen whose experience was all in the carving of their food. But you hold yourself as if you know what the blade is for – though perhaps that is just show?'

Sceberra reacted to the careful insolence as Orfeo had hoped he would, drawing his mouth very tight and staring at him with hot fury. But Sceberra's stance was *not* all show, and the minister clearly knew better than to let anger impel him into a careless sweep. Sceberra had paused, perhaps striving to think of a suitably cutting reply.

There was still much movement on the ledge behind Sceberra. One man was busy shoving others aside, apparently careless of the risk, in order to come to the head of the column of pursuers. It was the man at whom Orfeo had thrown the pincers. He, too, had a rapier, which he carried in his left hand – and like Sceberra, he carried it as though he had been carefully educated in its use.

'Who is that man?' said the newcomer, so calmly that the words seemed very strange, echoing in that eerie darkness.

'The player,' said Sceberra, whose own voice was as harsh as ever. 'The one who is too particular to call himself a minstrel.'

'But what quarrel has he with us?' asked the other, mildly. 'I thought him a friend of Cordova's – and my daughter speaks highly of his playing.'

Orfeo could see Sceberra's scowl, though the man behind him could not. That dark expression told him that Sceberra had acted entirely on his own authority in bringing him to the dungeons, and was now thinking that perhaps he had made a mistake.

'I had him safe in irons,' said the minister, sourly. 'And now I wish that I had made a wreck of his clever hands after all.'

'That would have been a pity,' said the other man – who could be none other than Marsilio diAvila himself. 'For I have not yet had the chance to hear him play. Do you think he might surrender, Estevan, now that his friend has vanished into the bowels of the mountain?'

'I have no quarrel with the diAvilas, my lord,' said Orfeo, loudly, 'now I know that you had no hand in my imprisonment. But I would not like to surrender meekly while I have a score to settle with your minister here. I would like to fight him – if you will grant me your permission.'

Sceberra's eyes flared again, and again Orfeo saw what Marsilio diAvila could not: an expression of animal hatred which would not be denied, whatever his master might permit or deny. Orfeo knew that if Sceberra quit this bridge alive, then he would not. But he was beginning to hope that if he could take care of Sceberra, he might yet save his own skin.

He was pleased, therefore, when Marsilio diAvila said: 'To be sure, Master Player, you have my permission. I am ever the man for a quick and violent settlement of quarrels, as anyone in my land will tell you. Cut away!'

Orfeo had not time to offer any thanks, because Sceberra had not waited for the speech to end – he had moved to action with all the expedition he could muster, and had darted a deadly thrust at the very centre of the bloodstain which marked Orfeo's heart.

Eleven

ORFEO TURNED THE thrust aside with his own blade, but once Sceberra had taken the offensive he was in no mood to yield the initiative to his opponent. His sword lashed out again and again, and each time Orfeo could do no more than parry. It would have been far easier for him to turn the advantage around had he been able to move sideways, but he dared not let Sceberra drive him to the very edge of the bridge – especially as the minister seemed uncommonly well-balanced for a fighter, coming forward and back very straightly, and very lightly on his feet.

Orfeo quickly saw that the greatest advantage which he normally had in fighting – his unusually long reach – was here cancelled out by Sceberra's unusual speed and fitness. Orfeo was ordinarily both dexterous and supple, but the wound in his chest was only one of half a dozen bumps and bruises which he had taken of late, and his body was feeling the strain of much ill-use. As he pushed Sceberra's blade aside for the fifth or sixth time he knew that he

173

would have to stretch his resources to the limit if he was to survive.

In the past he had always found that the longer a fight went on, the more his advantages were magnified, because most men used a heavier blade than he, and therefore tired more quickly – but if Sceberra's sword was any heavier than his own, the difference was more than compensated by the minister's freshness and freedom from minor injury.

Sceberra drove him back, inch by inch, and Orfeo saw the grimace of concentration which the other wore take on a hint of satisfaction. The minister was confident now, and Orfeo could do nothing for the moment to dent that confidence – but he was already thinking ahead, and knew that when he was driven back as far as the arch, he would have more scope for a move that might turn the fight around.

Had Sceberra been thinking as clearly as he should, he might not have pressed forward quite so aggressively, anticipating that he would be in trouble if he was stranded in the middle of the bridge while Orfeo had walls to either side of him – but Sceberra was obviously used to a fierce fight in which he overwhelmed his opponent with relentless pressure, and so he drove on. Orfeo allowed himself to be driven, though he kept his blade moving as fast as he could, to allow the minister no pause at all.

When he had almost achieved his object, by coming to the point where he could move more freely and launch a telling counter-attack, Orfeo was forced to a slight error which allowed the minister to prick his arm. It was a very faint hit, but it was not so faint as to draw no blood, and Orfeo heard the reaction of the watchers on the ledge, who were – not unnaturally – inclined to favour Sceberra. One or two of the men-at-arms called out encouragement, and Sceberra obviously thought that his time had come, for he pressed forward as urgently as he could.

Orfeo had felt the sting of the cut, but he knew how fatal it would be to let it disturb him – and he knew, too, that even the slightest wound in a man's sword-arm might prove a fatal disadvantage if its hurt were given time to work. He could not wait until he had come entirely into the tunnel towards which Sceberra was driving him, and he had to make his sideways move a litle earlier than he would have liked.

His rearmost foot, which should have come to a solid base at the angle of the floor and the tunnel-side, did not quite make that target, and Sceberra had no sooner reacted with alarm to the unexpected shift than he saw what grave danger Orfeo had placed himself in. The minister made haste to strike a mortal blow – but he made too much haste, for he had not entirely countered the riposte which Orfeo had set up, and instead of Orfeo's point traveling harmlessly past his shoulder it pricked his jaw and made his head flinch.

The tiny wound was no more serious than the one which Sceberra had inflicted on Orfeo – less so, given that it was on the face and not the sword-arm – but it stung enough to make Sceberra's arm tremble in its fierce attack.

There was but a tiny fraction of a second for Orfeo to respond to that tremor. The interval might have allowed him to take one more step backwards into the safety of the tunnel, but his reflexes took him along a different course, dashing his own weapon past the other's guard to put another and deeper cut into the muscles of Sceberra's shoulder. Sceberra, in his turn, was able to cut at Orfeo's breast.

The pain of the new cut, in the region where his flesh had already been torn and twisted by the pincers, sent a wave of shock through the player's whole body, and pushed his groping heel right back to the edge of the bridge.

Sceberra let loose a cry of triumph as he saw his opponent perched precariously upon the edge, and he thrust again, determined now that his enemy must fall – but the thrust which was meant for Orfeo's body missed, as the player pivoted and swayed.

There was another noisy reaction from the watching crowd, who plainly thought that Orfeo was certain to go over the edge, but as Sceberra's blade struck sparks from the edge of the archway behind him, Orfeo – with a trick which owed far more to his education in dancing than his practiced swordsmanship – came under the blade and up again, away from the edge over which he had so nearly toppled.

As he rose again from this remarkable crouch Orfeo found a far better balance than his opponent, whose wrist had been badly jarred by the carry-through and subsequent abrupt interruption of his thrust.

For just a second, Sceberra was all at sixes and sevens, unable to recover his defence. Orfeo was too close to him to bring his own sword up for an orthodox thrust, but he brought it up nevertheless, almost like an upward-thrusting dagger, and rammed the point into Sceberra's neck beneath the chin.

The minister's throat must have filled with blood on the instant, and the shock which echoed through his system convulsed him so badly that his flailing sword-arm went all awry. The force of the blow threw him backwards, and now it was he who was teetering on the edge, trying desperately to hold himself from a fatal fall.

It was hopeless; as Orfeo pulled back his blade, Sceberra seemed to crumple up, and he fell backward from the bridge, disappearing into the darkness of the pit. He emitted no scream as he fell, nor any to say that the fall had left him to face the rats alive. There was the dull thud of his landing, and then nothing.

Orfeo put out a hand to touch the arch, in order to balance himself. He could feel the warmth of the blood on his sleeve, and the stickiness of the reopened wound on his chest. He looked across the bridge at Marsilio diAvila, whose face was brightly lit by one of the several lanterns on the ledge, which was held close beside him by a man-at-arms.

The Duke's was a very handsome face, surprisingly youthful in its appearance.

Orfeo knew that the man must be at least as old as himself, given that he had two children nearly grown, but had Marsilio appeared with Tomas on one arm and Veronique on the other the three would surely be taken for siblings rather than father and children.

'Bravo!' cried the Duke. 'I swear that I have not seen such a fight with swords in all my days. I dare say that you could give even me a genuine contest, were you free of hurt!'

'I suppose I must try you, hurt or not, if that is what you wish,' said Orfeo, trying his best to stand straight.

'But why?' asked Marsilio diAvila, in all apparent sincerity. 'Your score is settled now, and I have no quarrel with you at all! What do you care about the lady Serafima? Come, man, you are not in this so deeply that you cannot stand aside. I extend my hand to you in friendship – take it, and you may still have your chance to play for me. Take it!'

Marsilio diAvila held out his right hand, while the left which held his sword hung limply by his side. But Orfeo did not move from where he stood. The voice of the Duke was pleasant enough, and there was nothing in it to betray insincerity – but Orfeo, now he had time to think, realized that he had heard the voice before, though he had not seen the man. He also saw that diAvila had not extended his foot by so much as a single inch from the ledge – as if he dared not trust its solidity.

Orfeo did not know how to reply, but while he hesitated, Marsilio diAvila was content to watch and wait.

Then, very suddenly, there was a rush of black wings as a huge bird swept out of the darkness beyond the angle of the stone, and zoomed low over the bridge as though in panic-stricken flight from some dread predator.

Before there was time for any of the watchers to register surprise, there came a terrible cry of pain and rage, which seemed to dwindle as its source – hidden somewhere in the darkness – descended precipitately into the depths of the crag. The cry was wordless, and might perhaps as easily have been the cry of a beast as the cry of a man, but somehow Orfeo knew immediately whose despairing cry it was. Before the echoes had died away, the bridge which extended from the place where he stood to the place where Marsilio diAvila waited had dissolved into dust, which drifted lightly down into the dark abyss.

The Duke of Zaragoz laughed softly.

'Poor player,' he said. 'You should have taken my hand while you had the chance. Now, I believe you must find your own way to the light, for Semjaza has certainly put an end to that troublesome priest with whom you came to my realm. I am told that it can be done, if the creatures which live in the lower depths will only let you alone. I hope you will find a way, and will come to the castle for the Night of Masks. I really would be pleased to hear you play.'

'Aye, my lord,' said Orfeo, having found his tongue at last. 'I believe you would, and I thank you for the invitation. I will not say that I am sorry to have killed your minister, but he was an intemperate man, and I have no doubt that his excesses have helped to tarnish the reputation of your reign.'

'Then I surely owe you thanks, sir,' answered diAvila, with a little mock bow. 'Give my love to the lady, if you find her, and do not be angry with her if she is not what you expected. Take this gift, that you may light your way to your destiny!'

So saying, diAvila plucked the lantern from the hand of the man beside him, and threw it across the gorge. He threw it so dexterously that it did not go out as it flew, and Orfeo caught it with equal grace, so that the flame became quiet again after fluttering madly for an instant or two.

Then diAvila, shadowed now – though there was light aplenty further along the ledge – signalled to his men to go back the way they had come.

Orfeo watched as the company of his enemies retreated. He was puzzled by diAvila's words – and, indeed, by his entire manner. The Duke had seemed to be amused rather than annoyed, not in the least concerned that Falquero had escaped, and must surely be somewhere far ahead with the lady Serafima in his arms. Perhaps, now that Arcangelo had been defeated, Marsilio diAvila was certain that Falquero and his mistress had no chance at all of escaping from Zaragoz. Orfeo had the disturbing feeling that he, too, was in a trap from which there was no escape, and that even if he managed to find a way out into the daylight again, there would be none waiting for him there but his kindly enemies, who would be happy to let him entertain them – until they grew tired of him.

But he was still alive, and could only take his problems one at a time.

He shrugged his shoulders, put his sword back in its scabbard, and made his way carefully forward into the darkness, holding up the lantern to light his way.

The tunnel soon began to descend, at first sloping gently, then more precipitately. There were no steps here, but the walls of the shaft were clean cut, and if the ceiling was too low for Orfeo's comfort that was no fault of the builders of the passage, who had presumably had none among their kind as tall as he.

He came to a division of the way, and hesitated, for there was no bright white mark such as Arcangelo had made at the higher junctions with his chalky stone. But when Orfeo held his lantern up he saw that there was a mark of a sort, where Falquero must have slashed at the wall with his blade before stumbling on into the darkness.

Orfeo was mildly surprised that the man had continued to run on into the mysterious depths, but Falquero could not have known that the pursuit would be cut off by the collapse of the magical bridge, and must have thought it necessary to go as far as he could before waiting to see who would come after him.

As Orfeo made his way on and down he felt desperately tired. The savage excitement of the fight against Sceberra had drained away now, and its absence left a void in his being. He felt weak, and the wound in his breast was hurting him again, wrenching at him as though the pincers had not quite surrendered their hold.

He came eventually to a place where the shaft widened,
and the corridor which the dwarfs had hewn gave way to a
natural cavern of some size. This, to his amazement, was
not without light, for there was a kind of fungus growing
on its wet walls which gave out a slight silvery glow. The
floor of the cavern was very uneven, with clusters of
humped stalagmites reaching up towards their sleeker
counterparts which descended from the roof. In between
these clumps was an assortment of loose boulders, all
smoothed by the occasional passage of floodwater. There
were also shallow pools of water.

It was surprisingly warm here – considerably warmer
than the corridors beneath the castle had been. Nor was
this a silent realm, for he could hear the fluttering of
winged creatures and splashing sounds made by small animals scurrying through shallow water as they fled from his
lantern.

The boulders and stalagmites were painted with bat- and
bird-droppings, dappled yellow and grey, and he could see
small reptiles with bright eyes watching him from cracks
and crevices.

If there were rats here, they seemed not to be here in very
great numbers – which might mean that this system of
caves was distinct from the one which connected with the
noxious pit over which Estevan Sceberra had mantained
his jail, and into which it had been the minister's fate to
tumble. More likely, though, the rats were simply too dis-
creet and incurious to expose themselves recklessly to the
light of his lantern.

Orfeo paused for a while, not knowing which way to go
across this strange subterranean landscape, but then he
saw a scar made by a sword upon a stalagmite, where the
encrusting droppings had been scraped away.

He knew then that Falquero had pressed on across the
floor of the cavern, and that he had continued to mark the
way for anyone who followed. Given this guidance, Orfeo
set off to weave his way between the columns of the stony
forest.

The light from the ceiling seemed to become brighter as he went on, though it was still faint by comparison with the glow of his candle. Leafless plants grew beside the stagnant pools and around the base of the stalagmites. They were tiny things, for the most part, some bulbous and some radiating countless rubbery limbs. There were also creatures like great grey slugs which roamed between the plants with exaggerated slowness, patiently feeding on their meagre flesh.

He had walked for perhaps three hundred paces when he caught sight of the yellow glow of Falquero's lantern reflected from the stalactites, and hurried towards it. Not until he was very close, however, did he catch sight of the two people he sought, in a small semicircular area of bare rock beside a pool of water.

Jacomo Falquero was supine on the ground, his limbs spread wide apart, and at first Orfeo thought that he must have collapsed exhaustedly when the force of the amulet he wore began to decline. The lady Serafima was crouched over him intently, and at first Orfeo thought that she was tenderly nursing her rescuer, deeply thankful for what he had accomplished in snatching her from the prison where her enemies had confined her for as long as they had confined him in his. But when he came closer, he realized that that was not what was happening at all.

Jacomo Falquero was bleeding from wounds about his neck which looked as though they had been inflicted by sharp talons – and the lady Serafima was dabbing her fingers in those bloody wounds, then carrying the blood to her lips, where she licked it off, with apparent relish.

When she heard Orfeo approaching, she lifted up her head, and she smiled.

The smile struck at him like a dagger. That such a pretty face should become so evil with merely a twitch of its muscles seemed to him too horrible to bear.

But then the face changed as its features flowed and altered. The smile remained as it was, but the prettiness and the semblance of youth vanished completely.

He remembered what Arcangelo had said about protecting his eyes from illusions – but only his own illusions. Not Semjaza's.

This, then, had been Semjaza's illusion, and even Arcangelo had not seen through it.

Suddenly, the obvious amusement of Marsilio diAvila, and his mockingly friendly manner, did not seem quite so odd.

This was not the lady Serafima at all. He was looking into the lascivious face of Morella d'Arlette.

'Orfeo,' she said, in a voice like the purring of a great predatory cat. 'I am so very glad that you were not hurt. But what are you doing with such a foolish fellow as this, when I thought you were my friend and darling lover?'

Orfeo felt quite numb, and strangely distant. 'It was all a trap,' he said, hollowly. 'Semjaza was alert before we ever set out. He knew exactly where we were from the moment we left the dungeons. Arcangelo thought that all was going to his plan, but he was only making a gift of himself to Semjaza's wrath.'

'Poor player,' she said. 'Did you really think that such as he could ever get the better of us?'

Orfeo shook his head. 'I had no choice but to believe him,' he said, tiredly. 'I did not want to reserve myself to Sceberra's tender care – and at least I have seen the end of that particular enemy.'

'Have you, now?' said Morella, with a chuckle. 'I never liked him. He was a stiff and sullen man, even when he played the lover. He was never truly one of us, you know.'

Orfeo could only shake his head.

'But now,' she said, standing up and licking one last drop of blood from her forefinger, 'everything is settled. That upstart priest can trouble us no more, and we will celebrate Serafima's betrothal to Tomas on the Night of Masks. You must play for us, Orfeo; it will be such a fine occasion, and afterwards – there are possibilities in pleasure which you have never dreamt of, my darling, and it would be a sheer delight for me to show them to you.'

'I think not, my lady,' he said, drily.

'Then you are wrong,' she said, lightly, taking a step towards him. 'For if I ask you to come, you cannot refuse me. You do know, Orfeo, that you cannot refuse me. You cannot, because in your heart of hearts, you would rather yield to me than run away – because there is something in your soul which cannot help but respond to my call. It is true, Orfeo, is it not?'

While she spoke she continued to come towards him, staring him in the eyes all the while.

He knew that there was magic in what she did, but he could not tear his gaze away. He could not avoid her stare, and as she spoke he realized that there was indeed something within him which responded to her, which could not deny her supernatural beauty, which somehow bound him to her like a slave. He had not the power in his conscious mind to reject the magical command which she was impressing upon his soul.

He knew then that if he had the power in his limbs to bring him to the castle at the appointed time, he would be there. He had knowingly let her work magic upon him when they first made love, and there was no way now to resist the demand which she made of him.

She saw it, and she smiled again. 'Fear not,' she said, 'for we will have such pleasure in one another in these next few months that you will not mind at all when the time comes to die. I promise you, you will not mind at all.'

And with that parting shot, she walked past him. When he turned, although it was only a moment later, she was gone. He did not think that she would have much difficulty returning whence she had come, if Semjaza came to meet her.

He knelt down beside Jacomo Falquero, and found that the unfortunate man was not quite dead. The stricken Falquero raised a cadaverous hand to touch his own fingers to the blood which leaked sullenly from his throat, and looked at it in terrified surprise.

'Serafima,' he whispered. 'Oh, Serafima, forgive me!'

'She will forgive you,' said Orfeo, softly. 'You have done what you have done, and there was not one whit less bravery in it because we were the victims of a vile deceit. Whichever god you pray to will know that well enough. You are a fine and good man, Jacomo Falquero.'

Whether Falquero heard any of what he said he could not tell – and by the time he had finished, the unlucky man was dead. Orfeo gently took the adamantine amulet from around the dead man's neck, and put it carefully away. If it still had virtue in it, it was too valuable to leave behind.

Then he stood up and looked about him, wondering which way to go. Even if his destiny would allow him no other choice than to seek the treacherously loving arms of Morella d'Arlette, he would far rather do that than die in the darkness with only a pale corpse for company. No matter how bleak his future might seem, it had still to be faced.

He went on into the eerie gloom.

Twelve

THE WAY BY which Orfeo had reached the dim-lit under-world had wound about so tortuously that he had no idea which direction was which, nor whether he had descended far enough within the crag to be on a level with Rodrigo Cordova's house.

That was undoubtedly the place of safety to which Arcangelo had intended to take Serafima Quixana had they succeeded in their attempt to rescue her from diAvila's clutches, but how the priest had intended to find his way there Orfeo had no idea.

He dared not extinguish the candle in his lantern – although the inner light of the cavern was bright enough to let him see his way – because he had no way of lighting it again should he once more find himself in total darkness. He estimated that the wax might last for another two hours – which would be ample time for him to traverse the distance which separated him from the Cordova house if only he knew which way to go, but which seemed all too

short a span for any lengthy exploration of this eerie
realm.

He had set off in the direction opposite to that from
which he had come, his eyes searching the gloom for any
sign that humans had ever passed this way before.
According to Arcangelo's story, enemies of the last
Quixana duke had made their way into the castle from
Cordova's house, and it was conceivable that some sign of
their passage remained – though the fact that there were
things living here, and that there was a continual leakage
of water through the caverns, meant that any such traces
would most likely have been obliterated long ago.

As he made his uncomfortable way across the broken
landscape he heard the sound of many creatures splashing
through the shallow pools as they sought to escape his
light. Once or twice he glimpsed the red glow of a rat's
eyes, but only the pale white lizards stayed still as he
approached, hypnotized by the light instead of frightened
by it. Bats and birds sometimes came close enough to
make him duck, because they only had clear air in which
to fly at, or just above, the level of his head; beyond that
was the inverted forest of densely-clustered stalactites.

Several of the birds which he saw seemed to be very ordinary – sparrows, finches and starlings – and he knew that
there must be cracks and crevices in the outer surface of the
rock which allowed them to come in and out. This gave
him hope that there might be more than one way out of
the caves, and that when his candlelight was gone he
might still be able to look for beams of sunlight or to follow draughts of fresher air in the hope of finding a means
of escape. And if all else failed... but the idea of trying to
feed himself by trapping birds and rats and eating them
raw was not a thought he cared to dwell upon.

As he went further the space above his head became
increasingly constricted, and he found himself dodging
the stalactites as well as the stalagmites. It was as though
he was walking into the many-toothed mouth of some gar-
gantuan monster – and this was another thought which he

found too uncomfortable to keep in his mind for long. The natural light of the cavern was weaker now, and he had obviously crossed the greater part of the entrapped space, but there was no sign of any exit ahead of him as the floor and ceiling gradually came closer. Many of the stalactites had here met up with their stalagmitic counterparts, to form great columns and pillars which often stood in pairs like gateways, but whenever he moved through these portals he found nothing beyond but more of the same.

It was difficult to maintain a straight course, and he decided that he would go to the left, keeping to this region in the hope of finding a path into the darkness which might conceivably lead to more dwarfish workings, and hence to a route into the cellars of one or another of Zaragoz's aristocratic houses.

When he heard more noises behind him he was not at first inclined to be alarmed, having become used to the shuffling sounds of shy and solitary rats and the fluttering of the birds, but his ear soon told him that there was something different in the pattern and texture of these sounds, and he turned to look back, holding the lantern out to see what was behind him.

The moment he stopped and turned the sounds also stopped – which, far from reassuring him, only reinforced the sudden conviction that he was being followed. He wondered briefly whether the rats which inhabited the caves might be coming together into the kind of horde which he had heard moving beneath the cell he had shared with Falquero, but that seemed unlikely – rats did not hunt in packs, so far as he knew, and came together in such huge numbers in that sewer only because the lure of food drew them from far afield. If there was anything here to draw them it would be Falquero's dead body, not a moving target like himself.

He remembered, though, that Falquero had spoken of other things which hunted the rats.

He continued, listening much more carefully now to see what could be deduced from the sounds which had made him anxious. Within minutes he became convinced that whatever was making the noises was much bigger than a rat, and that there was probably more than one. He unsheathed his sword, though the fact that both his hands were now occupied made it more difficult to move across the highly irregular terrain.

Once, he stopped abruptly for a second time, spinning on his heel and thrusting the lantern out into the darkness, but the light caught only the faintest flash of white at the limit of visibility, which might have been anything at all.

Orfeo knew that his sword was of limited use in his present surroundings, but he did not want to go back to the more open and brightly-lit centre of the cave – if he was to find a way out then he must find a passage leading away from that region, which he could only do by skirting it. He continued, therefore, to carry his unsheathed blade, trailing it behind him whenever he passed through a narrow gap so that if he were to be attacked from behind he would be able to bring the point into play with minimal inconvenience.

When the attack came, though, it came from the front. As he struggled to pull himself through a narrow gap he stood sideways, with the lantern before and the sword behind. Without any warning at all something reached down from a group of stalactites and snatched the lantern from his hand, hurling it away to bounce, splintering as it went, into a pool where its light was promptly extinguished.

Something white and huge then dropped down from above directly into his path, and came at him furiously. His eyes, accustomed to the candlelight, found it difficult to focus on the figure, but it seemed long-armed and apelike, with great oval eyes which caught the faint light, glowing like massive yellow gems.

Because he could not bring his sword around he tried to fend the marauder off with his free hand, but his reach, though long for a man, was unequal to that task, and he felt long-nailed fingers trying to close about his neck. The stench of the thing's breath was terrible, and left no doubt in his mind that what he faced was a beast of prey. As his fingers closed over the slender arm, attempting to pull it free, he felt thick coarse hair.

He felt another snatch, as something from behind tried to grab the sword from his other hand – but this second assailant found the advantage of surprise inadequate to ensure success, because Orfeo's hand instinctively clutched the hilt more tightly as soon as the blade was touched, and he was able to thrust the point at the would-be thief.

Where the blade caught the monster he could not tell, but he felt the force of the impact and there rang out a most appalling scream of rage and pain. He thrust again, blindly, while he still tried to force his other attacker back. As the strangling hands tried to crush his windpipe the fingernails drew blood from his neck, but the scratches were slight and he realized that the slender arms were not very powerful. Though he could not force the attacker's arms up and out he found that when he grabbed a good handful of hair and yanked powerfully downwards the arm gave way and the clutching hand came away from his throat.

Orfeo pulled his body backwards from the narrow cleft which confined him, stabbing all the while with his weapon. He struck home again, eliciting a second anguished howl, and this second cut was evidently sufficient to persuade the attacker that it was time to give up. The scream was drawn out into a long keening sound which dwindled as the beast fled into the darkness.

He pulled the other creature through the gap after him, at last positioning himself so that he could bring his sword into play. The thing was still groping for his throat, fighting against the grip which Orfeo had upon the hair of its arm, and Orfeo was able to bring the blade round and thrust upwards into its belly. The blow was a killing one, the point being driven through the internal organs towards the heart and lungs, and the beast went instantly limp. It had not even time to scream, but only emitted a faint, plaintive whimper which turned into a throaty death-rattle.

Dead and bloodied the thing was even more odorous than it had been when alive, but Orfeo nevertheless knelt to inspect the corpse. He had not seen its like before, nor had he ever heard tales of such a beast. It was vaguely humanoid in form, being capable of standing upright – though its feet were adapted for gripping too, so that it could live among the stalactites as easily as the stalagmites. It had hands not so very different from his own – but it was covered in hair and its teeth were the pointed daggers of a carnivore, shaped to rip apart a struggling victim.

For a moment he had thought he was beset by daemons, but now he saw the dead thing he recognized it as a strange freak of nature: a cave-dwelling ape, an eater of birds and rats. The way that the pair of them had attacked him simultaneously from front and rear suggested a rudimentary intelligence, but it was no kin to goblins.

He went to retrieve the lantern, but it was useless to him now and he let it lie. Like it or not, he would have to make what use he could of the faint light emanating from the roof of this little subterranean world.

He continued on his way, but now there was nothing to his right hand side but a vast confusion of dark shadows, and it was impossible to tell where a tunnel might begin if any did. He cursed the bad luck which had allowed the beasts to attack him – which had been bad for them too, given that one of them now lay dead. Perhaps the other would dine on its late friend's corpse, and bring its entire family to the feast, but he did not think that a cannibal orgy could really be counted to their credit or their good fortune.

He ran his finger over the scratches in his neck, but they seemed very trivial.

His eyes roamed everywhere, looking for a shaft of daylight penetrating the gloom, and periodically he stopped to test the air, hoping to detect a cool current which he could follow to its source – but there was nothing.

Now that he no longer carried his lantern the creatures of the cavern were not disposed to give him such a wide berth. The bats and birds zoomed close by him, making him move his head reflexively – bumping it once or twice as he did so. Whenever he stopped to look around he could see the tiny eyes of rats and reptiles, which seemed always to be pointed in his direction. There was no comfort at all in knowing that they could see him far more clearly than he could see them.

There was even less comfort in knowing that if he did pass close to subtle signs and marks which might otherwise have guided him out of this place, he would now be unable to detect them. His eyes adapted themselves as well as they could to the silvery radiance, but it was barely adequate to allow him to find a path between the great limestone spikes which grew up from the floor and down from the roof.

Eventually, he knew, he would pass by the entrance to the passage which had let him into this half-world, but he did not think he would recognize it, even if he were able to see it. The possibility that he might follow it in error, all the way back to the rim of the pit, was one he had to bear in mind – as was the possibility that any new passage which he found might be equally well-supplied with pitfalls. As he saw no passage at all, however, it was an anxiety which could be deferred.

He began to think of ingenious plans involving the unravelling of thread from one of his garments, which would at least allow him to know if he accidentally crossed his own path, but there did not seem to be enough profit in any such scheme to recommend it.

Hunger was beginning to make itself felt in his belly, but he ignored the pangs. He had been hungry before, and knew the importance of carrying on regardless of it.

He wondered, too, whether he would ultimately stumble across Falquero's body again – and what kind of feast he might interrupt if he did.

He stood still for a while, to rest his weary limbs. He still had his sword in his hand, and no intention of sheathing it again, but he was painfully reminded that he had enemies other than the apes when an unusually bold rat nipped his ankle. He cursed loudly and kicked out – and when he saw several pairs of red eye-lights suddenly switch off as their owners turned to run he realized how close they had crept while his attention had wavered.

He turned, uneasily, to see what was behind him, but the true danger was above him, and was upon him without warning. Another of the ape-creatures dropped upon his head and wrapped its long arms around his neck. Within an instant, two or three more were upon him, having swung down from the stalactites. He stabbed with his sword but it was already too late to make good use of the thin pointed blade – what he needed now was something heavier, with a long cutting edge.

He thrust outwards desperately with his arms, trying to dislodge the beasts which were clinging to him. The stench of their breath and their fur was dreadful, and he felt that he could not breathe.

He shouted, as loudly as his tortured lungs would let him, hoping that the sound would cause alarm where his enfeebled struggles had not – but these were not such stupid beasts as to be frightened when they had the upper hand.

The one which had an arm around his neck tightened its grip, while those which clung on to his arms dragged them down to prevent his fighting back.

He staggered and slipped, and was brought to his knees. A filthy hand groped about his features, and he shut his eyes to prevent their being scratched.

Teeth scraped his struggling body as they tried to fasten upon his left shoulder. Others gained better purchase, sinking into the flesh of his thigh.

He was convinced that the end had come.

Then the arm which gripped him about the neck was withdrawn, and he heard a yelp of pain from the ape which owned it. The other apes cried out, too – and their cries mingled with exclamations of alarm and horror which were definitely human.

When he opened his eyes he saw that there was light in plenty, cast by at least three bright lanterns. As the apes bounded from him, sped on their way by pricks and slashes administered by several blades, he collapsed to the ground, falling on his back. He felt utterly helpless, exhausted of all strength. But he found sufficient energy to raise a smile when he recognized the face which was looking down at him. It was the face of Rodrigo Cordova.

The joy of it made him want to shout again, but he could not find the necessary breath.

'Orfeo!' said Cordova, astonished and anxious. 'We searched day and night for you! How did you come here? We had to break down a false wall in order to pass from the cellars into the dwarfish workings – and by then our quest had become a different one, for we certainly did not expect to find you inside the mountain.'

'My friend,' said Orfeo, faintly, reaching up to grasp a hastily-proffered hand, 'I cannot tell you how glad I am that you found that path.'

'But did you come here of your own accord?' asked Cordova. 'If you did not, then I must have a traitor among my servants.'

'It is a long story, my lord,' whispered Orfeo, but could say no more, because a wave of giddiness swept over him. The relief of being found had ruled it unnecessary that he should any longer draw upon reserves of strength which were already much depleted.

It was Rodrigo Cordova who completed what he had tried to say: 'And this is not the place to tell it. We must take you to a bed now, and let you enlighten us when you are better.'

ORFEO DID NOT quite lose consciousness when he was picked up. Two of Cordova's servants carried him across the underworld, retracing the steps by which they had come to their fortunate meeting.

Orfeo was later able to remember, albeit dimly, their arrival in the cellars of the house and the ascent into the upper part. He remembered being laid upon the bed in the room under the eaves, and being stripped of his clothing so that his many wounds might be bathed. After that, however, his memories became blurred and entangled with nightmarish dreams in which he believed himself still to be trapped inside the crag, pestered by rats and chased by ghostly grey apes.

As these visions became more bizarre he dreamed that he saw Arcangelo's body tumbling into the pit, where it had been hurled by Semjaza's angry magic, and saw the rats crowd around it, fighting one another for the privilege of tearing at the spellcaster's flesh. In his dream, Orfeo tried to help the man, desperately grabbing at the rats to push them back, but wherever he pulled one rat away two more would take its place, and he felt as if he were submerged beneath a living deluge of the creatures.

Then, in his vision, he saw Arcangelo come to his feet, bloodied from head to toe by a thousand tiny bites, and stand as he had in Rodrigo Cordova's ballroom with arms outstretched, commanding their silence and obedience with the sheer force of his personality – and he saw the rats fall back then, confused and humbled.

He saw, too, another ragged army of the shadows, pale and yellow-eyed, prancing in the distant shadows, equally eager to hear the words of the preacher which their brutal gods had sent to them from the lighted heavens outside their dark and pitiful world. And mingling with this throng of white-furred apes were the indistinct forms of daemons, which seemed to be carved out of shadow – horridly unnatural things with limbs like spiders and stings like scorpions and heads like horned lizards. Some, though they went upon two legs and not four, were nevertheless used as mounts by humanoid figures whose faces the dreamer could not see.

All these denizens of the underworld beneath Zaragoz waited to hear what their prophet would say to them. And what he said, in his voice like terrible thunder was: *'Zaragoz is doomed!'*

The cry seemed to ring in Orfeo's ears until it saturated his whole being, and drove away all other sensation, so that when it finally dwindled away in a confusion of echoes, he was abandoned to peace and silence, and to the mercy of ordinary sleep.

When he awoke again, Marguerite Cordova was by his bedside, watching over him. She called for servants to bring him food, and stayed with him while he ate.

'You are safe now,' she said. 'You are a guest in this house, and our protection will not fail you a second time.'

He knew that she was sincere; but he also knew that something had been set inside him which would not let him stay in the house, and would take him back to the castle to please those who would make a toy of him. Whatever curse had been put upon the house to make it resentful of diAvila enmity and the magic of Semjaza's kin could not touch the obligation which Morella d'Arlette had inserted in his very soul. His friends had saved him from the white apes of the underworld, but he might need more powerful allies than the House of Cordova to save himself from Morella d'Arlette's destructive amorousness.

When he was fed, and his wounds had been tended, Rodrigo's mother left him, and sent her son to take her place.

Rodrigo asked if he was ready to tell his story, and Orfeo said that he was. Briefly, he described the events which had unfolded around him – his kidnapping, his torture, his imprisonment, his release, his involvement with the attempt to rescue Serafima Quixana, his duel with Sceberra, and his adventure in the dim-lit cavern.

'I will find the servants who betrayed me,' said Cordova, fervently. 'They will suffer for what they have done.'

'They did not move against you,' answered Orfeo, in a placatory manner. 'In delivering me to Sceberra, they were serving another loyalty, to their duke and his minister. It is not your servants who seek to harm you but your master.'

'What do you mean?' asked Cordova, uneasily.

'When I heard Marsilio diAvila speak, I knew that the order to kill Calvi and take you prisoner came from his own lips.'

'Are you certain of this?' asked the young nobleman, in obvious distress.

'He has a charming manner, has he not? But I think that what his people say of him is true – he is a cruel man beneath his finery, and one who does not care at all about honour and justice.'

'But why? I hope to marry his daughter, and he has never discouraged the match.'

'It was nothing to do with that. He wanted you made safe because he did not know whether the curse that was placed upon the House of Cordova would take effect in the walls which surround us or in the blood which flows in your veins. When Semjaza worked magic within its walls to hurt Arcangelo he awakened something – some power which had lain dormant here since the fall of the Quixanas. Semjaza has always known of it; it is not just the books in your library which have drawn him so often to this house. He knew that Arcangelo came here in order to awaken the force of that curse, and when the priest escaped from the cell where he was supposed to be safe, even Semjaza became afraid, and took what precautions he could. The war between the diAvilas and the Quixanas has always been fought with magic as well as with swords, and Semjaza had reason enough to fear whatever legacy the defeated Quixana wizards may have left behind them.'

'But it is over now, is it not?' said Rodrigo, uneasily. 'The sorcerer has been defeated and destroyed. He must have been killed, for I cannot believe that Semjaza would have let him go a second time.'

'Nor can I,' replied Orfeo. 'But there is a saying in the Empire, which says that although the honest strength of men dies with them, their magic may seek vengeance from the grave. Arcangelo's plans took account of the possibility of his death – or so he told me when he spoke to me.'

'But Serafima Quixana no longer needs saving! The cry-ers are out in every quarter of the town, declaring that her betrothal to Tomas diAvila will be celebrated on the Night of Masks.'

'Aye,' said Orfeo, in a low tone. 'And there is one in the castle who intends that my own betrothal will be cele-brated on that same eve – but I do not think that the lady intends a long and happy marriage, and I am not sure that Serafima Quixana's fate will be any less unpleasant. We are flies, my friend, caught in the tangled folds of two magical webs – and we may none of us escape if the spinners of those webs are to be drawn by their conflict to mutual ruination.'

'What would you have me do?' asked Rodrigo. 'My fam-ily has ever been loyal to the diAvila dukes, and I love Veronique diAvila. But even if I wished to do it, I could not use this house to launch an attack on the castle, as the diAvilas did in the distant past. I have no army, remember – nor any wizards either.'

'No,' said Orfeo. 'If I am asked for honest advice, I can say only this: go to the castle for the Night of Masks, as you would have if you knew nothing of this. Make love to Veronique diAvila, as you would have. Forget what I have told you about Marsilio diAvila, and behave towards him as if you had never heard it, seeking no revenge for the murder of Theo Calvi. If you are lucky, the Duke will con-sider that there is no further need to move against you, and will offer you hospitality that will make you as safe as any other of his subjects.

'But afterwards, take your mother to another city – and do not be in a hurry to return here. Once a man is sus-pected as the instrument of a curse, he is always in danger from those who fear the curse.'

'That is hard advice to take,' said Rodrigo, in a sombre way. 'For what is a man but the house he owns and the estates whose produce belongs to him? I was made to be a nobleman of Zaragoz, not a mere vagabond without a name or home.'

He meant no insult, and Orfeo took no offence. The player merely sighed, and said: 'Then stay, my lord, and wait for whatever comes. But see your mother safe, I beg of you – and do not let your affection for Veronique diAvila draw you into the wretched cult of which she is a part. And when you go abroad in this realm which makes your name a thing of quality, do not carry a sword which is a mere ornament – wear the best weapon which you have, and pray that when you are called upon to use it, you have more art than those who come against you.'

Thirteen

ORFEO REMAINED IN his bed for two days and two nights while the pain of his wounds eased and he recovered his strength. The third dawn brought the day whose eve would be the Night of Masks, and on that day he rose and dressed himself. Then he took up his lute to discover whether his injuries would affect his playing.

At first his arms were very stiff, and he was discomfited by the various scratches which had been inflicted by Sceberra's blade and the apes' sharp teeth, but as he drew pleasant tunes from the instrument – recalling memories of happier days in other courts and in the wild woods of Bretonnia – these pains were soothed away, and the stiffness with them.

The gentle magic of the music put new heart into him, and in the afternoon he left his room, intending to go down to the narrow garden which clung to the ledge beside the house, to bathe in the bright sunlight for a while.

As he made his way down through the house, though, he passed the room which was used to store the books and scrolls which had been deposited in the house by generations of scribes and petty wizards. He saw that the door of this room stood ajar, and could not resist the temptation to open it further and look inside.

On the far side of the table, with his back to the window, sat Semjaza.

The wizard looked up, and when he saw who it was in the doorway his strangely-contorted face moved into a grotesque parody of a smile.

'Master Storyteller!' he said, as warmly as his voice allowed. 'I am delighted to see you recovered.'

Orfeo, at first, could find nothing to say, but merely stared.

'Ah!' said the sorcerer. 'You are surprised to find me here. Do you think I should shun the house, because Arcangelo tempted me to awaken something which lay dormant in its walls? On the contrary – it is all the more reason to come. The study of magic has been my life's work. Please sit with me for a while. Do not be afraid of me, for I have never meant you any harm. I even gave you good advice, which you should have taken, and thereby saved yourself a measure of pain and grief.'

Orfeo closed the door behind him, and came further into the room. He did not like to be with the wizard, forced to look into that hideous face, but he knew that Semjaza was at the very centre of the secret society whose members included Morella d'Arlette, and must be the prime mover in the plot which had ensnared him.

'Had I taken your advice,' said Orfeo, 'I cannot imagine that my circumstances would now be very different. I would be appointed to play at the castle on the Night of Masks, and I believe that the lady Morella would still intend to place me under an obligation.'

Again Semjaza tried to smile.

'I believe she would,' he said. 'But you have been drawn into the game, and now must play it. There are only two ways forward – as a victim, or as a player. It would be a pity to waste a man like you in the mere slaking of Morella's lusts. Were you to ally yourself with me, you might be heir to a more enviable state. You have intelligence, and – so I am told – a very delicate touch with lute and blade alike. Most important of all, you have courage. You faced me well when I questioned you, and you do not shrink from me now, despite the horror which you feel for what you think I am. You pose as a gaudy man and a lover of women, but there is more to you than that, and you might make something of yourself if only you could raise your sights above the tawdry show which common men call the world.'

'I *am* a common man, my lord,' Orfeo replied, levelly. He remained standing, but he made no move to leave the room.

'And so was I, once,' said Semjaza. 'I had a father and a mother, and a brother and a sister. I bore another name and I wore another face. But that was long ago. I am not a common man any longer, and you know full well that I do not mean that some petty and vainglorious king or duke has dubbed me knight or marquis.

'There is another aristocracy, whose honours are not so lightly won, and whose authority far exceeds the petty power-play of wealth and lawmaking.'

'There are as many tales to tell of that aristocracy as of the other,' Orfeo said. 'It is my work to collect and make them. I hear and tell of necromancers whose play with the dead becomes by degrees an obsession with the grave and all things cold and grisly, and whose powers of destruction are in the end dissolved by madness. I hear and tell of those who make treaty with daemons, who become the most hated of men, and who are in the end destroyed by those Dark Powers they sought to conjure and control. It is difficult to envy those whose authority is bought at such cost. If the wisdom of lore and legend is to be trusted, the only happy wizards are those who bind themselves to the harmony of nature, who are as much servants as masters of the forces intrinsic to the material and living world.'

'And is it your opinion,' asked Semjaza, silkily, 'that the wisdom of lore and legend is to be trusted?'

'After its own fashion, yes,' answered Orfeo. 'I would not trust blindly what I learned from a tale, so that I could not recognize a plain truth which stood in contradiction to it, but I would be a sorry fool if I refused the lessons which have come from the lives and deaths of thousands of my forebears, on the grounds that I had not had the chance to learn them for myself.'

'The experience of common men,' said Semjaza, 'is shaped and spoiled by ignorance and fear. Whatever they do not understand they hate, and the lessons they pretend to learn are but the reflections of their own stupidity and cowardice. The so-called wisdom of lore and legend is a travesty of the truth, and I believe that you are too intelligent a man not to know that in your heart.'

'I am only a common man, my lord,' Orfeo replied, steadfastly, 'and I am heir to my fair share of ignorance and fear. But I know that there is pleasure enough in life, if only a man has enough to eat, women to love, and music for dancing.'

Semjaza shook his head. 'I do not need to touch you, Orfeo, to know that you are lying now. I can sense the feeling which is in your heart, and I know that for you, that is not enough. It is not even pleasure enough. You are a more inquisitive man than that – a man who finds fascination in questions and answers. You are a man who cannot discover a door which is ajar without wanting to look at the room within, especially if the room is full of books and scrolls.'

Orfeo could not deny it. He said: 'I am inquisitive, it is true. But I am not the kind of man who can take pleasure in hurting others. The power to do evil does not attract me.'

'You think that I am an evil man?' said Semjaza, seemingly more amused than annoyed.

'I do not know you,' said Orfeo, 'but I think that the powers upon which you draw are evil, and very dangerous.'

'Dangerous, to be sure,' acknowledged Semjaza. 'But it is not sensible to call them evil. Evil is a word which humans have made to describe what hurts them. It has no meaning in the greater world, which lies beyond and outside our own.'

'It is in our own world that we live our lives,' said Orfeo. 'Whatever daemons may be in their own world – of which I know nothing – I believe that their intrusion into ours is invariably evil, and that whoever calls them from beyond does evil's work.'

'You are wrong,' said the wizard, flatly. 'The way of thinking which deals in good and evil cannot contain the truth of what the world is truly like, and cannot measure the rewards of seeking that truth.'

'Advise me, then,' said Orfeo. 'Tell me the truth, and explain what rewards there are in the worship of forbidden gods and intercourse with daemons. I am, as you have argued, inquisitive enough to ask the question, though I may not like the answer.'

Semjaza leaned forward, intently, and the stink of his breath was suddenly sharp in Orfeo's nostrils. Though the closeness of the dreadful features seemed threatening, Orfeo knew that the magician was not trying to frighten or browbeat him. Whatever madness or malice was in the man was quiet now, and there was a sincerity in what he said. Orfeo realized that in a peculiar way, Semjaza was asking for his understanding, desirous that he should acknowledge the supremacy of the wizard's world-view as well as the power of his magic.

'Do you see the crack in the wall yonder?' asked Semjaza, pointing a thin finger at a place which was bare of shelves, where there was a line running across the stone, no broader than a hair.

'I see it,' said Orfeo.

'Within that crack there is a world. Just as there is a tiny world inside this crag, where the rats and the white apes live, so there is a tiny world inside every nook and cranny of the world which men call their home. In the world within that crack live tiny insects barely visible to the human eye, and each tiny insect has a rutted back whose every groove is a world where tinier things exist.

'Our world, Master Storyteller, is the merest crack in a world immeasurably greater, where there are powers which could grind it into dust with no more effort than you would need to draw a fingernail along that crevice. Every time you crush an insect beneath your heel you destroy countless tiny worlds, and this world in which we live might at any instant be obliterated by the casual, unthinking movement of some being too monstrous for our tiny minds to comprehend.

'I am not speaking of daemons, which would be equally trivial to such a being, nor even of gods; I am speaking of the true nature of things.

'While we speak, countless worlds tinier than ours are being born and speeding to their destruction. What seems but a trivial moment in lives such as ours is a near-eternity in the lives of tinier beings. By the same token, what seems to us a lifetime, or a vast reach of history, or the lifespan of a world entire, is but an instant in the greater time which measures that world of which ours is but a minute part. The eye which looks upon such a world cannot notice the blink whose duration contains the ages of a thousand worlds like ours.

'This greater world does not care at all about the things which occupy our little minds. All our dreams and follies are the merest nonsense to the eye which looks upon *that* world. Our conflicts are all absurd: diAvila and Quixana, Good and Evil, Law and Confusion – what can they matter? What significance can possibly be in them? It does not matter which side a man is on, Master Player. It does not matter whether he favours justice against malice, or love against hate, or the so-called Gods of Law against the so-called Gods of Chaos. The truth is that Chaos is everything, and that order is but a little accident, which happens here or there for the briefest instant, and then is lost as if it had never been.

'My friend, there is but one quest a man can have which makes anything of him at all, and that is to reach out into the greater world beyond our own, and draw upon its power to transform himself and – if he becomes wise enough and powerful enough – to transform the world.

'Tonight, you will see the people of Zaragoz put masks upon their faces, pretending to be other than they are – and at midnight they will take off those masks, thinking that they are revealing their true selves. You and I know that they are fools to think that their masks can possibly hide what they really are, and to think that their own faces are anything but masks of pretence. I am the one man in this realm who has abandoned his mask, to show his real face – which is not mine alone, but the face of truth, the face of real existence.

'In the coy stories which you tell of men who treat with daemons you roll your eyes and babble about the "unspeakable" and the "unnameable", but I know that you have heard the name of Chaos, and that you are not really too frightened to speak it aloud. You know that my magic draws upon the power of Chaos, and have felt it – just as you have felt the power of Morella d'Arlette. You are afraid of the power, and rightly so, but you need not be afraid if only you can grasp the truth.

'Put crude thoughts of good and evil out of your mind, and try to move beyond such silly ways of thinking – beyond even thoughts of Order and Chaos. In the true way of seeing, the authentic excitement of existence lies not in the feeding of the animal appetites but in reaching beyond the petty stupidities of ordinary life, in feeling the awesomeness of the greater world, and in bringing just a little of the intoxication of that greater existence into the narrow confines of our lesser one.'

Semjaza sank back into his chair as the high pitch of his excitement ebbed away. His bright eyes were fixed upon Orfeo's face, and Orfeo did not know how to reply. He wanted to conceal what he really thought, which was that he believed this strange view of things to be wrong and

perverse, but he dared not tell a bald lie, for he knew that
Semjaza could identify such lies.

In the end, he said: 'But there is power in Order and Law
as well as its opposite. You may have defeated Arcangelo
here, as he said you once did in Gualcazar, but still he had
power, and perhaps it was, in the end, only his cleverness
which proved unequal to your own.'

Semjaza seemed annoyed by this reply, which was certainly not the kind of speech he had hoped to elicit.
'Perhaps you are not so intelligent after all,' he said, 'if you
could not see what lay behind the masquerade of a priest
of Law.'

That was not the reply which Orfeo had expected, either,
and he started in astonishment when he realized what
Semjaza meant.

'Do you tell me that Arcangelo was not a priest of Law?'

'He was a priest of Law once,' answered the sorcerer. 'He
trusted in the power of Law to keep the lady Serafima safe
in Gualcazar, but it failed him. He saw then that if he was
to take her back, he must find greater powers than that to
aid him. I knew it when he escaped from the prison I had
placed him in, for there was only one way out of that
prison – and that was downwards, into the darkest recesses
of the crag. The forces which lurk in those depths are not
devoted to the cause of Law.'

Orfeo looked bleakly down at the wizard, trying to
fathom his unhuman expression. 'He went to make a pact
with your own daemons!' he said. 'He sold his soul in the
hope that he would buy Serafima Quixana's freedom –
and was betrayed!'

Semjaza made a disgusted noise. 'If you would put it in
the terms of your silly stories, yes! Arcangelo knew full
well that he could not fight power such as mine without
drawing from the same source. If you must think in terms
of scrolls signed in blood, then he set his seal to some such
contract. But your storyteller's language is only a mask set
to hide a subtler truth. He tried to draw upon the power of
Chaos, as do I – but he had not my knowledge or my skill.

In five years he sought to outstrip me, but in the meantime, I had gone further than he. He was fortunate not to be torn apart by the forces which he sought to control, as others have been, but he squandered his good fortune in trying to turn his new-won power against a master of the art. Did you really think that his tricks were gifts from the Gods of Law?'

'Yes,' admitted Orfeo, 'I did. I heard his cry on behalf of justice, and I felt that it rang true. I allied myself with him in order to be released from my prison, but also because I felt that his cause had rightness in it. I am sorry to be told that I was wrong.' But he did not deny what Semjaza had told him, for though he had not the wizard's power to detect a lie when he was told one, there seemed a certain dreadful likelihood in this account.

'I told you once before,' said Semjaza, 'not to confuse justice with Law. Arcangelo was not consistent in his pretences, and you should have seen through them. Like so many men, he had begun to confuse justice with his own self-interest and his own ambition. His determination to save the lady Serafima may once have been real, but in the end it was simply the mask which his hatred wore. Marsilio and his son mean no harm to the lady, and a loveless marriage is a small price to pay for an end to the hatreds which have torn this realm apart for centuries.'

But when this man says 'no harm', thought Orfeo, he does not count it harm that she will be brought into the untender clutches of those forces which he thinks he controls, and which may in fact control him.

'Perhaps,' said Orfeo, pensively, 'there is nothing which can be made of a man like me, after all.'

Semjaza only smiled, and said: 'If that is true, then I must abandon you to Morella's tender mercies. And if it is true that all that you value in life is pleasant meat and the tuneful measures of the dance, perhaps you will not be sorry to have a taste of ecstasy before she tires of you or consumes you with the heat of her passion. But when the time comes to choose, Master Storyteller, remember that there is one in Zaragoz more powerful by far than your greedy mistress or her playful duke!'

'According to your own account,' riposted the player, 'the thing to remember is that Zaragoz is but a tiny rut in a greater world, where there are powers which could crush us all without deigning to notice our passing. Arcangelo sought to stir those powers into violent action, and was willing to sacrifice his life as well as his soul to do it. I do not think, my lord Magician, that you are as sure of your victory as you claim to be.'

For a brief second, there was something dreadful to be seen in Semjaza's white-rimmed eyes – as though a shadow or a thundercloud had passed behind them. But the direction of the sorcerer's gaze never shifted, and his composure was quickly recovered.

'Arcangelo is dead,' said Semjaza, flatly. 'All that he achieved was to activate a protective spell within the walls of this house, which has only power to save and not to harm. Sceberra is dead, but we have a hundred who can fill his shoes, and his spies are rooting out all those who were moved to a spirit of rebellion by rumours of the prophet's cry and the murder of Theo Calvi. The betrothal of Tomas diAvila and Serafima Quixana will be announced this evening. All is well in Zaragoz, and so it shall remain.'

But in his head, Orfeo heard other words, as though from the lips of a dead man, which said: 'If justice cannot come again to Zaragoz, then *Zaragoz is doomed!*'

Whether that was true or not, he was sure of one lie that Semjaza had told. The sorcerer had lied when he said that he was the only man in Zaragoz to wear his true face. That shadow in his eyes, however fleeting, had betrayed him. His monstrous appearance was but one more mask – and behind that dreadful mask, fear still lurked, unconquered and unhealed.

IT WAS NOT until he descended to the garden that Orfeo realized how foul the air had been in that room where Semjaza sat.

It surprised him to recall how quickly he had ceased to notice the odour of the wizard's breath once he had been exposed to it.

Was it, he wondered, the same with evil? Did a man cease to notice the horror of what he did when it became familiar to him, and a matter of custom? Or was Semjaza right to say that the notion of evil was simply a meaningless phantom conjured out of men's fears of being hurt?

There was a saying in the Empire, he recalled, that vanity in excess was an invitation to destruction. Semjaza's dealings with the powers which he sought to command might be more reckless than he imagined. But the wisdom of sayings and fables was simply one more aspect of that wisdom of lore and legend which the wizard affected to despise – and which even Orfeo, in his heart of hearts, found it difficult to trust.

Orfeo found the invention of stories and pretty turns of phrase far too easy to put much faith in the ones which others had made.

While he was immersed in this turbulent sea of thought he went to stare out over the low stone wall which flanked the garden, looking down at the roofs of the houses in the town and the fields laid out between the city wall and the Eboro.

From this vantage-point the realm did not seem so very large, and the people in the streets were so tiny they might have been ants. How much tinier they must seem from the High Tower on the peak, from which Marsilio diAvila and his wizard could look down upon them!

But that tininess, he knew, was only apparent. The common people too were human beings, with the same needs, the same appetites and the same illusions as their aristocratic masters – even some of the same petty vanities. Tonight, all would wear masks and costumes, rejoicing in the temporary freedom of setting aside their identities... but when they took away the masks, they would still be the same people.

Semjaza's arguments, he decided, were nothing more than a mask which evil wore, which could not really conceal it, and which ultimately must be set aside, when the appointed hour came.

'Zaragoz is doomed!' he whispered, echoing again Arcangelo's defiant cry.

But he could not believe that, either, for the wisdom of lore and legend said clearly enough that a nation like Zaragoz would always be the same while its people could find no better way to live than to spill their blood in ceaseless wrangling over the fate of its shabby crown.

Fourteen

THAT EVENING, at sunset, Orfeo rode with Rodrigo Cordova's party up the winding road which led to the castle gate. Rodrigo had five servants in attendance, including the steward Cristoforo – all masked, as convention demanded, though they would play little part in the actual festivities, save to fetch and carry for their master. The lady Marguerite rode at her son's left hand, so that he was on the side where the sheer slopes fell away. Rodrigo had left his house in the charge of a dozen men-at-arms, who were instructed by him to be on guard and in readiness – though he could not say for what.

The party merged with others into an endless procession whose torches and lanterns made a lighted spiral around the upper part of the crag, drawing the noble blood of Zaragoz from all the houses which comprised the heart of the realm. Orfeo was one of very few common men on horseback; servants rarely had mounts of their own. There were but a handful of carriages on the road – perhaps because of the steepness of the hill, but more probably because the noblemen loved to let their horses parade and prance within the throng.

The servants in the crowd wore plain black masks which covered only their eyes. The gentler folk were by no means so minimal in their observation of the ritual of concealment; they wore full faces which were brightly-painted and sometimes studded with ornaments, and broad hats or scarves to cover their hair, so that only their eyes remained to say who they were. Some of the masks were smiling, others sternly impassive, but it seemed to Orfeo that the more such false faces sought to conceal by their size and prettiness, the more they actually revealed about their wearers. Whispers passed ceaselessly back and forth through the crowd as servants pointed excitedly at every fine display, and put a name to the person behind each mask.

There were many fanciful tales of the Estalian Night of Masks told in Bretonnia. Most were variants of a single plot, in which curious alliances and romantic attachments were made because kings and dukes were mistaken for commoners and serving-maids for women of quality – alliances and attachments which triumphantly withstood the test of unmasking. Orfeo saw that in Zaragoz no one but a fool could be so confused. Masked as they were, the servants were still servants and the nobles still their masters – it was in their bearing as well as the quality of their clothing, and there were no strangers here who could mingle unsuspected with the crowd. In the streets of a great city like Magritta it might be different, but in the little walled town at the foot of this hollow crag the shopkeepers and the artisans knew one another only too well, and kept their proper distance from the peasants, as they always did.

The space within the castle walls was lighted by candles and lanterns attached to every vertical surface, so that the gloomy terraces which had confronted Orfeo during his fateful ascent to the High Tower were utterly transformed into a scene far more delightful to the eye. While the horses were led to the stables – which would be crowded on this night as on no other – the people gradually filled up the pavements which extended from the western tower to the eastern. There were too many to fit comfortably into the Grand Hall, but that space would be reserved for the highly-organized dancing of the nobles, while their more numerous servants would find opportunities for their own casual performances out of doors.

Seven players, in addition to Orfeo, had been summoned to the castle to play for the dancers, including three pipers and two drummers. While the early part of the festivities – devoted to eating and drinking – took their course it was the Duke's pipers and lute-players who took turns to play in the Grand Hall, while Orfeo mingled with the crowd in the courtyard, awaiting his summons.

Though his pale smiling mask covered his face completely Orfeo was recognized wherever he went. Accounts of his duel with Sceberra had been widely circulated, and it was plain that neither servants nor men-at-arms could understand why he was free to walk among them. The paradox made them uneasy, and the crowd parted ahead of his path to let him pass.

Beneath the unease, however, there was an undercurrent of admiration – the minister had been the most feared man in the kingdom, and there were many even among the innocent who were not sorry to know that he was dead.

Orfeo ate little, drank less, and kept to his own company. This was a night for making assignations, but his was already made and though it was one that he could not relish, he was not free to make another. He had seen Morella d'Arlette briefly, in close company with Marsilio diAvila; she was dressed in scarlet, fiery with a jewelled mask, while he was in black and grey, ostentatious in his calculated sobriety. The sorceress had measured him with the barest of glances before turning to her conversation, but he knew that he was merely put away until later.

He had seen Semjaza too, in unexpected finery, with silver thread spun into confusing webs and whorls against a

backcloth of black silk – but the magician's mask was
shaped in the semblance of a grinning skull, hardly less
horrid than the face beneath.

When the dining-tables had all been moved back,
arrayed against the inner walls of the hall, preparing the
floor for the dance, the Duke's steward came to find Orfeo
and bid him do his duty. As Orfeo walked across the terrace to the doors of the hall he was uncomfortably aware
that every eye was upon him. Just as a path had opened
before him while he walked in the courtyard, so the gap
behind him closed now as the crowd drifted towards the
doors to watch the dancing within.

Orfeo consulted briefly with one of the pipers and one
of the drummers, who declared themselves more expert
than the rest in the music which was suited to the new
dancing. The piper was a traveller like himself, who had
been in southern Bretonnia.

When they had settled the order of their early pro-
gramme they began, with a formation-dance whose paces
were trod as prettily by the nobility of Zaragoz as any other
company which he had seen. He saw, though, that the gai-
ety and ease which had been obvious in Rodrigo Cordova's
house were missing. The location, the occasion, and the
fact that the present assembly had five or six times the
number of the earlier one, combined to make the dancers
stiffer and more precise in their movements. While they
concentrated on the neatness of their steps, the possibility
of true enjoyment was lost to them. Orfeo did not like that,
and determined that the energy and passion of his music
should loosen their manner a little, even if it could not
entirely swallow them up.

With this limited objective in mind, he applied himself
to his playing, and soon found the force of the music taking hold of his own heart and soul, so that the other
matters which hung heavy on his mind were gradually
brought into neglect.

When he led the throng in the first line-dance, winding
them around and around the hall to mimic the sinuous

movements of a lazy snake, he gradually increased the tempo of his playing and the vigour of his prancing, so that what started as a mere stately walk accelerated by degrees into a canter – and whenever the company reached what seemed to be a climax and an end he moved smoothly into another round, extending the dance to twice its normal duration, and then to three times, deliberately bringing their excitement to a far higher pitch than they had prepared for.

When the time came for them to dance in couples, the music which he played was licensed to be freer and he did not shun the opportunity. He sent the piper away, though he kept the drummer with him, having already built a rapport with the man. Though he began in an orthodox fashion his playing grew slowly more extravagant, and when he had passed the third pause he was plying his strings with a wildness which convention would certainly have disallowed had he not brought them to it by such a seductive route. It was not that he had tried to merge the careful steps of the noble dances with the rhythms of the peasant dances which would be plucked and piped in the streets of the town, but rather that he drew them into capers which were beyond the ordinary expressions of status and quality.

Always, in his youth, he had longed to play *real* music – the music of the elves – but he had been told that even if human fingers could ever be taught the way, human hearts could never fill the melodies with true feeling. He knew that it was so, and yet, when he was at his best, he felt that there was something in his music which was extraordinary, and if it was not truly elvish, at least it was a little beyond the merely human. He felt that now, as he tried with all his might to make magic with his playing – magic which would warm the hearts of these cool and stately people; magic which would would give them a taste of rapture.

There were some, he saw, who were thoroughly grateful for his efforts – who threw themselves with virtual abandon into the movements of the dance, forgetting protocol and surrendering to the tyranny of delight. He was less pleased when he realized that these were not his friends, but his enemies. The lady Marguerite had retired from the floor, and her son seemed hardly able to keep pace with his partner, Veronique diAvila. No matter what convention had to say about the male prerogative to lead it was clearly the flame-haired lady who was leading here, and her companion merely following. The same was true, it seemed, where Morella d'Arlette danced with Marsilio diAvila, for she was more possessed by the spirit of the music than any other, while he was the only man on the floor who was cool without being discomfited.

No other couple came close to reproducing the energy of these, including Tomas diAvila and the woman with whom he was dancing, whose mask and dress were almost identical to Veronique's, though her flowing hair was jet black. This, he knew, must be the authentic Serafima Quixana.

Orfeo saw that there was one more person who seemed to love his playing as much as any, though he had not danced at all. Semjaza, staring from the depths of his death's-head, was not moving in time to the beat of the drum, but was moving nevertheless, holding his arms wide and arching his fingers as though trying to catch and hold the insubstantial magic voice which spilled into the air from the singing strings of Orfeo's lute.

Orfeo was proud of all this – proud that he could stir the emotions of those who meant to do him harm; pleased that although he had no power to hurt them, they were not immune to his effects.

When he finished that round, and bowed to Marsilio diAvila's applause, he felt that he was in command of the moment. It was, of course, an illusion.

Rodrigo Cordova, with apologetic gestures, moved away from the lady Veronique and went to speak to his mother, who stood by a curtain beside one of the great doors. As he did so the crowd which was by the door parted, to let in a sergeant and four guardsmen. They were masked, and costumed, but the moment Orfeo saw them he knew that they were armoured beneath their bright tunics, and that the weapons they wore were by no means for show – two carried half-pikes, at the ready. One held a paper, which he gave to Marguerite Cordova. It was, in a way, a futile gesture, for neither the sergeant nor the lady could read – but its symbolism spoke volumes.

Orfeo looked around for the two men-at-arms who had come with Rodrigo's party to the castle, but they were nowhere to be seen. Force or higher loyalties had taken them elsewhere.

The lady had gone quite pale, and Orfeo realized that the warrant of arrest was for her and not her son. Marsilio diAvila had found a different way to subvert any threat which the cursed House of Cordova might present to him.

Orfeo saw that the move was a gentle one, more states-manlike than the duke's first bungled scheme – but he also saw that Rodrigo Cordova was not in any frame of mind to make subtle calculations of possibility, or to weigh the matter coolly in the balance. All that Rodrigo saw was a threat to his mother, and no thought of caution or danger stayed his hand, which went straight to the hilt of his sword.

There were men near enough to take Rodrigo's arms and hold him – and no doubt they had been charged by diAvila with exactly that duty – but they were taken aback by the suddenness and the fury of his reaction. Perhaps they too had been absorbed by the music of the lute, and had not quite recovered their quickness of wit. Whatever the reason, when Rodrigo snatched at his sword and they came forward to prevent him from drawing it, he sent them tumbling with an angry sweep of his arm, and while they fell over one another's feet the blade came free, and carved an open space around him as he lashed it back and forth.

The sergeant-at-arms transferred the warrant to his left hand and grabbed at his own scabbard, but Rodrigo slashed the tendons in the back of his hand, and he yelped

in pain. The blades of the half-pikes came down as their
carriers tried to force Rodrigo back by their threat – but
Rodrigo was not in any mood to give way. With his left arm
he swept one blade away and stabbed with his sword at the
throat of the man who held it, drawing blood.

As the man fell away Rodrigo caught the half-pike, and
used it to block the clumsy thrust of the other weapon.
Now the men-at-arms tried to fall back, to give themselves
room, but the crowd at the door was far too thick, and they
had to struggle for space to draw their weapons and bring
them into play.

Rodrigo whirled the half-pike around in a long, low arc
which cut at their legs like a scythe, and they could not
dodge the blow. Down they went like ninepins, all five of
them.

Rodrigo whirled to face the crowd within the hall, but
the men appointed to hold him were no longer enthusiastic to do the job, and they retreated, looking towards
Marsilio diAvila. Because the Duke's mask was full-faced it
was impossible to guess what expression was on his face,
but he drew his sword with practiced ease, and half a
dozen of the others on the floor – including Tomas – drew
theirs.

Orfeo saw Cristoforo struggling through the crowd, and
Rodrigo shouted at him to make the lady safe and take her
home. There was not the slightest possibility of his doing
so if diAvila's men moved to stop him, but the Duke signalled to them to let her go. Rodrigo had made his choice,
whether he had known there was a choice to be made or
not, and now that he had faced Marsilio diAvila with the
challenge of a naked sword, he had to be killed. His
mother no longer mattered.

Orfeo was not so far moved to wrath as to forget his ability to calculate, but mere arithmetic seemed not to matter
much in the present situation. To stand back now would
be to accept – indeed to welcome – the plans which the
diAvilas had for him. He laid down his lute and drew his
rapier, and found the sound of its drawing falling into a

sudden silence, where it attracted attention. Even Marsilio diAvila turned to look at him.

'To me, Rodrigo,' said Orfeo, who had a solid wooden table behind him and not a crowd. But Cordova did not move.

'There is no need for a melee,' he said, sourly. 'Far better to settle the matter between ourselves, my noble Duke.'

Marsilio laughed. 'But that, young sir, would falsify our relative strength – for we are half a hundred, and you are but two. And if you were lucky enough to kill me – why, there's another Duke beside me, and a dozen of my kinsmen nearer to the title than yourself. Would you duel with Duke after Duke, until you had slain us all?'

'Why not?' replied Rodrigo, sullenly. 'If a dozen Dukes are bent on taming me, let them try in their turn until one of them can do it.'

'Any one of them could do it,' said Marsilio diAvila, his voice hard-edged. 'I doubt that more than two or three could best your player friend, who outfenced Sceberra as prettily as one could wish, but you are a boy facing men, and you know it.'

'My lord,' said Orfeo, before Rodrigo could reply, 'this is the Night of Masks, and at midnight we are all required to show our faces. Until then, we are privileged to be anyone we pretend to be. A player may pretend to be a warrior, a boy may pretend to be a man, a Duke may pretend to be... whatever he wishes. Your people say that you are a cruel man, but tonight your cruelty is masked. Why not let the mask remain, and let the boy fight as a man. Appoint one to fight him, not six.'

Marsilio shook his head. 'The dancing is done,' he said. 'If Don Rodrigo lays down his arms I will not have him killed, but this is play no longer.'

That would have settled matters, but for two interventions which the Duke had not looked for. Tomas, his son, said: 'I will fight him, sir – and when I kill him, none can say that it was man against boy.' And Veronique, his daughter – perhaps upset by the unexpected turn of events, of which she could have had no warning – said: 'Boy or man, he is not a dog. Let him fight, father, as he demands to be fought.'

Perhaps the Duke scowled blackly beneath his mask; perhaps he was amused – but he could judge the mood of the crowd. The aristocracy of Zaragoz was gathered here in its entirety, with a hundred servants looking on. This was no ordinary night or ordinary arrest, and if judgment were being pronounced on anyone, it was the state of Zaragoz which stood to be judged, not Rodrigo Cordova.

Outside, there was a clatter of hooves, and Rodrigo tried to look over the heads of the servants gathered in the doorway, to see whether his mother had been allowed to go. Orfeo could not hear what was said, but he judged by Rodrigo's manner that the news had come back that the lady Marguerite was gone.

Rodrigo said nothing, but simply waited calmly.

After half a minute's silence, Marsilio diAvila shrugged his shoulders and said: 'If we must make a tournament of this, so be it. But if Rodrigo Cordova claims a man's right, he must have a man to fight. And if the Duke concedes that right, then the Duke must be the man.'

So saying, he levelled his blade, and moved into a fencer's stance. Rodrigo hesitated for a second, then cast the half-pike away, and copied him. The pairing looked odd, because one was right-handed and the other left, but when the Duke came forward and the blades clashed the sense of incongruity was quickly dispelled.

Although Rodrigo tried with all his might to turn the attack around Orfeo saw at once that Marsilio had spoken the simple truth. Rodrigo had been schooled in the art of swordsmanship, but he had been educated more as a sportsman than as a killer. He had the show of skill, but not the force of it. Marsilio, on the other hand, was as swift as any swordsman Orfeo had ever seen, and knew his business completely.

When Marsilio broke off the first engagement to draw back, Orfeo knew that the Duke could have pricked his opponent already, but had elected instead to make a display for his loyal subjects. Orfeo grimaced behind his mask.

Rodrigo came forward furiously, determined to make up by sheer fervour what he lacked in technique, but the desperation of his thrusts made them less effective rather than more, and diAvila parried them easily, rejoicing in his control of the situation. Orfeo could only wonder how long the Duke would let the duel go on, and whether he would kill the boy with a flourish or content himself with cutting him, then sending him to the dungeons. He gritted his teeth, and tried to decide what he should do – if, indeed, there were anything he could do.

There was no sound but the clash and click of blades, which echoed oddly in the high-roofed hall. Time seemed suspended by that near-silence, so great was its contrast with the noise which had earlier filled the hall and the courtyard with the hubbub of celebration.

Marsilio diAvila came smoothly forward again, teasing his opponent's blade with his own. Rodrigo parried, tried to counter-attack, and was suddenly bested. The Duke's blade drew a line of blood across his chest, and the swift spread of the stain showed that it was a deep cut. Rodrigo staggered back, and though he did not fall his sword-arm dropped until the blade rested on the floor. With his left hand he swept the mask from his face to reveal his frightened eyes, and the gesture brought a gasp of alarm from the crowd.

There was a moment when the Duke might have struck again, delivering a fatal blow, but he hesitated. Orfeo ran forward to his friend, and Veronique diAvila moved forward at the same time. They reached him at the same moment, in time to catch him and help him stand up. The wound in his chest was not a fatal one, but the shock and loss of blood made it impossible for Rodrigo to continue.

Orfeo looked at the Duke's masked face, and said: 'He cannot harm you. Let him go home, I beg of you.'

But Marsilio diAvila shook his head, and said: 'He offered himself in place of his mother. He must go to prison now.'

'And if I offer myself in his place?' asked Orfeo, loudly.

But Marsilio diAvila only laughed, and said: 'You are not of his quality, and we have you already, have we not?' As he said it, he looked towards Morella d'Arlette, who was standing with Semjaza at the other side of the hall. Their masks, one gaudy and one horrible, were impassive.

'My lady,' said Orfeo to Veronique, 'I beg you help me carry him to yonder table, where we can lay him down. There is a door beyond it, by which he may be removed without going through that crowd.' He could see her eyes through the bright, smiling mask, and knew there was genuine affection in them for her damaged lover.

She nodded, and looked at her father. Marsilio diAvila put up his sword, and signalled to her to do as she was asked.

Rodrigo was hurt, but he could still walk, and they had no difficulty in leading him away from the middle of the floor. The crowd, seeing that it was over, grew suddenly murmurous, and the Duke of Zaragoz turned to them, and said: 'It is a shame that blood has been spilled tonight, for this was to be a night when wounds were healed instead of opened. I say now, so that all of you may hear me, that the troubles and anxieties which have plagued Zaragoz for many generations are laid to rest. Though the news was to be sent abroad at midnight, I see no reason to wait. I ask you to rejoice for my beloved son, Tomas diAvila, who is this night betrothed to the lady Serafima Quixana, and to rejoice also that their marriage will put an end forever to the enmities which have been the bane of all our lives. Rejoice, I say, for the future Duke of Zaragoz, and for the future of Zaragoz itself!'

As these words rang out the murmur in the crowd, which had initially been silenced, swelled again, and Orfeo thought that their intention was indeed to rejoice, or to put on such a display as would please the man who ruled them – but when the murmur grew and grew it became very clear that its clamour was of a different kind, and when Marsilio diAvila stopped speaking there was a sudden gust of chilly wind which blew about the hall, causing a hundred candles to flare and then to die, sending shadows dancing madly about the walls and the ceiling above them.

Those shadows should have died with the wind, but somehow they did not, and though only one in ten of the flames which illuminated the room had been extinguished, there was a darkness in the air which shifted and stretched, as though erupting out of nowhere.

There was a great sound of screaming, then, which came from the open space outside. It grew within a few seconds to an astonishing volume as voice after voice took it up, howling in pure terror.

The crowd which had been crammed into the doorway had been held back as though by an invisible barrier – a wall which separated the arena of the nobility from the space where common men were permitted to walk – and no matter how many people had pressed forward in the determination to see the duel that barrier had held. Now it broke, and so great was the pressure which had been upon it that it burst with a tremendous force, hurling people across the dance-floor in every direction like a human tide.

There soared into the room above the heads of the maddened throng a great black bird, which seemed for a moment as huge as an eagle, though it was in fact a raven. It dived at the man in the death's-head mask, screeching like an angry daemon, and met the taloned fingers which were raised to ward it off with talons of its own.

Marsilio diAvila leapt backwards, drawing his sword again – but so quickly did the cataract of human flesh consume the space of the floor that within an instant he was surrounded by jostling commoners too terrified to know or care that he was there. The crowd was irresistible as it flowed to surround the others who had drawn their swords in support of their duke.

Orfeo and Veronique, backed against the table at the far side of the room with Rodrigo Cordova between them, had more time than anyone else to react. Orfeo leapt up on the table-top, and pulled Rodrigo up after him. The lady Veronique wasted no time in following this example.

Orfeo had time for one cry of alarm as the crowd swept over the lute which he had laid upon the floor – but then, over the heads of the crowd, he saw what it was which drove them to such panic and produced those screams of animal terror.

The courtyard outside, which had been brightly lit by thousands of candles, was much dimmer now, as though all but a few had been snuffed out by some invisible hand. The grey stone of the terraces was stained black now, and seemed to have come to life, agitated like dull pondwater rippled by a sudden fierce shower of rain.

The tide of humans which had burst into the ballroom was followed by a tide of rats – rats by the thousand, red-eyed and thick-tailed.

They ran and leapt and bit as though driven by some inner madness which had overridden their every instinct, bringing them forth as a furious legion from their own world to destroy the greater one that contained and confined it.

And as Orfeo looked up from the rats to the dark things whirling and capering upon the air like shadows come gleefully to life, he knew that the rats had not come alone from their secret abyss, and that whatever bargain Arcangelo had sealed with the daemons which lurked within those depths was only now to be brought to its conclusion.

Fifteen

FROM HIS STATION atop the table Orfeo looked out on a sea
of confusion.

At least two hundred and fifty people were now crowded
into the room, each one lashing out in blind panic as he
or she tried to run away from the black horde which
seethed around their feet and leapt up to snap at their
clothing. Not a single face could be seen; all the fright and
horror was hidden behind grinning masks, and all the
screaming merged into one colossal voice which seemed
to have no lips or tongues to shape it.

Orfeo could see men with swords hacking about themselves to the right and to the left, but their wayward blades
seemed to strike their fellows more often than the beasts
which harried them. Everyone in the room was looking
wildly about for a way of escape, but the rats had herded
them into a veritable trap, because all three of the smaller
doors which led from the hall into the inner corridors of
the Duke's palace were blocked by tables which had been

moved back to make way for the dancing. There were five
glazed windows in a row above the double doors through
which the throng had poured but they were far too high to
be reached without ladders.

The door which was behind the table on which Orfeo
stood was the one which had been used to bring the food
for the banquet from the kitchens. Veronique diAvila was
already reaching down into the gap behind the table, trying to turn the handle which was hidden from view.
Rodrigo Cordova was clutching his chest, too weak and
dazed to help her. Orfeo took out the adamantine amulet
which he had taken from Falquero's body, and placed its
chain about Rodrigo's neck, hoping that it had power left
to save his strength. There was nothing more he could do
but wait for Veronique to wrestle the door open; in the
meantime he stood helplessly above the turmoil, watching
the tragedy unfold.

Orfeo reached out a hand to a man nearby, hoping to
help the other climb up beside him, but the crowd had
pushed all the way across the floor by now, and was all
about him. The man was so crazed with fear that he nearly
pulled Orfeo down to the floor again; he let go too soon,
and tumbled back across another's shoulders.

Orfeo was searching with his eyes for Marsilio diAvila –
but the costume which caught and drew his eye was the
vivid scarlet worn by Morella d'Arlette, whose fingers were
spitting sparks as she recoiled in dread from the beasts
which swarmed around her. She too was backed against a
table, at the further end of the room, but the space around
her was empty of people. Alas, it seemed that her magic
could not keep back the rats, for they came at her with
insane enthusiasm, undeterred by the tricks which she used
to hurl them back.

Semjaza, who had been beside her only moments
before, had clambered up on to the tabletop to be out of
reach of the rats, but the raven still fluttered about his
head, groping with its claws at the edges of his mask – and
though he summoned magical force enough to blast it

into a cloud of feathers, Orfeo saw that when it was hurled away it left something on the sorcerer's head – something like a long black worm which clung to the death's-head mask like a great leech.

Orfeo remembered that he had seen it before, and knew now that it was Arcangelo's familiar, given to him by the forces with which he had made treaty as an earnest of their dark intent.

If anyone could send this plague of monsters back into the depths from which they had been strangely roused it was Semjaza, but as Orfeo watched the magician over the heads of the panicked crowd he saw that he had spoken more truly than he knew when he told the wizard that he could not be as confident of his victory as he liked to appear.

Whatever sacrifices the sorcerer had offered to the hungry evil which lurked beneath the citadel, they had been less than Arcangelo had in the end been willing to give. And how could it have been otherwise, when that agreement gave both wizards entirely to the daemons, body and soul?

Orfeo glanced towards the great doors, and saw that the rats had not come alone – for in the terraced courtyard, where half a hundred men-at-arms were fighting off the rats with pikes, torches and swords, other figures were moving now, white as snow save for great oval eyes which caught the light of the guttering candles and glowed eerily yellow in the descending dark. And with the white apes came darker things, like shadows struggling for substance: two-legged steeds and sinister riders.

There were at least two dozen of the ghostly apes, capering madly as they leapt from level to level, striking out with their long arms. They were not hunting now, after the fashion in which they had hunted Orfeo within the crag – they were not one whit less mad than the rats which they had chased from the depths. Orfeo knew immediately that they were not the herdsmen of this horrid invasion, but merely part of the herd, and that the shadowy riders which had driven the rats across magical bridges to penetrate those parts of the castle where they had never come before were their masters.

But the shadows were not merely behind the horde – they were also above it.

There was a living darkness in the air, hovering above the courtyard and the dancing-floor alike, drowning out the light of the stars and the feeble flames of the candles – an obliteration which erupted from the cracks and crevices of space itself, roiling and writhing as if in indecision over what shape to take, or whether to take any shape at all.

The blackness was filling the air, with a fierce cold and a foul graveyard stink of which Semjaza's odious breath was but the merest echo.

Orfeo's lips formed again the saying which he had repeated to Rodrigo Cordova: *Though the honest strength of men dies with them, their magic may seek vengeance from the grave.* He had heard that it was easier by far to destroy by magic than it was to build, and now he saw with his own eyes what destruction could be released by hatred and recklessness combined.

He saw that Semjaza's death's-head mask had become still once the raven had been hurled away. The sorcerer stood boldly upright, almost as though he were surveying the scene without any panic or urgency at all. But the mask lied in that implication, and the lie was written across it by the writhing coils of the dreadful worm, which had begun to insinuate itself through an eye-hole to reach the disfigured face within. Though the wizard put out his arms as if to issue a command, there was no authority now in the blindly groping hands which clawed the air in desperate futility.

Semjaza had been certain that he had turned Arcangelo's daemonic conjurations against their upstart would-be master, but Orfeo saw now how true was that wisdom of lore and legend which said that the more a wizard demanded of unearthly servants, the more he made himself vulnerable to their revenge.

Chaos was come to the castle of Zaragoz – and it came not to serve Semjaza, but to claim him.

It was as though a flock of invisible hands swept through the courtyard and the hall, killing with icy blasts the warmth which had been in the air. The candles in every high-stacked column flickered and died. The room had seemed filled with light while the nobles danced, swirling their finery about them in cascades of brightness, but now the darkness which grew and grew in the empty reaches above the heads of the crowd brought a true Night of Masks to Zaragoz, and it was no longer possible to tell noble and commoner apart in the desperate throng where everyone was reduced to the madness of pure fear.

No scaly or chitinous being appeared with livid eyes and savage teeth, to gloat and rejoice in the maelstrom of suffering – these daemons were as much an absence as a presence: an absence which seemed to suck up the life of the people as it sucked up the warmth and the light from the room. It sucked in Semjaza, too, plucking him hungrily from his place upon the table to bring him flying into the maw of the dark maelstrom.

The arms which the wizard had raised to direct his power flew wide as the force gripped him about the middle, and his legs flailed as madly as the legs of any rat-gripped kitchen-maid. His body seemed to glow within its star-spangled silks, which rippled as though there were a plague of rats inside them.

But Semjaza did not vanish utterly into that unnatural emptiness just yet; instead he wriggled and whirled, and fire flashed from his fingers in fountainous arcs, repairing for a second or two the gloom which had been cast over the battle of the rats.

Orfeo reached down again to help another join him on the tabletop – a woman this time, who was lifted up by someone else, so that as he bent to catch her she could put her arms around his neck. He put her down beside him, gently enough, and brushed a clinging rat from her skirt with his knuckles. The fragrance of her hair took him by surprise, but in the dimness he did not see at first what colour it was, and thought that it was Veronique diAvila. But Veronique was still behind him, and by now had contrived to open the door for herself and Rodrigo Cordova. The newcomer was Serafima Quixana.

Orfeo, seeing the doorway yawning wide, thrust her quickly towards it, calling to her to jump and run. He did not follow her immediately, but turned back towards the crowd, thinking to help others to pass over the table – there was a connecting beam between its legs which made it very difficult for anyone to pass beneath.

The man who had held up the lady Serafima had been swept away by the struggling crowd, who were pulling one another back as they competed for a place at the table's edge. One man and one man only was able to leap from that mass on to the table-top, and he turned quickly enough to Orfeo, reaching forward with the blade of his slender sword as though to drive the player over the edge and into the sea of frenzy. It was not the mask which the man wore but the fact that he carried his sword left-handed that told Orfeo who it was. He was facing the Duke of Zaragoz himself.

Orfeo, knowing what an absurdity it was that the strongest men in that troubled throng should begin hacking at one another with their weapons, cried, 'Peace!'

He could not tell whether his cry was unheard or not, but Marsilio diAvila cut at him again, and he had to parry the thrust, moving backwards the while.

Then, as though compelled by that same strange reflex which had taken hold of Rodrigo Cordova, Marsilio swept his mask away with a jerking movement of his right hand – and Orfeo gasped in astonishment and alarm.

The face which had been Marsilio diAvila's when he put on his mask – the extraordinarily handsome, unnaturally youthful face – was Marsilio's no longer. It was as though a talon had reached out from another world, before whose deft caress the Duke's hard flesh had been as soft as butter, and had drawn five grooves across it from the right temple to the left part of the jaw, drawing not a single drop of blood but pressing every feature out of shape, making the right eye into a ghastly shrunken thing and the nose into a twisted wreck.

And yet, as Marsilio stared at Orfeo, he clearly had no inkling of what had happened, for Orfeo still wore his impassive mask, and the horror in his own face was quite hidden from view.

A cataract of light fell upon them from that place high above, beneath the roof-beams, where Semjaza still struggled desperately against whatever thing it was which held him. So few candles were burning now that the light seemed dazzling, and Marsilio diAvila blinked in a curiously quizzical fashion, as though he could not decide what was happening to his eyesight.

Without warning, the Duke thrust again at Orfeo – a blow launched with speed and art, yet not the sort of blow which a fencer would have delivered – it was too frantic for that. Orfeo diverted the strike with his own blade, and this time he struck back, hitting the Duke above the left breast.

It was a deep cut, but it drew no blood.

Marsilio hesitated for just an instant, and Orfeo thought that the Duke might cry 'Peace!' and devote his actions once again to the vulgar cause of survival. But the cry, if it was ever intended, was stifled by a darkness which came upon his twisted features, not as though it fell upon his face from the air above, but rather as if it came from within, lazily removing itself from an envelope of flesh which it had briefly possessed.

The Duke of Zaragoz tried to turn then, as though in search of a different opponent, and Orfeo could have dealt him a mortal blow – but he did not, for there was no need. Marsilio's tortured features were scored yet again by that same daemonic hand, so that both his eyes were shrivelled and the two rows of his fine white teeth stood out from his melting lips and cheeks, which were dissolving into vacuous craters.

Marsilio diAvila was shrinking, as if something inside him was pulling his body in upon itself, as a sleeping man might huddle tightly within a blanket to save himself from the cold.

The Duke of Zaragoz toppled sideways, falling from the table to the floor where the wrathful rats awaited his delivery.

Orfeo did not wait to see his fate, but turned and leapt into the gaping cavity of the open door. Once there, though, he paused and looked up, to see what had become of Semjaza.

The magician was still struggling in mid-air, but he too seemed to be collapsing in upon himself, his hands and feet dwindling to threads – and the death's-head mask was falling from his head into the crowd below.

Behind the mask there was no face at all; it had already been swallowed up into the darkness, devoured by that hungry leech which the raven had brought to feed on him.

The last brief blaze of light from that place where the sorcerer had been devoured by emptiness lit up the silver braid on his robe as it fluttered and drifted in the turbulent air, floating hestitantly downwards to follow the mask. Orfeo could not help following the fall of the garment with his eyes, which brought his gaze again into confrontation with Morella d'Arlette.

Her mask was gone, and though the rats still leapt at her and tore at her gown her fearful eyes were directed elsewhere. She had been searching for him, and now had found him. As their stares met and were locked together Orfeo heard a dreadful screaming inside his head: a wordless cry for help, more agonized than anything he could ever have imagined. The hold which she had on him prevented his flight, and though he put up his hands to shield his eyes he could not set aside the power of her command. With every fibre of his being he tried to hurl himself through the doorway and into the corridor beyond, but his flesh would not obey him while his soul was in thrall to the sorceress. He felt certain that her magic would snatch him up, as Semjaza had been plucked from his tabletop, and draw him into the yawning crack of darkness, to accompany her to whatever hell her daemons had prepared for her.

He drew his unavailing hands away from his eyes again, and looked to see what state she was in. Despite the distance between them her features were quite clear to him, and her colourful eyes were aglow with some inner light. There was a lust and craving in her expression which was absurd in its avidity.

As he watched, the air which thickened around her head like a halo seemed to take the form of a host of faces – every one as perversely beautiful as she; every one transfigured by that same miraculous lust.

And as those faces crowded about her, to destroy her utterly with their kisses and caresses, her hold upon the player was abruptly severed – whether by accident or by design, he could not tell.

Orfeo jumped down into the corridor beyond the door just as the rats began to spill into the new space which had thus been opened to them. He did not wait to see if any other man or woman had contrived to scramble on to the table – he grabbed at the door and slammed it shut behind him, stamping his feet upon a rat which tried to bite him. Then he turned and ran.

He nearly ran right over someone who was hurrying along the corridor in the opposite direction. It was the boy who had brought him food in the dungeon, and had earlier been struck about the head by Morella d'Arlette. He had once carried the stricken boy through the very same door which he had shut behind him.

'Not that way, little fool!' he said, urgently. 'Which way did the others go? Which way from here to the gate?'

The boy shook his head, dumbly.

'The stables, then – we must find horses, if there are horses left which have not been driven to madness!'

The boy collected himself then, and nodded vigorously. Orfeo turned him about, and he began to run along the

ill-lit corridor. Orfeo followed him, first downwards and
then to the left, then up a flight of stairs and across a
landing. Wherever they ran they found rats, but only in
ones and twos, and Orfeo had no difficulty driving them
off with his blade. The boy stumbled once or twice, but
he was a nimble runner and did not seem to mind the
rats as much as those who had been panicked by them.
As the lowest of the low within the castle walls, he was
probably better acquainted with the beasts than anyone
else.

The way they took brought them eventually out on to the
ramparts of the castle, where there should have been men-
at-arms – save that on the Night of Masks they had all come
down to take their share of food and drink, or to follow
their luck with serving-maids and street-girls who had
sneaked in from the town. Now the only guards by the battlements were great white apes ranting and raving at the sky
which they had never seen before.

Orfeo looked over the wall to see if there was any chance
to make an immediate descent, but the drop was sheer for
two hundred feet and more, so he followed the boy along
the narrow path, heading for the gate beside which the stables were extended.

When they went down the stairs into the stables it
seemed that this quest too must be in vain, for there were
rats rattling in the straw, and every box seemed to have
been kicked open. The lamps which had been suspended
from the roof-beams had been cast down, all save two, and
one had started a fire which was extending slowly to the
feed-store. A great many of the horses which had been
brought to the castle by the guests had broken free and had
joined the tumult on the terraces, but those which had
been trained for military use had been taught to withstand
both noise and fire, and though they did not like the rats
they had held to their stalls.

Not thirty yards away Orfeo saw Veronique diAvila struggling to secure a saddle on one such horse, with Rodrigo
Cordova still beside her, pale and injured but alive and

conscious. Serafima Quixana was nearby, evidently having followed the other two in their flight.

Rodrigo cried out when he saw Orfeo, but Orfeo ran instead for a corner which neither the smoke nor the rats had reached as yet. There he found two horses, as quiet as any in whole place, with saddles ready in the stall. When Orfeo made haste to throw one of the saddles on the broad back of the nearer beast it did not try to smash him with its hooves, but responded to his calming call as a well-trained horse should.

When the saddle was on, Orfeo looked round for the boy, and found Serafima Quixana beside him as well. He lifted the lady in his arms and hurled her into the saddle. Though she probably had not ridden for several years she had been taught in childhood, and knew enough to cling to the rein. He thrust the boy up behind her, and told him to hold tight – then he smacked the animal on the rump, and sped it on its way to run the gauntlet of fire and madness, all the way to the castle's gate. He saw as he sent it forth that Veronique diAvila had succeeded in saddling her own mount, and had paused to pull Rodrigo Cordova up with her, so that they too could ride together into the gathering darkness.

Orfeo would have leapt upon the second beast's bare back had he dared, but he had seen too much of the road which led from the top of the mount to the bottom, and he knew that there was no way he could ride around the spiral without the means to guide his mount and cling tightly to its back. He put the other saddle on, and pulled a bridle over the horse's head, then hauled himself up by the side of the stall to set himself astride it. The others were long gone, and the fire burned brighter now. When he urged the horse to run, it did not pause, but galloped forward with all possible haste, scattering a group of men who tried to halt it, intent on fighting for the privilege of using it.

Orfeo had dropped his sword in order to wrestle with the horse's livery, and both his hands gripped the reins –

but once the horse was given its head there was no way to pull it back, for it was stronger by far than he was.

The gate was yawning wide, and those who could reach it were already running from the castle as fast as their legs could take them. So far as Orfeo could see they were mostly servants, and he could only presume that the Duke's men-at-arms were standing their ground as best they could, using their pikes and blades to oppose the creatures which had invaded their realm.

Orfeo held on as best he could while the beast which he had mounted pleased itself about the course which it took, and when they hurtled on to the perilous road at full gallop he was sure that they must plunge over the edge and tumble down the crag. But the horse, like that ancient animal which he had earlier borrowed from Rodrigo's house, had gone that way a hundred times, and though it had surely never gone as fast, it knew its way. It drew as close as it could to the side of the mountain, and kept its balance at every twist and turn.

Orfeo wished at first that the horse would slow down once it was free from the tumult in the castle, for he did not believe that the rats or the apes could bother them any more, but when he glanced up at the towers looming above them he saw that the danger was by no means passed.

There was a darkness growing in the sky which hid the stars, and there was a monstrous sound as if the stony fabric of the walls themselves were being squeezed and rent. He saw a stone from the battlements dislodged, setting loose a sliding mass of little stones as it careered down the nearly-vertical slope. Whatever daemons had been unleashed upon Zaragoz were not content, it seemed, to swallow up their former worshippers.

Yet again he heard the phantom voice of Arcangelo crying in the lonely depths of his mind: 'Zaragoz is doomed!' And he knew that behind the mask of the priest of Law there had been a heart and mind as twisted as Semjaza's naked face, which had been willing to sacrifice everything in the cause of vengeance and hatred, and that had unleashed upon Zaragoz a force which would not stop at swallowing up the diAvilas who had worshipped it.

Orfeo's senses reeled as the horse swerved around another bend and he came terrifyingly close to being tumbled from its back. But he no longer prayed that the beast would stop; instead he prayed that it might find pace enough to outdistance whatever it was which gripped the peak of the crag like a huge black spider, and whose dark exhalations were drifting down through the still air, raining destruction upon the fleeing crowds.

When he looked up again, and could not see the stars, he felt such anguish in his heart that it seemed to him that nothing less than a miracle could save him.

But then, in that very instant, the miracle was granted, for he saw ahead of him another gate looming above the precipitous road, lit by half a dozen lanterns – and it was a gate which he knew.

It was the gate of Rodrigo Cordova's house – which, if its long dormant magic had power enough to oppose the deadly forces Arcangelo's battle with Semjaza had unleashed, might be the one place on the mountain which was safe from the agents of destruction.

The gate was already wide open, and there were men waiting for him, who had begun calling and waving as soon as he came in sight. Cristoforo was there, and Rodrigo Cordova himself, still standing despite the great bloodstain which soaked his tunic. He was not the only fugitive to whom they were signalling, for some of those who had fled from the castle as soon as the rats had emerged from the depths – those who had not been drawn irresistibly to the spectacle of Marsilio diAvila's duel with Rodrigo Cordova – had already come this far on foot, seeking sanctuary.

For one awful moment, Orfeo thought that the horse would not be turned from its headlong flight, and would take him helplessly down the mountain, all the way to the streets of the town at its foot. But the horse, too,

could recognize safety, and it galloped gladly through the
gate, already pulling up as it clattered into the narrow
court within. As grooms ran to intercept him Orfeo saw
that there were armed men swarming about – Cordova's
men rallied to the cause by earlier arrivals.

Orfeo jumped down from his saddle and raised his voice
as high as he could, trying to shout above all the other
shouts, telling everyone who could hear to go inside the
house. He pointed desperately at the sky, trying to show
them what it was that they must hide from, and when he
looked up to follow with his eyes the direction of his own
pointing finger he saw that matters were worse than he had
thought. The blackness was no longer spread across the
whole sky – instead, it was gathering itself to form a thick
and grotesque cloud, which was descending steeply upon
this house and no other, pursuing those who ran to its protection.

He stumbled then, knocked over by a running man, but
hands went out to him instantly, to pull him back to his
feet. As he was brought upright again he heard a wild cry,
and thought for a moment that the monstrous dark had
come about them with its foul minions in train, but the
cry had only been a cry of joy, when Rodrigo Cordova
found his mother safe, brought here by his trusted men
before the panic had even begun. She was standing in the
open doorway of the ballroom where Orfeo had played,
and the crowd was rushing past her now, carrying Rodrigo
with it, and Veronique diAvila. Orfeo was glad to see that
Serafima Quixana and the kitchen-boy were with them
too, clinging together as though they were brother and sister.

Orfeo struggled to Rodrigo's side as they passed through
the doorway, and when all those who had been in the yard
were inside they tried together to take hold of one of the
two doors, intent on closing it. But more running figures
were coming through the gate, racing into the very heart of
the awful black shadow which was descending there, and
they hesitated to close the newcomers out.

As they stood there among the crowding figures, it seemed inevitable that the foul black void would sweep past them into the hall, there to work its will with those who had fled from it – but as the crowd of awful shadows came to the threshold it met some invisible barrier which held it back, and though the darkness sealed off all light from without, it could not reach the candles which burned within the room.

It was as if the empty space between the far-flung doors became a wall of solid black, mere inches away from Orfeo's face, and though all those who were crowded about him – save for one – fell back in alarm, he did not. Although he knew full well that he did a very dangerous thing, he actually reached out a hand to touch that wall, to see how solid it was – and when he touched it, it was as though it seized his hand, not to pull him away from where he stood and consume him, but rather as though it was welcoming him with a fond and seductive caress.

He looked into the darkness, and once again he saw the faces which had crowded about Morella d'Arlette in the ballroom: faces as beautiful as they were bizarre, whose glamour made an urgent appeal to his senses and his desires. He remembered that Morella had warned him that there was something of Chaos already in his being – and also that she had aspired to show him an ecstasy so intense that he could never again be content with a merely human lover.

But there were other things in that convoluted host of shadows, whose forms were incompletely hidden by the darkness – things with horned heads and huge bovine features, and insectile creatures with glaring compound eyes. When he looked into those eyes, he seemed to be staring into an infinity of horrors where the mere and meagre desires of the flesh counted for nothing at all.

The vision lasted but a fraction of a second; then the blackness became and remained absolute; but still there was a strange thrill which surged through his body, and though he saw nothing, it was as though some inner part of himself still looked through that wall of shadow into an awesome lighted world beyond: a world of fire and blazing light, a world without form or landscape, a world unimaginably greater than his own.

When he took his hand back, it came easily, without resistance. Then he turned to look at the other person who had stood her ground, who had likewise reached out to touch that frightful shadow while it was held at bay by the armour in which the house was clad.

It was Veronique diAvila, her red hair declaring her identity even though she wore a decorated mask.

The mask, at least, was smiling.

'Midnight is past,' she said, in a voice hoarse with excitement. 'It is time to lay our masks aside.' And she reached out to lift Orfeo's false face away, and looked at him, as though relieved to find that what was underneath was only what her reason told her would be there.

EPILOGUE

'AND IS THAT the end of your story?' asked Alkadi Nasreen, sourly, as Orfeo's voice lapsed into silence.

Orfeo could not tell whether the sourness was simply the result of lack of sleep, or whether the tale which he had told had annoyed the man severely.

'It was the story's climax,' he replied. 'Were it an invented tale, climax and end would be one and the same, but this was a phase in the unfolding tapestry of life itself, and there are parts of it which extend beyond its climax. I know a little more of what became of the survivors of that night, but I went on my way within a week, in search of a happier place.'

'Then tell me what remains to be told,' said the Caliph. 'Were all those who did not escape to Rodrigo Cordova's house killed by the things unleashed upon the castle? Did the castle walls crumble away entirely?'

'By no means,' replied the story-teller. 'Many stones were dislodged from the ramparts, and the High Tower was felled, but the castle was not destroyed. Nor were all who were trapped there killed. Some forty or fifty men and women were brought down by the rats and the apes, and bitten to death. A hundred more had only minor wounds, though a few died of fevers in the days which followed. But the dark shadows – the daemons, if that is what they were – claimed for themselves less than a hundred men and women, who were swallowed up so completely that they left no trace behind. Included in that number were all but one of those who had sought to steal their power and control them. I have named the exception.'

'Why did the Chaos spawn turn on those they had formerly served?' asked the Caliph.

Orfeo sighed, feeling that he had already made adequate explanation of the fact, but he had no choice but to be patient when his freedom hung upon the telling of the tale. 'Arcangelo had not the power to win them to his own cause,' he said, 'but by using his own flesh as an instrument – in such a manner that it cost him his life – he could cast a spell which dissolved the bonds by which Semjaza's followers had held them captive and forced them into servility. Though Arcangelo could not free the lady Serafima in the way he had intended, still he succeeded in breaking the shackles which mattered, and some kindly god took the trouble to number the lady with those who lived.'

'Did you go to the castle again?'

'Eventually. But there were others braver than ourselves. For many hours that night, and throughout the day which followed, Rodrigo and his mother received in their house the injured servants and nobles who limped down from the peak. They continued to arrive in ones and twos, while others went to their own houses, and the occasional troop of men-at-arms rode down to the town on their well-schooled horses. When we had lent to those who came to us what help we could, we went to the castle. There we found that the fittest and the strongest of those who survived had looted what they could before they fled. The bodies had been stripped of their jewels and silks, and the treasures heaped up by the diAvilas had gone. Much of the gold must have been carried out of the realm by soldiers of fortune, but enough remained within its borders to double the price of bread within five days.'

'But you did not leave without your purse, I'll wager?' said the Caliph.

Orfeo smiled, but rather mirthlessly. 'Rodrigo Cordova was a good and generous man,' he said. 'His people will love him, now that he is proclaimed Duke of Zaragoz. He will go down in their annals as a man of honour, and if ever he is treacherously slain, the act will leave such a legacy of bitterness that some diehard champion of the people will surely appear to demand vengeance in his name, and will threaten the town with doom if justice is not done.'

The Caliph laughed, but there was no more mirth in his laugh than there had been in the player's smile. 'At least,' he said, 'the feud between the diAvilas and the Quixanas is ended. It will take time for the House of Cordova to find an enemy which hates it as fiercely as those two families hated one another.'

Orfeo hesitated before replying, but then said: 'No. Nothing is ended. Rodrigo Cordova has Veronique diAvila and Serafima Quixana in his house. I cannot tell whether the love he once had for the one will in time be transferred to the other, but this I believe – that one day he will marry one or other of them, and in the calculations of his people he will then become diAvila or Quixana, while the woman he rejects will carry bitterness and envy into exile.

'It does not matter which one he chooses – red hair or black – for in a hundred years it will all be the same. There will be harder Dukes, and resentful subjects... and always there will be the word – the word of power which signifies a change of allegiance and a plot to seize the crown. When a man of justice sits upon the crag of Zaragoz, the pain of that country's disease is soothed for a generation... but as long as the crag is there, and the castle, and the houses of the nobles arrayed upon its slopes, there can never be a proper healing. Are matters any different upon this crag of Arjijil? Is this impregnable fortress any safer from the corrosions of envy which seethe beneath the surface of its daily affairs like rats in its sewers?'

The question which he asked of the hearer of his tale was no mere taunt. What Orfeo was really asking the so-called Caliph to consider was whether he had really left Zaragoz behind when he sent himself into his distant exile. Was there any place in all the great wide world where the sicknesses which were in Zaragoz could not be found?

He knew that the Caliph himself was pondering that question when Alkadi Nasreen said: 'What of these daemons of darkness which came traitorously from the depths of the crag to turn the tables on those who had sought to use them? Have they been laid to rest forever?'

'I would like to say that they were,' Orfeo told him, 'but I cannot believe that either. They are still there within the mount, dormant now like the force which which was bound within the walls of Cordova's house.

'Now that Semjaza is dead, some other magician will come to Zaragoz craving knowledge and craving power. If he cannot become Rodrigo's friend he will become his secret enemy. There is an instrumentality of temporal power which consists of kings and noblemen, and there is an instrumentality of magical power which consists of wizards and priests... and in our world their fortunes are inextricably bound up with one another. Just as kings and noblemen generate their own opposites, as diAvilas produce Quixanas, so the magicians who seek power from the Gods of Light and the Gods of Law generate rivals who seek power from the opposing forces of Darkness and Chaos. So it goes on, pausing for a while, then bursting forth in blood and fire, but never ending... never *truly* ending.'

'In Araby,' said Alkadi Nasreen, 'we acknowledge only One God, and no others. One God who rewards, and One who punishes. Where there are daemons – in the searing heat of the desert and the black shadows of the night – the priests and prophets of our One God go to bind them... to seal them in bottles of brass and bury them in the sand or throw them into the sea. I do not know what you mean when you speak of Chaos but the priests of Araby know well enough what is meant by evil, and will stamp it out wherever it appears. I think this is a better land than Zaragoz, though I do not know how matters go in Bretonnia or the Empire.'

'There are men of Araby in Estalia,' said Orfeo. 'I met some in Magritta, who told me many tales of the power which your priests and prophets have, which some use to bind evil. It was that which put it in my mind to travel in Araby, for I am a collector and a teller of tales, and I believed that there was much that I might learn in the Sultan's own city, and a little that I could teach, after my own poor fashion.'

'The wisdom of lore and legend?' asked Alkadi Nasreen, sarcastically.

'I believe in that wisdom,' said Orfeo, evenly. 'I believe that there is a truth in tales, which is not the everyday truth of actual events, but a truth without which actual events cannot be seen for what they really are. I am a servant of that truth, and I am proud of what I am.'

'In Araby,' said the Caliph, 'we have a higher truth than that, which is the truth of our prophets and our priests – the truth of the One God. It is a truth which binds daemons, and will one day cleanse the world of evil.'

Orfeo did not know how to reply to that, for he could not guess how honest a believer Alkadi Nasreen really was in the faith to which he had been converted. His acknowledgement of the One God might be merely a ploy, to allow him to live among these folk and lord it over them as a pirate king... but it might, on the other hand, be the overzealous faith of the genuine convert, ever anxious to justify itself.

Because of this doubt, he only said: 'Every exercise of power produces resentment. If Araby grows too ambitious to convert the world, what begins as a cleansing may end as a nightmare of blood and fire. If, on the other hand, it grows too complacent in its wealth, and turns to the pursuit of luxury, what begins as pleasure may end as decadence. Your story-tellers know that, if your priests and your kings do not.'

'Storytellers have been hanged or burned for sedition in many different lands,' said Alkadi Nasreen, darkly.

'Aye, my lord,' replied Orfeo, softly. 'I know it. I have been a prisoner myself, condemned to death and lucky to escape.'

The Caliph laughed again, still without much humour.

'I might get a good price for a man like you,' he said. 'But the buyer might one day come to me and say that I had sold him an annoying thing.'

'It is only too likely, my lord,' agreed the storyteller. 'And I believe that I have your promise that if the news which I brought you was good, you would set me free – and the boy too.'

'I remember what I promised,' said the pirate. 'And I would honour my word, if only I knew for certain whether I should weep or rejoice in consequence of what you have told me.'

Orfeo was disturbed by this, for he thought his tale plain enough. If this man had fled Zaragoz because he was Quixana, or an ally of the cause of the Quixanas, then the fall of the diAvilas should have been news that he was glad to hear. If he was not Quixana, then what interest had he found in what he had been told?

'I have told you the truth, my lord,' said Orfeo. 'All that I know has been set forth before you. It is a grim tale, I know, but I think that it ended as well as it could have ended. Rodrigo Cordova is a good man, and he will rule as justly as any king or duke that I have ever encountered in my travels.'

'I am not concerned with Rodrigo Cordova,' said Alkadi Nasreen. 'And in the matter of justice, I am inclined to side with my brother's opinion, that much of what is said and done in its name is mere hypocrisy.'

'Your brother?' asked Orfeo.

'Like me, he took another name. I became Alkadi Nasreen – he became the man you have called Semjaza.'

Orfeo's heart sank, as he remembered not only his account of Semjaza's death, but also the manner in which he had reproduced his conversations with the sorcerer. One spoken sentence now resurfaced in his memory: *I had a mother and a father, a brother and a sister...*

Even the most vicious of magicians begins life as an innocent, as a child.

'You took very different paths, my lord,' said Orfeo. 'What he had become–'

'I know it,' said the Caliph, interrupting him. 'I know that we took very different paths. Even between brothers, there can be strife, and hatred, and an opposition which grows into intolerance. Even between brothers... and yet, when all is said and done, we *were* brothers.'

Alkadi Nasreen stood up, his hands lying limp at his side because he did not know what to do with them. He walked to the wall, and then turned on his heel, his brow deeply furrowed by anxiety. He had meant what he said when he told Orfeo that he did not know whether he should weep or rejoice. Orfeo waited patiently, not stirring in his seat.

Several minutes passed, which seemed to weigh heavily upon the smoky air; and when Alkadi Nasreen turned again to face the storyteller he seemed no nearer to a settlement of his inner turmoil.

'At least,' said the Caliph, 'I know what became of him. I believe that you have told me the truth, Master Player, and I am a man of my word. I will not sell you, or the boy either. If the price which you have paid for my mercy is not entirely to my taste, it was no fault of yours.'

Orfeo let out his breath with only the slightest of sighs.

'Thank you, my lord,' he said.

'Do not call me that,' said the Caliph. 'You are a free man now.'

Orfeo said nothing, because the other man had not quite finished. There was something else which he intended to say, but he could not immediately find the words. In the end, the Caliph only said, in a voice near to a whisper: 'He was my brother.'

'The wisdom of lore and legend,' said Orfeo, quietly, 'says that all men are brothers. It is true, in all that it implies.'

ABOUT THE AUTHOR

When asked why he dressses entirely in black, Brian Craig claims to be in mourning for H. P. Lovecraft, but the real reason is too dreadful to reveal. The rumour that he joined the British Antarctic Survey in 1993 to 'to get away from it all' is false; he failed the medical and had to join the French Foreign Legion instead. He is not allowed to discuss the reasons for his dishonourable discharge therefrom in 1999, but he is glad that he will now have more time to write and play cricket.

Brian Craig is the author of the three Tales of Orfeo – *Zaragoz*, *Plague Daemon* and *Storm Warriors* – and the *Wine of Dreams*, as well as the Warhammer 40,000 novel *Pawns of Chaos*. He has contributed short stories to a range of anthologies, including the *Dedalus Book of Femmes Fatales*, edited by Brian Stableford. He is 28 and only looks older because his troubles have aged him.

More Brian Craig from the Black Library

THE WINE OF DREAMS
A Warhammer novel

THE SWORD FLEW from Reinmar's hand and he just had time to think, as he was taken off his feet, that when he landed – flat on his back – he would be wide open to attack by a plunging dagger or flashing teeth. As the beastman leapt, Sigurd's arm lashed out in a great horizontal arc, the palm of his hand held flat. As it impacted with the beastman's neck Reinmar heard the snap that broke the creature's spine.

As soon as that, it was over. But it was not a victory. Now there was no possible room for doubt that there were monsters abroad in the hills.

DEEP WITHIN THE shadowy foothills of the Grey Mountains, a dark and deadly plot is uncovered by an innocent young merchant. A mysterious stranger leads young Reinmar Weiland to stumble upon the secrets of a sinister underworld hidden beneath the very feet of the unsuspecting Empire – and learn of a legendary elixir, the mysterious and forbidden Wine of Dreams.

More Brian Craig from the Black Library

PAWNS OF CHAOS
A Warhammer 40,000 novel

GAVALON HAD ALREADY begun thinking of the bulk of his forces as 'gunfodder', even though they had never faced guns before. The guns produced by the Imperium in their planetary-based factories were by no means as powerful as those they had brought from the star-worlds, but they were guns nevertheless and there was nothing in Gulzacandra that could compete with them – except, of course, magic. If the Imperium was to be stopped, magic would be the force that would do it.

IN THE GRIM future of Warhammer 40,000, mankind is engaged in an eternal conflict with the armies of Chaos. On the medieval world of Sigmatus, the hated Imperium is flexing its power with ruthless efficiency. The rebels have a plan to fight back: summon a powerful daemon from the warp and unleash it upon their enemies!

More Warhammer from the Black Library

The Gotrek & Felix novels
by William King

THE DWARF TROLLSLAYER Gotrek Gurnisson and his long-suffering human companion Felix Jaeger are arguably the most infamous heroes of the Warhammer World. Follow their exploits in these novels from the Black Library.

TROLLSLAYER

TROLLSLAYER IS THE first part of the death saga of Gotrek Gurnisson, as retold by his travelling companion Felix Jaeger. Set in the darkly gothic world of Warhammer, TROLLSLAYER is an episodic novel featuring some of the most extraordinary adventures of this deadly pair of heroes. Monsters, daemons, sorcerers, mutants, orcs, beastmen and worse are to be found as Gotrek strives to achieve a noble death in battle. Felix, of course, only has to survive to tell the tale.

SKAVENSLAYER

THE SECOND GOTREK and Felix adventure – SKAVENSLAYER – is set in the mighty city of Nuln. Seeking to undermine the very fabric of the Empire with their arcane warp-sorcery, the skaven, twisted Chaos rat-men, are at large in the reeking sewers beneath the ancient city. Led by Grey Seer Thanquol, the servants of the Horned Rat are determined to overthrow this bastion of humanity. Against such forces, what possible threat can just two hard-bitten adventurers pose?

DAEMONSLAYER

FOLLOWING THEIR adventures in Nuln, Gotrek and Felix join an expedition northwards in search of the long-lost dwarf hall of Karag Dum. Setting forth for the hideous Realms of Chaos in an experimental dwarf airship, Gotrek and Felix are sworn to succeed or die in the attempt. But greater and more sinister energies are coming into play, as a daemonic power is awoken to fulfil its ancient, deadly promise.

DRAGONSLAYER

IN THE FOURTH instalment in the death-seeking saga of Gotrek and Felix, the fearless duo find themselves pursued by the insidious and ruthless skaven-lord, Grey Seer Thanquol. DRAGONSLAYER sees the fearless Slayer and his sworn companion back aboard an arcane dwarf airship in a search for a golden hoard – and its deadly guardian.

BEASTSLAYER

STORM CLOUDS GATHER around the icy city of Praag as the foul hordes of Chaos lay ruinous siege to northern lands of Kislev. Will the presence of Gotrek and Felix be enough to prevent this ancient city from being overwhelmed by the massed forces of Chaos and their fearsome leader, Arek Daemonclaw?

VAMPIRESLAYER

AS THE FORCES of Chaos gather in the north to threaten the Old World, the Slayer Gotrek and his companion Felix are beset by a new, terrible foe. An evil is forming in darkest Sylvania which threatens to reach out and tear the heart from our band of intrepid heroes. The gripping saga of Gotrek & Felix continues in this epic tale of deadly battle and soul-rending tragedy.

INFERNO! is the indispensable guide to the worlds of Warhammer and Warhammer 40,000 and the cornerstone of the Black Library. Every issue is crammed full of action packed stories, comic strips and artwork from a growing network of awesome writers and artists including:

- William King
- Brian Craig
- Gav Thorpe
- Dan Abnett
- Barrington J. Bayley
- Gordon Rennie

and many more

Presented every two months, Inferno! magazine brings the Warhammer worlds to life in ways you never thought possible.

For subscription details ring:
US: 1-800-394-GAME   UK: (0115) 91 40000

For more information see our website:
http://www.blacklibrary.co.uk/inferno